PRAISE FOR SECRET MARRIAGE

Ms. Dearen's prose ensnares the reader from paragraph one and keeps up the pace with admirable dexterity... Stephanie and Bran are layered characters who develop throughout the book, and Bran's disability is sympathetically and realistically portrayed.

— JANICE MATIN, IND'TALE MAGAZINE

Rarely do I become emotional to tears. In this book, I started with tears and ended with tears. So many great elements in this book.

— RANDY TRAMP, AUTHOR OF NIGHT TO KNIGHT

I loved the new twist on the billionaire love story idea. Can't wait to see how the whole series turns out!

— LIA LONDON, AUTHOR OF THE NORTHWEST ROMANTIC COMEDY SERIES

There are wonderful characters, deep issues, humor, intrigue, and great chemistry! There's raw honesty in the character of Bran, the blind billionaire.

— TINA MORLEY, AMANDA'S BOOKS AND MORE

THE BILLIONAIRE'S SECRET MARRIAGE

BOOK ONE OF THE LIMITLESS CLEAN BILLIONAIRE ROMANCE SERIES

The Billionaire's Secret Marriage hardback version

Copyright © 2018 by Tamie Dearen

All rights reserved.

No part of this book may be reproduced in any form or by any electronic or mechanical means, including information storage and retrieval systems, without written permission from the author, except for the use of brief quotations in a book review.

ISBN 9781720785590

Cover by Tamie Dearen Arts

The Billionaire's Secret Marriage

To my grandfather and my grandson, who taught me that we see each other with our hearts, not our eyes.

FOREWORD

Glaucoma took my grandfather's eyes by the time he was forty years old. He never saw my face, but we were the best of friends. I used to get up before sunrise so we could drink hot tea together on the back porch of their tiny farmhouse. I followed him around as he fed hay to the cows and collected the chicken eggs. In the eyes of a ten-year-old girl, there was nothing he couldn't do. He wielded a saw and a hammer to build new outbuildings on their property. He killed chicken snakes with his bare hands. He knew every cow by touch. That he could do these things without the benefit of sight never seemed anything but ordinary to me.

And so, when our blind grandson was added to the family, my expectations for him were high. Yet, he is even more amazing than my grandfather. He is fluent in three languages, and he can read and write Braille in multiple languages as well. He has read more books (mostly audiobooks) than I have. He leaps fearlessly from cliffs, trusting only our word that there is water below. You should hear him play the drums in the school jazz band!

When I told him I was going to write a romance book with a blind hero, he asked me why. I explained I wanted to show that people are basically the same, whether or not they have the benefit of vision. He agreed to talk with me and give me advice about my character. The most remarkable thing about that conversation was not the insights he shared, but the fact that a fifteen-year-old boy took the time to chat with his grandmother about her writing. Once again, he taught me that what makes him special is not his disability, but his heart.

I hope you feel the same way about Branson...

CHAPTER 1

Stephanie Caldwell winced at her reflection in the mirror, snatching a tissue to wipe the smeared mascara from under her eyes. She wasn't about to let anyone know she was bothered by the announcement her boss just made. No one else had been surprised. Why was she? She knew from the start there could never be any kind of relationship between her and Branson Knight.

I'm twenty-nine... too old to have a silly school-girl crush.

A few wispy brown curls escaped her bun, the only adornment of her neck. She hadn't worn her typical costume jewelry, knowing the other female guests would be sporting genuine diamonds.

The jiggling doorknob, followed by a few sharp knocks, jerked her back into reality. There had to be a dozen bathrooms in Bran's mansion. Why did someone need to use this one, in the far back corner of his darkened private library? Most people didn't even know it existed.

"I'll be out in a minute," she called, hoping whoever it was would simply go to another empty restroom. A glance in the mirror revealed red-rimmed eyes and a matching red nose. Maybe she could explain it away as an allergy attack.

The doorknob rattled again. "Stephanie?"

Bran's voice. She laid her hand over her chest as her heart performed a haphazard flip. Just her luck—the one man she most wanted to avoid at the moment.

"Yeah. Sorry, boss." She forced a relaxed tone. How could she explain why she'd chosen his private restroom, hoping to hide away until she pulled herself together? "The hall bathroom was taken, so I didn't think you'd mind. But I'm coming out, now."

She turned out the bathroom light and whipped the door open, planning to slide past him and escape, but his imposing form blocked her exit, silhouetted by the dim moonlight trickling through the library window. He towered over her, though her three-inch pumps boosted her to a respectable five feet seven. She hated the way her chest clenched so close to him, glad for the moment she couldn't see how enticing he looked in a tuxedo. But he was one of those guys who looked hot in anything he wore, whether he was dressed in jeans and a t-shirt, with his muscles stretching the thin fabric, or draped in an expensive designer suit.

"I was looking for you. I sent a text."

"Sorry. I had my phone on silent during the party." She hoped he couldn't tell from the wobble in her voice she'd been crying. "Technically, I'm not working tonight."

Her boss was driven and would probably work around the clock if he could. He even dictated to her while he was exercising in his private gym, not that she minded the scenery.

She must've done a poor job of hiding her frustration because his voice went contrite. "I'm sorry, Stephanie. I wanted your take on the reactions when I made the merger announcement. I should've warned you ahead of time, so you'd notice the details. Were you watching?"

Her stomach fell into her gut as she realized why she'd been invited in the first place. She'd been so thrilled to find her name on the exclusive guest list for the annual spring gala, thinking he was finally beginning to see her as more than an employee. He'd even insisted she buy a new dress at his expense. She'd purchased the exquisite designer gown with growing excitement, especially when he asked her to describe it to him in detail and suggested she come early to the party. For a few days, she'd allowed herself to believe the fairy tale might come true. Hoping Branson Knight was actually interested in dating her.

She'd swallowed her lumpy pride when she arrived, only to be greeted by Bran's girlfriend, who looked her over as if her clothes had come from the refuse pile. Carina was one of *those* girls—beautiful, rich and successful. No doubt she'd been homecoming queen, head cheerleader, class president, and valedictorian. Only the remembered words of Steph's MawMaw kept her from creating a Carina voodoo doll and sticking it with pins. *"Now Stephanie... don't judge people. Every mean person has a sad secret hidden inside."*

But it wasn't Carina's snobby attitude that had hurt Steph's feelings. What tore her apart was recognizing the obvious truth. Bran wasn't interested in her. He simply wanted her to be his "spy." The new dress was only part of her disguise, because Branson assumed, correctly, she had nothing in her closet that would allow her to blend in with the other, affluent guests. As usual, with Bran, it was strictly business.

"I was watching. I paid attention, even though I didn't realize I was still on the clock." More perturbed by the second, she couldn't resist a dig. "But which merger announcement were you referring to? Your takeover of Reston Incorporated? Or your engagement to Carina Parker?"

He seemed to wince, though the moonlight didn't illuminate his face clearly. She didn't need to see him. She knew his face by heart, from the arch of his brows to the angle of his carved jaw, which was smooth-shaven tonight, though his customary style sported a slight beard, one she thought made him look even more rugged and masculine.

"The business announcement, of course. My engagement isn't important."

"Not important? You're getting married, and you don't think that's going to impact your life?"

His hand came up and pushed through his dark hair, leaving the ends sticking up like pieces of straw in his shadowed silhouette. She almost reached up to smooth them, but caught herself at the last second.

His head was shaking slowly back and forth. "The marriage will be mutually beneficial to both of us. Living together won't change anything."

He spoke as if it were a business transaction. Her next words spilled out before she could stop them. "Wouldn't it be cheaper to hire someone by the hour?"

When she saw him stiffen, the hair stood up on the back of her neck. This time she'd gone too far.

"Perhaps you're right, *Ms. Caldwell.*" He spoke as calmly as if he were reciting a grocery list. "Were you volunteering for the job? What are your hourly rates?"

All the oxygen rushed out of the room, leaving her so lightheaded she had to grab the doorframe to stay upright. Her chin lifted as she glared at him, ineffectually. "You couldn't afford me, *Mr. Knight.*" Gaining her composure, she tried to push past him.

"Wait." Her arm was in his iron grip, as he bent down to mutter in her ear, his breath sending electric impulses rippling down her spine. "I'm sorry. I didn't mean that. Please forgive me."

"No apology necessary." She jerked at his unrelenting grasp. "I was out of line. It's none of my business."

"I should've told you about the engagement."

Dagnabbit... he sounded repentant. She grasped at her anger, catching it before it disappeared.

"Why didn't you?" Another tug of her arm produced no results.

"Honestly, it slipped my mind, with the Reston deal on the line."

Really? Business made him forget his engagement? She ought to feel sorry for Carina.

"Let. Me. Go." She stumbled back when her arm slipped free at last. An engagement could simply slip his mind? She wondered, not for the first time, if there were any feelings inside his impassive exterior. How could she be attracted to someone so cold and calculating, so much her opposite? She must've imagined those times when she'd caught a glimpse of the real Bran Knight, the fantasy man she was in love with.

"I've apologized. Now can we get back to business?"

"Yes, we can." She pushed back the storm of emotions

threatening to explode from her fragile hold. "As the first order of business, I'm giving you my two-weeks' notice."

"Why?" He took a step toward her, holding out an open palm. "I told you I'm sorry. What else do you want?"

"I don't want anything." *Nothing you're willing to give me.* "But you'll have a wife to pick out your clothes and check your appearance and coach you on your expressions. You won't need me anymore."

"Your job entails a great deal more than that."

His detectable irritation gave her a sense of satisfaction. He hardly ever displayed his emotions, so he was impossible to read. She had to face reality—Branson Knight was never going to think of her as anything but a personal assistant, no different from any of the dozens he'd probably employed through the years.

Maybe his engagement and marriage would help her douse those flames she'd been trying to suppress for the last two years. She shouldn't have let herself fall for him.

The timing couldn't be worse. Ellie's new medication was incredibly expensive, and the insurance wouldn't cover it. She couldn't afford to lose this job, no matter how much her pride stung. But what if his new wife wanted him to fire her? Carina had always given Steph the cold shoulder, making her feel invisible.

"I apologize, Mr. Knight. I was totally out of line. The truth is, I need my job, and I don't want to quit. But my head's killing me, so I think I'll call it an early evening."

Though her words were stiff she managed to sound genuine. At least she thought she had. Yet he stopped her before she could get away, his hands firmly grasping both shoulders as he bent his head toward her. For an instant, she thought he was going to kiss her, and her chin lifted toward him, lips parting of their own accord. But he turned his head at the last minute, his face contorting in frustration.

"I'm blind, Stephanie, not deaf and not dense... at least not usually. I don't want you to leave until we fix things between us. You're the best personal assistant I've ever had. You take care of every part of my life, personal and business. I'm willing to consider a raise, if that's what you want."

"I'm not asking for a raise." She swallowed a lump in her throat. A raise would be life-saving right now, but she couldn't accept it under these circumstances. "Why do you make everything about money?"

His hands dropped to his sides. "Because, in my experience, that's how things are."

"I'm not like that." His words hurt so much, even though she knew it was his own life experiences that made him so cynical. "Don't you know me by now? We've been together two years."

"Are you volunteering for a pay cut?" The corner of his mouth twitched, a grin threatening to emerge, and she briefly considered stomping on his three-thousand dollar Ferrinos.

"Of course not," she sputtered. "I need money, like everyone else. But that's not what this is about."

"Then enlighten me." In the shadows of his face, his eyebrows lifted. "Why are you upset?"

She struggled to explain her reaction without revealing her feelings for him. "I guess my feelings are hurt because you usually share everything with me." Her voice dropped to a hoarse whisper. "I didn't even know you and Carina were serious."

"You knew we were dating exclusively." His eyes widened in innocence.

"You didn't even pick out her birthday present. You said, and I quote, 'Get her anything. It doesn't matter. I'm sure you'll pick something suitable.'"

"You know I never hide anything from you. I didn't mean to do it tonight."

"That's debatable."

The man hid behind a mask. Sure, she knew about most of his business dealings. Yet she never had personal contact with his closest friends, other than Carina, who sometimes barged in during work hours. Of course, he worked so much, he didn't have much time for leisure activities.

"I planned to announce the engagement in June at the shareholders' meeting, but Carina said it was too impersonal. Right before the party, she talked me into pushing the date forward. I didn't have a chance to tell you."

"And you just happened to have that diamond and ruby ring lying around?"

He waved his hand in the air, as if erasing her objections. "That's not even the real engagement ring. It's one my mother left to me. Carina would never settle for another woman's ring."

"I understand." She threw the lie out with all the resentment she felt.

"If you'd moved into the estate, like I've suggested all along, you would've known the last minute details."

"I have a daughter. One I barely see, as it is—"

"You and Ellie would have your privacy inside the estate. There's an entire empty wing where you could hide, along

THE BILLIONAIRE'S SECRET MARRIAGE

with your nanny." His voice dripped sarcasm. "You could keep your precious time away from me."

She bit her lip to keep from crying, glad he couldn't see her face. All this time she'd resisted his offer to live at his mansion complex, for fear of becoming even more dependent on him. But the past few months, the medical bills had increased to the point she was seriously considering moving in to relieve the financial pressure. Now she didn't know what she was going to do.

"It doesn't matter now. Your new wife wouldn't want another woman living in her house."

"There are dozens of people who live on the grounds. She wouldn't even notice you. And it doesn't matter what she thinks, anyway."

"I think her opinion matters. You're getting married."

"Nothing will change. My life will continue as always."

"You've got to be kidding. Of course your life will be different. You'll have a wife. And someday, you'll probably have children, right?"

"Children?" Why did he sound like her suggestion was outrageous? He was only thirty-two years old, and he loved kids. He'd poured millions into charity work for children. "We haven't had time to work out these details," he muttered, sounding disgruntled.

"You've been dating for a year."

"Exactly." He gave a sharp nod. "After a year, why were you so shocked we got engaged?"

She gaped at him, unbelieving. "Maybe because you never said you were in love with her."

His mouth opened and then closed, as if he was debating what to say. "No. I didn't tell you."

They both jumped when the library door clattered open. A man wearing a tuxedo and a cowboy hat stepped inside, flipping on the light. "There they are." A broad smile creased his face as he pointed toward them, the ice clinking in the glass grasped in his fingers. A blond-haired man pushed his way past the first, while another, with swarthy features, followed behind, moving with a slight limp.

Bran groaned, scrunching up his face. "Come," he ordered, grabbing Stephanie's hand and dragging her behind him as he strode toward the door like a madman trying to escape an asylum.

"Oh no, you don't." The blond stepped in front of him, barring the way, while the first man shut the door.

Stephanie couldn't help the grin that slipped onto her lips. She knew exactly who the men were. She'd been dying to meet them since she'd learned of their existence, but Bran had always given her time off when this group got together. For some unknown reason, he didn't want her to mingle with his three close friends and business partners.

"You must be the mysterious Stephanie." The blond man spoke with a slight English accent. He stepped forward, lifting her free hand to gallantly brush his lips across the back of her fingers, like something out of a movie. On her other hand, Bran's grip tightened like a vise.

She felt her cheeks heat. "I'm hardly mysterious."

"Yes, you are." His brows bobbed up and down. "Bran's been hiding you for two years, and that makes you a mystery."

"We need to get back to the guests," Bran spoke between gritted teeth.

"Go back to your party," said the cowboy, swooping

around Bran to wrap his arm across Stephanie's shoulder and wrench her away from her boss. "We'll stay in here and get acquainted with Stephanie." He took off his hat. "I hope that's all right with you, ma'am. My name is Cole."

"Not happening." Bran's voice sounded like grinding gears.

Stephanie ignored his growl, addressing Cole with a wry smile. "Yes, I know who you are, Mr. Miller. In fact, I recognize all three of you from your pictures. I know all about you."

"You know all about us? Even how we met?" The dark-haired man tilted his head, glancing at Bran from the corner of his eye.

"Yes, I know you're Jarrett Alvarez from Denver." Then she addressed the other two. "Cole Miller from Texas. And Finn Anderson, from New York. I know how you met and what you all have in common, besides the corporation."

"And what do we all have in common?"

She flinched at the sharp edge in Cole's voice.

"Unless I'm mistaken, you all have a love for kids with disabilities, and that's why you started *Limitless*, to help those kids." She lifted her chin, refusing to be intimidated by Cole's towering stature or the wealth and power he represented as one of the four kingpins in Phantom Enterprises. After all, she dealt with his equal on a daily basis.

"And how we met?" Finn Anderson asked in his charming accent, though his brows drew together with suspicion.

"You met at the computer camp you all went to every year from age thirteen on," she announced, triumphant in her knowledge.

"Computer camp?" Finn glanced over his shoulder where

Bran's shoulders drooped as if he were resigned to the death chamber.

"It *was* computer camp," Branson defended.

"For kids with disabilities," Finn clarified.

With great difficulty, she stopped her jaw from dropping open, but her eyes must have gone wide. Unbidden, her gaze darted to the three, surreptitiously searching for their hidden flaws. Each one was drop-dead handsome in his own way, though none of the others held a candle to Bran. She'd noticed Jarrett limping earlier, but she forced her eyes away from his feet.

"I can't believe you never told her the truth." Cole aimed an ineffectual glare at her sullen boss.

"It's not like she doesn't know I'm blind. I had no reason to give her details about the three of you—especially you, Cole." She saw a tell-tale twitch on Bran's lips, and suspected he was holding back a grin. "I always said we shouldn't have let you in the group. You're only missing your left hand. *And* you have a prosthetic replacement that works better than the original. Hardly counts."

Her furtive glance at his hand didn't expose any clue that it was anything but natural. She almost wrote off Bran's comment as a jest.

"It counts." The impatience in Cole's voice told her they'd repeated this argument a thousand times. He turned and gave Stephanie a knowing look, extending his hand for examination. "This one is fairly useless... just for looks. I prefer my other one. It looks like a colorful robot arm, but the function is impressive."

She marveled at the realistic prosthesis, though close

inspection revealed its artificial nature. "Why not wear the other all the time, if you like it better?"

"Social settings. It makes people uncomfortable." Cole used his elbow to push her boss back when he tried to edge around him. "Bran, I see you've been trying to keep her sympathy all to yourself. Too bad, buddy."

"Sympathy?" She let her disbelief show. "He gets no sympathy from me."

"Good. He doesn't need it." Jarrett lifted his pant leg to show a metal prosthesis with a dress shoe. "I'm the one with the fake leg. Osteosarcoma. I lost it when I was thirteen."

"I see." She plastered a smile on her face and nodded, all the while, thinking of the trauma that must have been involved in fighting childhood cancer, and secretly wondering what his longevity might be.

"It's cystic fibrosis for me," Finn said. "I guess I'm the least disabled. I don't struggle with anything but breathing. But I'm thirty-two and living on borrowed time."

Steph felt a sting in the back of her eyes and blinked fast to keep tears from spilling out. She understood cystic fibrosis all too well.

"Shut up, Finn." Jarrett gave his shoulder a friendly shove. "You'll probably outlive all of us."

"It makes sense, now." Steph tucked her head down, to hide her trembling chin. "I mean, I get why you're all so determined to do something for those kids out there. *Limitless* is an awesome organization."

"Yeah, but that's not why we want to talk to you." Finn herded her toward the couch and settled her onto the buttery soft leather, where she found herself flanked by him and Jarrett. "Tell us all Carina Parker's dirty secrets, so we can stop this disastrous marriage."

"Leave it…" Bran's voice gurgled a warning. The only time she'd ever seen him this emotional was when he got off the phone with his father. "This isn't your business."

"Of course it's our business." With his arms crossed and shoulders squared, Cole faced Branson. "You're one quarter of Phantom Enterprises. You're risking everything, marrying this woman we don't even know."

"It doesn't matter," Branson retorted. "She'll sign a prenup. And we don't need to discuss this in front of Stephanie. She has nothing to do with my personal life."

His careless words hurt more than she expected, and her anger flared again. "I'm afraid he's right, guys. He didn't even bother to tell me they were serious, much less on the verge of engagement and marriage."

The three stared at Bran like he had an extra head. Jarrett was the first to recover. "You didn't even tell your PA? Branson, you really are a jerk-wad, aren't you?"

"I didn't have the chance." He sounded even more desperate to convince his friends than her. "I have my reasons, but I can't talk about it right now."

Carina chose that moment to glide through the door in five-inch spike heels, with the grace of a ballet dancer en pointe. *"Darling…* everyone's been looking for you."

A deep crease between his brows, Branson turned his head toward his friends and muttered from the corner of his mouth. "Are you coming with me or not?"

"What do you think?" came Finn's glib reply.

Branson marched to the door, snatching his fiancée's arm as he went. Pausing, he glared their direction with such

14

ferocity in his steel blue eyes Steph could've sworn he actually saw his friends' smug expressions. He flipped off the light switch and slammed the door, the thud echoing from the library shelves as her eyes once again adjusted to the dim moonlight filtering into the room.

Jarrett let out a low whistle. "Whew! Bran's ticked off, isn't he?"

"Yep," Cole agreed. "Most fun we've had since the last Star Wars premiere."

"Maybe even better," said Finn.

CHAPTER 2

*B*ranson woke in a foul mood. No surprise. It was Sunday—Stephanie's only day off. And today, of all days, he needed to talk to her. His friends had grilled her for at least forty-five minutes, and he had to find out what she told them. More importantly, he worried what secrets his friends might have revealed about his past.

He gave himself a mental kick. He should've known it was a trick when all three of his Phantom Enterprise partners told him they weren't coming to the annual gala. He was furious they'd found a way to gain access to Stephanie, though he wasn't quite sure why he'd been so determined to keep them apart.

"Where are my socks and shoes?" Bran snapped, leaning from his perch on the bench at the foot of his bed to grope on the floor.

"As always, your shoes are on the shoe rack in your closet, and your socks are in your second dresser drawer," Fordham replied, in an unperturbed tone.

"Stephanie always lays them out for me," he complained.

"Ms. Caldwell indulges your laziness. I do not. You're a grown man, perfectly capable of fetching your own socks and shoes."

"I can't be sure what color they are." He let a petulant tone creep into his voice. "Someone could've put them in the wrong compartments."

Fordham wasn't buying it. "As you only allow Stephanie and me to put them away, you've the same odds, whether you're trusting us to sort them properly or fetch them for you."

"Remind me again, Fordham, what do I pay you to do?"

"To listen to your endless complaints, I suppose, and then remind you you're a man and not a child. Let me know when you're ready to forgo your tantrums. I'm certainly prepared to retire at any moment when you admit I'm no longer needed."

"No." Bran ground his molars together. "You know I still need you. I don't do well with change. I need consistency."

"So you said the last fifteen times we hired a personal assistant," Fordham said with a yawn. If he looked as bored as he sounded he would be lying flat on his back, the gray hairs trembling on his chin as he snored. Not that Bran had seen his gray hair, but Fordham described it on a regular basis, saying he was too old to work. "And yet that didn't stop you from firing each one the moment he or she did something to displease you. That is, until you hired Ms. Caldwell." He added another vocal yawn at the end of his discourse.

"You seem more tired than usual. Are you okay?" Bran asked, only partially in jest. He didn't like the sick feeling in his stomach at the thought of Fordham's possible infirmity. As his primary caretaker, even before Bran's mother passed away, Fordham had been the most constant fixture in his life since he could remember. During college and graduate school, it was Fordham who played the role of father, as his own was too busy traveling around the globe, checking on the resort properties that had made him a wealthy man.

Fordham answered, "I may have had a bit of indigestion last night—a consequence of too much of that decadent dessert concoction from the dinner. We had our own version back in the kitchens. So delicious. Though I suppose you didn't taste it."

Bran ignored Fordham's jibe about his aversion to sweets and all things he considered unhealthy. "You could've joined the main party. It's not like you aren't invited every year."

"But I've nothing in common with *those* people." He said the word like it tasted bad.

"Because they're rich? Privileged? Snobby?"

"Because most of your rich friends have nothing of interest going on inside their brains but to fabricate lies to impress others who, like them, have nothing of interest inside their brains."

A hearty laugh slipped out before Bran could stop it. "Is that how you see me, too? What about Cole and Finn and Jarrett?"

"None of you four fit in with that group, and I can't conceive why you'd want to. It was a lucky thing your friends showed up and saved Stephanie from either a slow and painful death of boredom or being skewered to death by judgmental stares."

"I guess you were in on that surprise visit, huh? Not sure where your loyalty lies these days."

"Your friends don't need my help to plan their pranks. But that didn't stop them from bragging about their success when I showed them to their rooms last night. Quizzed me about your reasons for keeping them away from Stephanie. And why you didn't tell anyone you were getting engaged."

"And what did you say?"

"The truth." Fordham let his statement ride in the silence that followed, as Bran wondered at his meaning, his stomach churning.

"I thought I could trust you, Fordham."

Fordham made an exasperated sound. "The *truth is* I have no more idea than anyone else why you do what you do. But thanks for letting me know what you think of me after all these years."

Bran hadn't meant to hurt his feelings. He groaned in frustration. "You know better. You're family to me, more than my own father."

"Then explain it to me. Why've you kept Stephanie away from your friends for two years? When you announced your engagement to Carina Parker, it blew away my longstanding theory."

"What theory?"

"That you were secretly in love with Stephanie Caldwell."

Bran's chest tightened. Though he originally chose Stephanie from fifteen other candidates because he'd discovered her child had cystic fibrosis, his feelings for her now were confusing at best. Yet he knew he was incapable of love, just as he knew no one would ever love him. Women didn't see him as a man. They saw him as someone to be pitied. And used. His value lay, not in who he was, but what he had. Money.

"You know I picked Stephanie because she needed my help."

"Because of the medical bills. Yes, I know what you said."

"And I've tried to talk her into moving to the estate, but she won't do it. I can't understand why."

"I imagine your reputation for firing your assistants preceded you. Or perhaps she simply resented your attempts to control every aspect of her life."

Bran grunted. "I'm not that bad."

"Keep telling yourself that," Fordham needled. "But only last week, she approached me about the possibility of moving in. She might be changing her mind."

Hope bloomed in his chest. "Really? She didn't say anything to me about it. I mentioned it again last night."

"Last night? Was that *before* or *after* your engagement announcement?"

"My engagement has nothing to do with this."

"Whatever you say, Master Knight."

Fordham's voice drizzled even more sarcasm than usual, and Bran decided to change the subject. He hoped he could persuade her to move to the complex. *Because I like order in my life. It's not that I have feelings for her.*

"You're really not going to bring me my socks and shoes, are you?" Without waiting for an answer, Bran padded his way to his closet, the plush carpet making his progress silent. Emerging with his running shoes and a pair of athletic socks, he went back to the bench to put them on.

"How did Carina's father respond when you announced your engagement?"

"With enthusiasm. I got a pat on the back and a hearty handshake. My fingers are still numb." He worked to tie his shoe, his nimble fingers having no difficulty with the task.

"Sounds like he's glad to be rid of her," Fordham remarked.

"Ha! You may be right." Carina could certainly be a handful. "I'd call the party a success. After I announced the merger, Kingsley and Johnson pulled me aside to talk about investing. Soon, our resorts will be the largest chain in the world." *Larger than dad's. He'll be furious.* The thought brought a grin to his face.

"Bully for you. You've done an excellent job fitting into the group. You're more like your father every day."

Bran knew the last remark was meant as an insult. "I don't try to fit into *the group*, as you call them, but I keep them happy and well-fed."

"Like pets?"

"No. More like livestock."

"I see."

"That's why I need Carina. She speaks their language."

"You don't need another goat to take care of your goats. You need a goatherd."

"Carina's not like the others. She's smarter than you think."

"No doubt that woman is smarter than *you* think. Mark my words, you will not control her. She will as soon cut your throat as the steak on your plate."

Bran finished tying his shoes before responding. "Then I better not give her anything sharper than a table knife."

A creak of the chair indicated Fordham's rise to his feet, and Bran wasn't surprised when his voice moved. "Having one's carotid sawed open with a dull blade hardly sounds more pleasant than a quick slice with a razor."

Bran reached up and clasped the hand he knew was offered, though he didn't need help standing. He paused, turning his face square to Fordham's. "You think she hates me that much?"

"On the contrary, I believe she loves you a great deal… as one loves a trust fund."

Bran strode into the hallway, snatching his cane where it leaned against the door jamb without breaking stride. "I have my reasons."

"I don't trust her." Fordham kept pace with him.

"Me, neither. I thought you'd watch her for me."

"A formidable task that will be, when she becomes the mistress of the household."

Pausing at the door to his workout room, Bran put his hand on Fordham's shoulder. "But you'll do it?"

His long-suffering sigh was loud enough to carry all the way down the stairs. "I will try."

"Thank you, Fordham." Bran squeezed his shoulder. "If the guys are up, tell them I'll be down for breakfast after my run."

"Not necessary. Most reasonable people don't awaken two hours before the sun rises."

"I feel sorry for all the rest of you, tied to a ball of fire ninety-three million miles away."

"Every person needs to sleep—even you. Your health will suffer if you continue to operate on four hours of rest at night."

"Sleep is a waste of time, like this argument."

To avoid any further discussion on the subject, Bran

strode to the treadmill to start his daily run. Though he tried to concentrate only on exercise—pushing his body to the limits—thoughts of Stephanie kept inching their way inside his head.

He remembered the day, several months after she started working for him, when she'd started an awkward conversation.

"Branson? Can I make a suggestion?"

He could hear the nervous tinge in her tone. *Something's up.*

"You can try. I probably won't take your advice," he joked, hoping to put her at ease.

"You told me once you don't sleep very much. Is that from being blind?"

"Yes. Without light and dark stimulation, your body's circadian rhythms don't work right. It's pretty common in people who are totally blind."

"Isn't there something you can take for that? Because some days you look so tired. I don't think it's good for your body to live on so little sleep."

Some remote part of his brain registered she was concerned for his health, and he tucked that tidbit away to mull it over later.

"I don't like taking drugs of any sort. Anyway, I get a lot done if I don't sleep."

"That's not a good answer. I'd rather have you healthy, even if you get less work done. I'm going to do some research about sleep issues with blind people."

"Knock yourself out. I doubt I'll listen to you any better than I listen to Fordham or my doctors."

She went quiet for a moment and then said, "You don't

have to tell me if you don't want to, but how did you lose your eyes?"

He'd been waiting for this question. Everyone was curious.

"Cancer. Retinoblastoma." He said the words like it was no big deal.

"Was it painful?" Her voice was tight with some emotion stronger than curiosity.

"I guess so. I don't remember. I was a baby at the time." This was all the information he intended to share, but something made him go on. "My mom told me it was her fault I lost both eyes instead of one. She said the doctors explained I could've had radiation in one eye. It was risky, but maybe I could've kept my sight in that eye. Mom argued it was better to lose both eyes and know for sure I'd survive. Dad said something to the effect that I might be better off dead."

He heard her sniffling. *Why did I tell that story? I made her feel bad.* He hurried to make an awkward apology. "Steph, I'm sorry. I shouldn't have—"

"No, I'm glad you told me." Her voice cracked. "I hope your mom waited until you were grown before she told you that."

"Mom died when I was seven."

He heard a muffled whimper, like she was covering her mouth with her hand.

"Oh, Bran! I'm so sorry."

Next thing he knew, he'd spilled the whole sordid story of his childhood, from birth through his mother's death. Though Steph never moved from her chair across the desk, he felt her soothing empathy as if she were holding his hand.

Dry-eyed as always, he gave every detail, including the rumors he overheard at the funeral.

"They were whispering that it wasn't an accident. That she jumped off the balcony on purpose. I was sitting right there, but I guess they thought I was deaf, too. Or maybe too dumb to understand." He didn't say what he'd always suspected— always known—that his mother was escaping the horror of having a defective child.

"That's so terrible."

It was then he noticed the sniffling and the distinct sound of a tissue being pulled from the box on his desk. *I've got diarrhea of the mouth. What's wrong with me?*

"I'm sorry, Stephanie. I shouldn't have gone on like that. You can see why I'm so screwed up."

She responded in a shaky tone, "No child should have to deal with *any* of the things you've had to face, much less all that baggage put together. It could've turned you into a bitter man. But it didn't. You channeled it all into a good thing. The work you do for disabled kids. I think you turned out amazing, after all you've been through."

Her words made him swell up, wishing so badly to be the man she described. But deep inside, he knew she was wrong.

"I'm more bitter than you think." He snatched his stress ball from a tray on his desk and squeezed with all his might, thinking of his dad.

"I wouldn't have been able to deal with all that." Her wobbly voice steadied a bit. "My life was easy. My grandmother raised me, and she loved me with every bone in her body. She died three years ago, but her voice is still in my head."

"Fordham's voice is in mine." He put the stress ball back in its proper place.

"A good voice to have."

His fingers itched to touch her face. To know the shape of her nose, the line of her jaw, the slope of her forehead, the contour of her eyelids, the softness of her lips. He wanted to know her form as he knew her soul, to *see* her the only way he could. He pushed the yearning back inside, where it belonged.

From that point on he had wanted not only Stephanie's presence, but her approval, though he knew it was based on pity. He craved it, like an addict. And he would take it any way he could get it.

Irritated at his lack of concentration, Bran increased the speed on the treadmill until his only thought was finding the strength to land one foot in front of the other. On and on he pounded, unrelenting, sweat dripping from his body. At last, a beep sounded to indicate he'd reached his ten-mile goal, and the machine gradually slowed to walking pace.

He followed with a round of one-handed pushups, once again proving to himself he was in complete control of his body. And his life.

∼

Bran sat alone at the breakfast table. Hearing occasional laughter rising from within the kitchen, Bran grew more irritated. He pushed his food around on his plate and took a few bites, finding his customary steel-cut oatmeal with a side of fruit and Greek yogurt to be tasteless.

When the laughter broke out once again, he recognized

one of the voices. *Finn.* In an instant, Bran was out of his chair and striding to the kitchen door to jerk it open.

Stunned silence greeted him. Then Finn's guffaw echoed in the tiled room, and Bran recognized the answering chuckles of his other two friends.

"Good morning, Mr. Knight. Have you ever had these homemade cinnamon rolls?" Finn spoke in a garbled voice. "They're unbelievable. I might steal Mindy away from you."

As Mindy mumbled an embarrassed protest, Bran made a mental note to make certain she got a raise, though he knew Finn was teasing him.

"Didn't your mother teach you not to talk with your mouth full?" Branson didn't bother to state the obvious fact that he'd refrained from eating anything with processed sugar in it since the age of sixteen.

"Yes, she did. But Mum's not here. And I'm glad, as she'd probably eat my share."

"And mine, too," Jarrett added, a reference to Finn's mother's reputation for a robust appetite. Finn described her as *built like a lumberjack*. It was true. When she first met Bran, her hug had crushed the air from his lungs.

"You three use me for the rooms and the food, but you can't eat breakfast with me?"

"We avoid you like the plague until you finish your morning routine," said Cole. "Since when do you like company for breakfast?"

"Or any other meal, as far as that goes?" Finn added, his curiosity tinged with a hint of humor. "Is this the new Branson Knight? You're engaged, and you're not a hermit anymore? If so, we welcome Carina with open arms."

Bran's face heated, knowing Mindy and her assistant

were listening in. His staff knew his habits had changed when he started eating lunch with Stephanie. "Why don't we go in the other room to talk?" Bran stomped into the dining room, his friends shuffling behind him. "The truth is, I read it's better for your digestion if you don't eat alone."

"Only you would base a conversation on health benefits," said Cole, as his chair scraped on the granite-tiled floor. "Heaven forbid you just wanted to talk to someone."

"I talk to you guys all the time," Bran defended, dropping into his usual chair at the dining table, directly across from Cole. "Mostly on the phone, but that's because we all live in different states."

"We never hear from you unless you want to discuss business," Cole said.

"So what?" Bran shook his head, trying to follow his friend's reasoning. "Why else would I call?"

"Because we're supposed to be friends." Jarrett took over the argument, but Finn and Cole muttered agreements.

"We *are* friends. You're my only friends." Branson failed to keep the frustration from his voice. Jarrett wasn't making any sense.

"Friends talk about more than business," Jarrett continued. "They talk about what's happening in their lives. We used to get together every month, but the past couple of years you've been gradually cutting us off. It's like we barely know you."

"And friends tell each other upcoming major life changes, like engagements," Finn added.

"That's what this is all about?" Bran asked. "You guys are mad because I didn't tell you I was getting engaged to Carina?"

"Not mad, exactly," said Cole. "More like shocked."

"It was a last-minute decision."

"I don't believe that for a minute," Finn sputtered. "You don't make last-minute decisions. You and Carina have been dating for a year."

"This is just like the argument I had with Stephanie. First you say you're caught by surprise. Then you complain I've been dating her for a year. What do you want from me? Seems like you all could've seen it coming."

"Maybe we could've, if you'd ever called to talk about anything besides business or let us get to know this woman," said Jarrett.

"It wouldn't have helped," said Cole. "Stephanie was surprised, and she's with him almost every day."

"Yeah... poor Stephanie." Jarrett's tone was dramatically sardonic. "I'm sure she deserves a raise, putting up with a boss like you for two years. But I guess you'll have to fire her since you're getting married."

"I'm not letting her go."

"When's Carina moving in?" Finn ignored his words. "I might like to hire Stephanie. Do you think she'd mind living on the east coast?"

"I'm not firing Stephanie." Bran slapped his hand on the table, rattling the silverware. "In fact, Stephanie's moving into the complex." He hoped his words were true. Fordham hadn't reported back yet.

You could've heard a pin drop. Finally, Cole broke the silence. "Uhmm... Bran? Does Stephanie know that? Because she didn't say anything about it when we talked last night."

Bran didn't want to consider the possibility it might not happen. His hands wadded up the napkin in his lap. "That's

30

another thing. You had no right to question Stephanie like that."

"Branson…" This time Finn's tone was soft and filled with sympathy. "You're withdrawing from everyone. It's not good for you, and you know it. We had to trick you. It was our only chance to talk to Stephanie. We had to find out what was going on."

"And did you?" Bran asked, scrunching his eyebrows.

"Not really," Finn confessed. "She didn't even realize what you used to be like. You should've seen her face when we told her how you used to travel all over the world with us and do every single extreme sport."

Finn paused, but Bran fumed silently rather than respond.

"What happened to the old Branson Knight?" Finn asked. 'You used to shake your fist at society and prove you could do anything a sighted person could do—usually better. Now you hide away with your treasure like an old dragon in his cave, and all you think about is business."

"Maybe I don't have anything left to prove," he said, sullenly. "Maybe I don't need that anymore. I'm happy here, and I don't need anyone else."

"Not even us?" asked Cole, his words tinged with hurt.

Bran groaned. "That's not what I meant. You guys are my brothers."

From across the table, Jarrett's voice came closer. "Then, as your brothers, we're telling you to stop shutting everyone out. You've written advice to our disabled kids, and that's one of the things you always warned them against… cutting themselves off from society."

Is that what I've done? Why didn't I recognize it?

"Next weekend, we're going to Vegas," Finn announced.

"Vegas?" Bran's heart pounded in his chest. He couldn't handle the crowds. The noise. "I think I've got meetings—"

"Sorry, bud. Stephanie checked your schedule, and you've nothing important planned," Jarrett said.

"I don't think—" He choked, his mouth as dry as if he had a mouthful of flour.

"You can even bring Carina. Make it a trial run, of sorts." Finn's hand gripped his shoulder and his voice lowered. "You can do this, Bran. We'll be right there with you. You need to let loose and have fun again. You've got to get back out in the world."

Bran's throat constricted, and he felt like a vacuum had sucked all the air from his lungs.

"It's going be a regular thing," Cole added. "Phantom Enterprises is going to hold a corporate meeting at a different location every month, just like we used to, and you're going to come. No excuses."

Footsteps announced the entrance of a fifth person in the dining room. Bran recognized Fordham's gait. "Mr. Knight, I have a report for you. Two items."

Bran rubbed his aching temples. "I hope it's good news, Fordham. I don't think I could handle any bad."

"We'll let you be the judge."

From his buddies' chuckles, he could assume Fordham made a funny expression.

"First," said Fordham, "Ms. Stephanie has reluctantly agreed to move into the complex. I believe she used the term, 'financial rock and a hard place.'"

"I pay her well," Bran stated, wanting to defend himself before his friends.

"Yes, but she tells me her doctor recommended a new prescription drug for CF, and her insurance doesn't cover it."

"Stephanie has cystic fibrosis?" Finn asked, incredulous. "I would never have guessed."

"Not Stephanie," Bran explained, inexplicably worried this piece of information would cause Finn to pursue her on a more personal level. "It's her six-year-old daughter, Ellie."

He could almost hear his friend swallowing hard before whispering back, "Stephanie's right. There's a new breakthrough med, and it's costing me about three hundred grand a year. I was planning to bring it up at our next board meeting. We can't afford to give that much money to every CF kid, but how do we decide which one gets it and which one doesn't?"

I don't know. But I'm making sure Ellie gets the drug she needs. Bran pressed his lips together, keeping the thought to himself. To Fordham, he said, "When is she moving in?"

"I hope I wasn't presumptuous, but I convinced her to move this week, on Tuesday. Her lease renews this month, so it's now or next June. She was concerned about missing a morning of work, but I assured her you'd be accommodating."

"Excellent." Bran rubbed his hands together briskly, imagining how his life would improve with Stephanie close by. "Hire a moving company. I don't want her to lift a finger. Give them connecting suites in the east wing, by the rose garden. Ellie ought to like that. All girls like roses, right?"

"And Ms. Fields? Where do you want her to stay?"

"Ms. Fields?"

"Laurie Fields, their live-in nanny."

He faltered, embarrassed to have forgotten the nanny's

name, since Stephanie talked about her almost every day. "Yes, Laurie Fields. Right. She'll need to be next door in the same wing."

"And Ms. Parker?" Fordham inquired, in the same impassive tone.

"Carina? What about her?"

"She's here, waiting for you."

"What?" Bran choked, gasping to catch his breath as his mind spun. *Why is Carina here?*

"She's in the parlor, asking where she can put her things. Shall I have her trunks moved to your master suite?" This time, Bran noted the edge of a laugh in Fordham's voice.

"She can't move in here."

"Evidently, she's unaware of that restriction. She was quite perturbed to be kept waiting. I believe my ears are still burning."

What a disaster. We haven't even drawn up the prenuptial agreement. "No. I'll deal with her. You can go, Fordham."

"With all my heart, I thank you." As Fordham fled the room, Bran's traitorous friends howled their laughter.

"I'm guessing you weren't quite prepared to live together," Finn remarked, the direction of his voice rising as he stood. "That's what you get when you sleep with a woman. Of course she expects to move in once you're engaged."

"We aren't sleeping together."

"Sure, you aren't," Finn said, with unwelcome sarcasm.

"We aren't. At least, not anymore." Bran's head throbbed, as he tried to explain the complicated relationship. "It only happened once."

Bran flinched as a hand clasped his shoulder.

"Good luck, Bran," said Finn. "We'll see you at lunch, if you're still alive."

"Where're you going?" Bran demanded. "You can't leave me at a time like this."

He heard the other chairs creaking and scraping and retreating footsteps. Cole's voice answered from the kitchen door, "I'm off to your workout room. Gotta burn some calories after scarfing all those cinnamon rolls. Later, bro."

The door clicked shut, muffling the laughter and leaving him alone with his scrambled thoughts. With hardened resolve, he pushed away from the table and strode out, down the hallway to face his formidable fiancée.

What have I gotten myself into?

CHAPTER 3

"This place looks like a country club. Or maybe a resort." Laurie's eyes bugged out of her head. "I can't believe we're actually going to live here."

Stephanie glanced around with fresh eyes, taking in the polished marble floors of the entrance pavilion, with an ornate carved ceiling and rich furnishings. She remembered her own awe at her initial visit, the day she came for her interview. When she received the phone call to set up the meeting, she'd almost accused the caller of making a mistake. She'd only applied out of desperation, thinking she had nothing to lose. In her wildest dreams, she hadn't thought she would actually get an interview, much less a job offer, especially since the position called for a master's degree, and she lacked six hours of completing hers.

Steph had never heard of Branson Knight, though practically everyone on the planet knew about Phantom Enterprises. No one had warned her that her potential boss was blind. For the first part of the interview, he seemed to look right at her with those intense blue eyes, and she'd had no idea he couldn't see. What she did know was he was the most beautiful man she'd ever seen. The moment he strolled into the room, the temperature rose about ten degrees, and she found herself fingering her top button, wishing she could pull her blouse out and back to fan herself.

With her attraction pushed to the back burner in light of how much she needed this job, she'd swallowed hard and concentrated on presenting herself in the best possible light. She still remembered how her heart had pounded with confusion and anger as he'd explained her duties would include arriving early to lay out his wardrobe for the day. She should've kept her mouth shut, but she barked her disapproval at the assumed insult to women, knowing she could never work with a chauvinist, no matter what the pay.

"I thought you were interested in my brain, Mr. Knight. But I suppose, because I'm female, you think I should perform these menial tasks."

She sprang to her feet, ready to march out, but he rose with her, unperturbed by her outburst.

"Your gender has nothing to do with this. I need a personal assistant to help me with all the chores I find difficult to complete on my own. They aren't menial to me. Since I'm fully blind, choosing my wardrobe is one of those tasks. But if it's above your station—"

"You're blind?" She stared at him in disbelief. The lighting was dim, but there was no way this man was totally sightless. She would've seen it in his mannerisms. She barked her accusation. "You walked straight to your desk and sat down. And you've been looking right at me this whole time."

"That may be so, but it doesn't change the fact I'm blind."

One corner of his mouth twitched, as if he might be on the verge of a smile.

"Prove it."

His supposedly-sightless eyes opened wide. "I... uhhh.... Ms. Caldwell, you've actually shocked me beyond speech. I've never been asked to prove I can't see, and I'm not sure how to go about it. I don't suppose owning a white cane would do it for you."

He popped up, moved unerringly to the open door and pushed it closed, revealing two white canes propped behind it.

"Anyone could own a white cane." She left her chair and stomped over to stand directly in front of him, her hands on her hips. "You could have low vision or something. You can't be totally blind."

Still confident, she lifted her right hand and wriggled her fingers silently in the air, her stomach knotting when his eyes didn't follow the movement. She repeated it with her left hand, but his gaze never wavered.

"There's one sure way I can prove it," Branson said, "though most people can't stomach it if I remove my prosthetic eyes."

"No, that won't be necessary." Heat rushed to her face as she realized what a fool she'd been. And a rude one, at that. *What kind of person makes a blind man prove he's blind?* She choked out, "I'm so sorry, Mr. Knight. I'm not usually so insensitive. Thank you for your time."

She scurried back to her chair, intending to snatch her purse and escape before her cheeks burst into flames.

"What are you doing?" he asked, his gaze somehow

following her as he stepped in front of the door, barring her exit.

"I can't apologize enough. I'm really sorry." She scrambled, trying to squeeze past him, but his well-muscled, six-foot-two form wouldn't budge. Stepping back she put her hands on her hips and scowled, only to remember her expressions had no effect on the man. His piercing blue eyes, though apparently artificial, somehow penetrated into the depths of her soul, leaving her vulnerable. Every flaw, every thought, every insecurity was laid bare for his leisurely inspection.

His lips curved upward. "Why are you leaving? Do my prosthetic eyes make you that uncomfortable?"

"No, but it's not too comfy having my foot in my mouth."

"And that's the only thing bothering you?" His arms folded over his chest, muscles rippling under the fabric.

"Yes." It was a small lie. She couldn't tell him how her throat went dry imagining how it would feel if his arms were wrapped around her instead of wastefully crossed over his chest.

And then it happened. His hand touched her bare elbow and sent a chilled ripple in every direction. When she jerked her arm away, his hand found the small of her back, a gentle pressure guiding her back to the interview chair. She sat stiff, like a rod was planted in her spine, while he leaned against the desk in front of her. She kept her gaze down, using a critical inspection of what must be her first close-up sighting of designer leather shoes to distract her from his magnetism.

"When could you start, Ms. Caldwell?"

"What?" With all her breath suddenly gone, the word came out as a whisper.

He bent toward her, matching her whisper in return. "I said, *when could you start?* I was wondering if you're available right away."

"I'm available." She felt hope blooming. Even after her blunder, she might still get the job. She couldn't stop her enthusiasm. "I'm available any time, if you want me."

His eyebrows arched and his lips jerked at the corners, as if he were stifling laughter. Only then did she realize the implications of her answer.

Mortified, she sputtered, "I didn't mean available, like *available*. I meant I can start work any time. Today, if you want."

When he threw his head back and laughed, unguarded mirth melted years from his face. She realized he was probably in his early thirties, rather than forty-plus, as she'd originally thought. An intense desire overwhelmed her. She wasn't fantasizing about his arms around her, like she was before. This time she only wanted to keep him laughing, to smooth away the worry lines on his forehead. Though she barely knew him, she could spend the rest of her life making him happy.

"Earth to Stephanie..." Laurie's voice jolted her back to the present.

"Sorry. What did you say?"

"The movers are outside, asking where to take our things." Laurie rubbed her hands together briskly. "I can't wait to see our rooms."

"Fordham said we'll be in the east wing, but I have no idea where that is. I've never been in this part of the mansion."

A shrill, harsh voice interrupted. "You won't be staying in the east wing. That's for family and guests. You'll be in the west wing with the other employees."

Startled, Stephanie turned to face the intruder. "Carina? What are you doing here?"

She released a grating cackle. "What am *I* doing here? I'm soon to be Branson's wife. I live here. The question is what are *you* doing here?"

"I'm here because Mr. Knight needs me." She jutted out her chin, hoping it wasn't shaking.

"He won't need you for long, so I wouldn't get too comfortable, if I were you."

Even though the same thought had occurred to Stephanie when Bran announced his engagement, hearing the idea from Carina made the blood pound in Stephanie's ears. This woman would never be able to take care of Bran the way he deserved.

Spying Laurie's clenched fists from the corner of her eye, Stephanie put a hand on her rambunctious friend's arm, lest she punch Carina's lights out. "It's okay, Laurie. I've got this."

Stephanie squared her shoulders and faced Carina. "I have a signed contract promising room and board at the Knight estates for my daughter, our nanny, and me, along with my wages for a full year."

Carina's eyes widened, but she retorted, "Don't be surprised if that changes. Contracts are made to be broken."

"I'm afraid Branson Knight's contracts are clad in iron, as you would know if you'd signed your prenuptial agreement. You might be surprised, instead of me."

Carina bared her teeth in something no one would mistake for a smile. "We'll see."

"Ah, Stephanie. You've arrived."

Stephanie turned a grateful, though weak, smile to her rescuer. "Hi, Fordham. Carina was just explaining that our housing assignment has changed from the east wing to the west."

"Really? Branson didn't mention the change to me." Fordham's hand slipped inside his coat pocket and retrieved his cell phone. "Let me check with him."

Carina pushed his phone down. "That won't be necessary, Fordham. You see, Branson gave me permission to choose my suite of rooms, and I've already moved into the east wing."

"The entire east wing?" His chin dipped low, and he gazed at her through bushy gray eyebrows.

"Not the entire wing, of course, but I don't want some noisy kid around."

Fordham went rigid, but Stephanie didn't want Carina's ire aimed at him. "That's okay, Fordham. We'll be perfectly happy in the west wing. To be honest, I'm pretty protective of Ellie. I don't want her around people who don't like children."

"Good choice." Carina didn't object to the intended slight. "You probably know Branson detests children as much as I do. He and I are alike in so many ways."

I can't think of one.

∽

"THAT WOMAN IS A WITCH."

It was probably the nicest thing Laurie had said about Carina in the past two hours since their encounter. She didn't normally employ the colorful language she'd been using to describe Bran's fiancée, and Steph was glad Ellie wasn't around to hear it. She could always count on Laurie to come to her defense, kind of like a protective bull dog. That was one of the reasons she loved her so much. That, and the fact that she'd adopted the two of them as her pet project.

"Yes, I know," she explained for the umpteenth time. "But my boss has chosen to marry her for whatever reason. My job is to support him, no matter what. I don't get to judge him, and I sure don't get to give him advice."

"But what could he possibly see in her?" Laurie asked as she shoved a cardboard box into the closet. "I could understand if he wasn't blind. She's got flawless skin and blond hair."

"And perfect boobs," Stephanie added, wistfully.

"You've got decent boobs." Laurie unloaded books onto the bookshelves in random fashion. "At least they're perky."

"Ha! Perky is another word for tiny. Hers are big, even though she's skinny." Stephanie pulled a pile of books back off the shelf to sort them by genre and size.

"Probably fake."

"Come to think of it, they're bigger than when I first met her, so she must've had some work done." The thought brought a smile to Steph's face. Carina wasn't *naturally* perfect.

"But appearance shouldn't be important to Bran, since he's blind. Right? So what's the attraction?" Laurie ripped the tape off another box.

"She's from a wealthy, well-respected family. She has lots of influence in important social circles."

"Seems like an awful reason to choose a wife."

"She hates children. She said Bran hates children, too." Steph paused to open a book and flip through the pages. "This is yours, I think. Murder mystery. May I borrow it?"

"Sure." Laurie pushed another haphazard group of books onto a shelf. "We're never going to finish if you stop to sort and read the books, you know."

"I know." Steph pushed the books back onto the shelves and grabbed a pair of scissors. "I need a different job. I'll break down the boxes."

"How can Bran hate children? He gives away half his money to help disabled kids. Does that sound like a child-hater?"

"Not really. But he's never asked to meet Ellie, even though I talk about her all the time."

"Oh." Laurie made a weird upside-down smile that showed her teeth.

"*Oh?* What does that mean?"

"It means *oh*, maybe he might like kids in principle, but not in person."

Steph's heart sank into her stomach. "Oh my gosh. You're right. No wonder he was so awkward when I asked if he and Carina were going to have children. And he gives his money all the time, but he never delivers it in person or has anything to do with the kids." She collapsed onto the leather sofa and dropped her head into her hands. *Another reason Bran and I could never be together. Why can't I get it through my thick skull?*

The cushion dipped beside her, and an arm slid around her shoulder. "I shouldn't have said anything, Steph. It doesn't matter. He knows you have Ellie, and that didn't stop him from insisting you move in here. You have an *iron-clad* contract, so it's not like you're going to lose your job."

"I may have exaggerated that iron thing. It's more like a thin, soft metal sheeting."

"Like aluminum foil?" Laurie suggested.

Steph nodded, dread welling deep in her belly. "Truth is, Carina has all the power. She hasn't even signed her prenup. If she convinced him to fire me, we'd be gone so fast our heads would spin, contract or not."

"We can't let that happen," Laurie declared, her mop of tight dark curls bobbing. "We already let our apartment go."

"At least Fordham likes me." Stephanie stood up and started pacing, her boots thudding on the polished wood floor. "All I have to do is get on Carina's good side and keep Ellie away from her and Bran."

"How're you going to get on Carina's good side?" asked Laurie, as she drummed her fingers on the arm of the couch. "I hate to tell you, but I think she hates you."

"For starters, I can't confront her or criticize her. I'll have to talk her up to Bran, whenever I get the chance." She wouldn't let petty jealousy jeopardize her job, her only means of providing Ellie the care she needed. "And I'll swallow my pride and apologize to Carina as soon as I get the chance."

"Ugh. I don't know how you're going to stomach it."

She stopped pacing and turned to face the door, gathering her nerve before leaving to face her boss, who would undoubtedly be grumpy since she missed most of the morning during the move. "I'll do whatever I have to do… for Ellie."

CHAPTER 4

Bran attempted to control his impatience. After all, he was the one who insisted Stephanie move into the estate on Tuesday, rather than wait until the next weekend. He'd been awake since four a.m. Exercise, a shower, and breakfast had only passed two hours of time. He managed to reply to about fifty emails without Stephanie's aid, though he saved them for her to proof. He checked the time... ten o'clock. How long could it possibly take to get settled? He'd sent a team of professional packers to do the work. Most of her things were going into storage, since all the rooms in the estate were furnished. He'd secretly hoped she would report in as usual and let the movers take care of everything without her supervision.

Fordham had already reported Carina's antics, forcing Stephanie out of the preferred rooms. And Branson had blasted her for it, though it barely fazed her. Her behavior served as a warning for what might come, and he was already reconsidering his decision to marry her. If only he could find another way to procure the stocks he needed.

His ringing cell phone interrupted the sound of his fingers drumming on the table. His phone's dulcet feminine voice announced, "Call from Finn Anderson."

"Yeah?" Bran answered with impatience.

Finn's laugh rang in his ear. "Good morning to you, too. How's it going? Has Stephanie moved in yet?"

Since their surprise weekend visit, Finn had been pestering him for details, calling multiple times each day.

"I told you yesterday, she's moving in this morning."

"And Carina? What did she say when you told her Stephanie was moving in?"

"It doesn't matter what Carina thinks," he growled. "This is my house and my life and my decision."

"Ha! That from the man whose brand new fiancée moved into his house without signing a prenup agreement."

"She'll sign one." Bran's fingers tightened into a fist. "If she doesn't, the wedding is off."

"Whatever you say." Finn chuckled. "Are you feeling better about Vegas? Did you invite Carina to go with you?"

"I mentioned the possibility to her. But I may not be able to go." He forced a cough. "My throat's getting scratchy."

"Oh, no you don't! You're going to Vegas, even if you come from the hospital with an IV pole."

As it did every time he thought about the upcoming trip, his heart hammered in his chest. "I think I need more time to prepare."

"We were all planning to meet you in Vegas, but I can come there and fly on your jet, if you like."

Bran wiped his sleeve across his perspiring forehead.

"Maybe that would be a good idea. Carina hasn't committed to going, anyway."

"You never did say why you're getting married. You don't act like you're in love with her."

"Who said love has anything to do with marriage." The subject made Bran angry, but anything was better than the panic he was feeling before.

"I can't believe I'm hearing this from you. I thought you wanted to be different from your dad."

"I *am* different. Phantom Enterprises proves it. I do good things with my money instead of spending every last dime on myself. And my resort business is expanding like wildfire. I'll have even more money to give to our pet project."

"But that's your *business*, Bran. That's only one part of your life. Don't you want to marry for love? You always said how much you admired my folks and their marriage."

"You've got no room to talk," Bran retorted. "You're thirty-two years old and you seldom go on a date."

"That's different." Finn's voice went quiet. "I can't get married. It would be dishonest to do that, when I only have a few years to live."

Bran's throat went tight. He never liked being reminded of Finn's diminished life expectancy. "You could outlive all of us. Aren't you the same man who told me I shouldn't waste a moment of life, because no one is promised to live another day?

"That's not an excuse to hurt someone. I don't want to marry a woman, knowing I'll leave her a widow."

"What about me and Cole and Jarrett? You don't think we'll be hurt when you die?"

"That's different." Finn's words were distorted, like he was talking without moving his lips.

"It's the same thing," Bran insisted.

"How did we get off topic? We were talking about why you should marry for love instead of whatever this is with Carina."

Bran blew out a heavy breath. "It's not that I don't want to marry for love, but I'm a realist. There's only one reason a woman would want to marry me, and that's my money and station. Carina and I laid out all the advantages and disadvantages and made the decision together."

"Gee. Sounds like you're purchasing stock options instead of planning a life together."

"Jeer all you want, but at least we have an honest relationship."

"Honest?" Finn scoffed. "I don't believe that for a second. But let's go back. Who told you no woman would marry you except for your money? Your kind and benevolent father who's given you such a fine example of marriage and family?"

"It doesn't matter who said it." Bran deflected, since Finn had guessed accurately. "Unlike you, I've dated a lot of women, so I've seen it for myself."

"Every one of those women went out with you because you're rich? Not one mentioned being attracted to you for some other reason? Your personality? Or maybe your looks?"

His looks? Bran knew better. Sure, his body was in impeccable shape from his relentless training. Yet he knew his fake eyes were frightening to observe. His father had told him so, as had Carina. More recently, the terrified cries of a baby had confirmed it. His friends tried to shield him from the truth, but Bran had accepted it as one more strike among many. "Yeah, I've heard some women like my muscles. Doesn't mean much to me. Is that a better motivation? Thought it was considered shallow to date someone solely because of their appearance."

Finn made a strangled noise of frustration. "Okay, let's start over. Why are you attracted to Carina?"

Bran didn't hesitate. "She's poised, beautiful, and influential. And she says exactly what she thinks."

"Wait a minute... how do you know she's beautiful?"

"You don't need eyes to detect beauty. I sense the confidence that comes with it. I verify with Fordham, and I've never been mistaken."

"You enjoy spending time with her?"

"Not particularly, but I'm prepared to play my role. So is she."

"What about your personal assistant. In your opinion, is she beautiful, as well?"

Bran knew the answer, but he paused, pretending to consider the question. "She's very confident in a lot of ways, so I'd say she's beautiful. She tries to show deference, but I sense her pride pacing in the background, ready to pounce. Sometimes she can't control it." The thought brought a smile to his face. He loved goading her, keeping her a bit off balance.

"Considered marrying Stephanie, instead?"

Bran's pulse skyrocketed. "I could never ask Steph to marry me."

"Why not?"

"She'd think it was an ultimatum—marry me or lose her job. She might say yes to protect Ellie, but she'd hate me for forcing her into the relationship, taking away her choice. Steph wants love. She believes in it. She's always oohing over some romance book and declaring she won't make the same mistake twice. Said she has no desire to marry again."

"So she was married before?"

"To a real jerk," Bran confirmed. "Cheated on her from day one and left her because he couldn't handle Ellie's CF."

Finn's expletive mirrored Bran's feelings on the matter.

"She deserves someone who'll give her all the love and romance she wants," Bran said.

"And why can't that be you?"

Bran didn't address the most obvious reason. Steph respected him as a boss, but would be disgusted at the thought of a physical relationship. "Like I said, I don't believe in love. Plus, she needs the security my job provides. I'm not going to risk screwing up our relationship."

"Maybe it's you who needs the security Steph provides. Maybe you're afraid to rock the boat."

His breathing stopped. *Is it true? Am I using Stephanie as a security blanket?* He'd spent thirty years proving his independence. He covered his panic with anger. "Maybe you're sticking your nose where it doesn't belong. *Again.*"

"I'm worried about you. Okay? All three of us are. This whole engagement thing doesn't make any sense."

Bran blew all the air out of his lungs. "Fine, I'll tell you the deal, but it stays between the two of us. I own thirty-five percent of Parker-Aston Pharmaceuticals. Carina's agreed to sign over her shares. That gives me fifty-one percent."

The phone went quiet as this information sank in. Parker-Aston's ground-breaking new cystic fibrosis drug would be under Branson's control. "Are you telling me you're going to control the company that makes Decolyde?"

"That's right. Hopefully, we'll be able to reduce the price to something the insurance companies can stomach."

"I can't believe it."

"Satisfied, now?"

"Not quite." Finn dragged the two words out like he was thinking hard. "I suppose you already tried every other source to gain the majority stocks?"

"Yep."

"Here's the obvious question. Why get married? Why not just buy her out?"

"Believe me, I tried. It's the only way around her father's stipulations on the Parker family shares. She can't sell them. On paper, she's giving them to me as a wedding present."

"Out of the goodness of her heart?" was Finn's droll question.

"She'll be getting an equally nice wedding present from me—ten percent of Escapade Resorts."

"What comes after that? A divorce?"

"Can't. Not for three years, anyway. My ownership is only provisional. I can't sell them. If we divorce or she dies, her family has the right to buy back the shares for a third of market value."

"You're really going to marry this woman?"

"On paper. Yes. You sound like I'm walking the plank. I'm getting married to a beautiful woman." *A woman who's willing to play the part of blissful bride, blinded by love to her husband's physical appearance.*

"Bran, we can find another way. Don't sacrifice your happiness for me."

"Not just you. Steph's daughter, Ellie. And the other 15,000 kids with CF, in this country alone."

Finn was silent again.

"Don't think too hard," Bran jibed. "You'll hurt yourself."

Finn answered with a chuckle. "I only have one more question."

"I feel like a genie who's already granted you way more than three wishes."

"Just one more. I promise. It's about Stephanie. You plan to keep her on as your personal assistant indefinitely, even after you're married?"

"Yes," Bran pronounced, with a tone of finality he hoped would end the conversation.

Finn let out a low whistle.

"What now?" Bran barked.

"Wonder what's going to happen when Carina gets jealous of Stephanie."

"Why would Carina be jealous of a paid employee?"

"Branson Knight…" Finn said his name like he was speaking to a child. "Sometimes it's hard to believe you have an IQ of 165."

∼

WHEN STEPHANIE FINALLY ARRIVED, an hour before lunch, Bran could tell something was off. She seemed quieter than normal, only answering direct questions.

His irritation at missing her for most of the morning had faded in the wake of a new worry, emerging from Finn's earlier line of questioning.

Am I really dependent on Stephanie?

"How was the move?" He closed his laptop and leaned forward, turning his face directly toward her so she would know she had his attention. "Sorry about Carina and the room change."

"Our rooms are great. Don't worry about Ms. Parker. It was no big deal. The furniture is finer than anything I've ever had." The conversation drifted into an awkward lull, until she spoke again. "Congratulations on your engagement, by the way. I didn't say it Saturday night. Sorry, I made a scene at the party. It's none of my business."

The tense muscles in his shoulders relaxed as he settled against the back of his desk chair. That's why she was so quiet. She felt awkward about their argument, and they hadn't cleared the air yesterday. In fact, yesterday had been business as usual, as if nothing had happened. Exactly the way Bran wanted it. "No problem. I've already admitted I shouldn't have surprised you like that." He stopped short of telling her the wedding might never happen.

"About Ms. Parker..." She shifted in her chair, her pants squeaking against the leather.

Here it comes. She's going to criticize Carina. To prove he wasn't dependent on Stephanie, he should threaten to fire her in response to any criticism. His stomach churned at the thought. *I only have to threaten—I don't have to go through with it.*

"What about Carina?" He kept his tone and his posture neutral, taking a sip of water from his thermal cup, his muscles tense, as he waited for her response.

"I think she's a great choice."

If he hadn't already swallowed, he would've spewed water everywhere. "You do?"

"Yes." Her voice was firm, as if she had given the matter a great deal of thought. "She's intelligent and attractive. Socially, she's a good match."

"Interesting. You've never said anything nice about her in the past." *Why was Steph complimenting Carina when they'd just had a big confrontation?*

She hesitated, clearing her throat. "Sorry if I wasn't encouraging before. You don't need my approval, but I ought to support you in every decision you make."

"Instead of expressing your honest opinion?" he asked, wryly.

"I changed my mind. Women are allowed to do that, you know. I was harsh and judgmental before. Decided to look at her the way you do."

Who was this woman? Certainly not the Stephanie he'd come to know over the past two years. "And how do I *look* at her? Since I can't *see*," he prodded, hoping to provoke a bit of ire and bring back the old Stephanie.

"You know what I mean. There's a reason you're attracted to Carina. You could've had any woman you wanted, and you chose her."

"Right. Any woman I want. Any woman willing to marry for money."

"Branson Knight!" It was her scolding schoolteacher voice. He'd succeeded in irritating her. "You know, good and well, money isn't your only asset. It's not even your best asset."

"Then what is my best asset?

"I can't believe you're fishing for compliments," she barked, in an obvious sidestep. "How can someone be so generous and caring in one instant, and conceited and selfish in the next?"

He painted a scowl on his face, though he was ridiculously pleased she'd called him generous and caring. He jumped when he felt her standing beside him. He lifted his face toward her. "Why the heavy sigh?"

"Mr. Knight, can I be honest?"

"Always," he said, and he meant it, though he cringed at her formal address.

"I need this job... now, more than ever."

"So?"

"So, you're wasting your time asking me these questions, because I'm bound to say what I think you want to hear."

"Then let me tell you what I want to hear." He stood abruptly, frustration rising in his gut, lapping at the edges of his control. "Just this one time, I want you to have the gall to say it to my face."

"Say what?"

Her tone was small, like a small child cowering at his fury. But he didn't care. Only his father, who cared nothing about him, had ever been straight with him. He couldn't trust anyone—none of his friends, Stephanie, or even Fordham. He faced her and glared in a way he knew must be terrifying. Her feet shuffled away from him.

"I want the truth. That's one thing I get from Carina. She's blunt—honest to a fault."

"I don't know what you're talking about."

Her voice shook, but he continued his tirade. He jerked his hands up to point to his eyes. "Tell me to cover these with shades, so you don't have to see them. Say I'm a monster.

Admit when I get close, you turn your face or shut your eyes to avoid looking."

"No." She'd scrambled four or five feet away from him.

He heard a frightened gasp escape her lips. He ought to back off, but he couldn't. Not when he was so close to hearing the truth. Now, more than ever, he needed someone he could trust implicitly. Why couldn't Stephanie be as brutally honest as Carina?

"The truth, Stephanie. I want the truth, or I want your resignation. I'm tired of playing games. I can handle rejection. I'm used to it."

"I don't understand," she cried, and took a shuddery breath.

He closed the distance between them and gripped her shoulders. "I want you to look into my eyes and tell me what you feel. I can handle whatever you say. What I can't handle is dishonesty."

Her entire body trembled in his grasp. But he knew from the direction of her voice, she hadn't turned her face away.

"I feel... I feel vulnerable. I feel misjudged. And most of all, I feel..."

He waited, holding his breath. *Sickened. Petrified. Go ahead. Say it.*

"Alone... Desperate, unloved, and *alone*."

Her arms shook free of his grip, and her footsteps receded from the room at a running pace. The door slammed shut, the sound reverberating in his ears.

Alone? What does that even mean?

CHAPTER 5

*S*tephanie was still shaking when she made it to the end of the hallway. Fighting a wave of dizziness, she bent over and put her hands on her knees, leaning sideways against the wall for support. What now? It's not like she could run home—she lived here, now. She wiggled her toes inside her well-worn flats, a reminder of her tight budget. An hour ago, she'd declared she would do whatever it took to keep her job. She had to get a hold on her emotions and march back inside his office.

She heaved a deep, calming breath and straightened her spine, pivoting to face the long hallway with his intimidating office door at the end.

"What are you doing?"

Carina's voice made Steph jump out of her skin. She whipped around to face a smug smile.

"Hello, Ms. Parker." Stephanie dipped her head in a gesture she hoped was sufficiently humble. "I was... I was headed to the kitchen to grab some coffee for Bran—I mean for Mr. Knight. Would you like for me to bring you a cup?"

Her eyebrows only twitched a millimeter, but Stephanie knew she'd been caught by surprise. "Certainly. I like it with—"

"A teaspoon of cream. No sugar."

This time, the brows arched high. Carina had to wonder how Steph knew, since they'd never spent any time together. Steph didn't reveal that she'd overheard Carina ordering coffee at the party Saturday night.

"Ms. Parker, I'd like to apologize for my attitude earlier this morning. I'm afraid the stress of the move made me forget my place. I'm loyal to Mr. Knight, so I'm loyal to you."

Her arms folded, slender fingers with perfectly manicured French nails tapping an impatient rhythm. "Forgive me if I think you're lying through your teeth."

With Ellie's needs at the forefront of her mind, Steph bit her sarcastic tongue and forced a fake smile on her face. How she wanted to jab splinters under Carina's impeccable fingernails! "The two of you are obviously in love. I want what's best for my boss, and I'm smart enough to know that's you."

"Or..." Carina lifted a hand to her chin and tapped a finger against her lips. "You want what's best for you, and you're wise enough to know you need me."

Steph let her smile fade. "Either way, I'm committed to support your relationship in any way I can. I'm not claiming to have much influence, but what little I have will be going your direction. I won't criticize you or try to interfere. I promise."

"Believe me, I'm not worried about your influence." A

mocking sneer slid onto Carina's face. "I'll take your promise, though I'm not making any. My moods change so quickly. You know how it is."

Stephanie stood speechless as Carina turned her back and glided down the hallway with smooth strides like a model on a runway. When she disappeared into Bran's office, a chill assaulted Steph's spine. Her Granny used to say when you felt that, it meant someone was walking on your grave. Steph shook her head, turning toward the kitchen. "In my case, Carina would probably dance on it."

⁓

Though she only needed sixty seconds to prepare the coffee, Stephanie took her time. Carina had rejected her peace offering, so Steph needed to be even more careful to stay in Branson's good graces. Unfortunately, she had no idea what he wanted from her.

Did he suspect her attraction for him? Had it been a trick to force her to admit to it? He'd certainly set every nerve-ending on fire when his hands grasped her arms, examining her with magical, x-ray vision.

He had to know. There was no other reasonable explanation. He knew she was hopelessly in love with him. He knew, and he didn't return the feeling.

Balancing the mugs on a tray, she returned to Branson's private office, her expression revealing none of the private turmoil she felt. "I've got your coffee."

Branson paused, his racing fingers on the Braille keyboard. "Great. Here." He patted an empty spot on his desk and returned to his typing, as if nothing had happened between them. As if she hadn't bared her soul to him and experienced agonizing rejection. Okay, maybe she was exaggerating a little bit, but she was irritated he seemed unaffected by the whole ordeal.

Ignoring everyone, Carina sprawled on the leather couch, designer shoes carelessly tossed on the floor, her eyes glued to her phone screen. Steph placed Carina's coffee on the table beside her, with the distinct impression of being invisible. Was this going to be the new norm? Carina lurking in the background while they were trying to work? *I guess she wants to be sure nothing illicit is going on between Bran and me.*

"Stephanie, are you ready to start? I've already recorded two hours of dictation. You'll have to wade through it, because I went back and corrected things."

Was Bran's tone more gentle than usual, or was that Steph's imagination? She slid into her customary chair beside Bran's desk and opened her laptop, diving into the day's work. Soon she was engrossed in transcribing Bran's dictations playing in her earpiece, and at about two p.m., her stomach gurgled to complain of missed lunch.

"Was that your stomach?" asked Bran. "Or a pack of werewolves on the hunt?"

Stephanie pressed her hand on her rowdy abdomen, to no avail. "I guess I'm hungry."

"Let's go to lunch. Mine is getting noisy, too." His hand swept toward the door.

A quick glance around the room revealed Carina was missing. "What happened to Ms. Parker?"

"I can't believe you missed all that." He rubbed the back of his neck. "Didn't you notice when she dragged me outside into the hallway?"

"Kind of. But I had my dictation earpiece in. I was working on those communications you recorded earlier today, and I can't hear much else.

He shook his head as if he had a hard time swallowing her explanation. "She complained she was bored and demanded I take her shopping."

Steph almost laughed out loud, imagining how that went over. "I guess she learned you don't respond well to demands."

As a crooked grin appeared on his face, she warmed all over, knowing she was responsible for it. "Needless to say, Carina is now shopping on her own."

His hand nestled in the small of her back, as if he were the one guiding her down the hallway. She realized if the interior was pitch black, she would totally trust him to lead her through the dark. He never erred.

By the time they were both seated at the table, with lunch in front of them, Stephanie had done her usual thing, describing in detail all about the move and how excited Ellie was that she would have a new home when she returned from school. She was most excited that she would have her own room with a big bed, instead of sharing a bedroom with her mom.

Swallowing his last bite, Bran sat back and pushed his plate away, patting his lips with his napkin. Steph suddenly wondered if Bran's dislike of children extended to hearing stories about them. She talked about Ellie way too much.

"I'm sorry," said Steph. "I always run at the mouth. I can't seem to stop myself."

"I enjoy your stories," he said, politely.

But Steph wasn't fooled. She scrambled to change the

subject. "Are you excited about the Vegas trip? The guys said you love it, and you used to go all the time. I can't picture you there."

"No? Why not?" came his tight-lipped reply.

"I don't know. I guess because you don't drink alcohol or eat rich foods. And I can't see you gambling your money away in Vegas. You're such a..." She let her words fade as his expression hardened.

"Go ahead. Finish the sentence," he urged, his jaw muscles bulging.

"I wasn't being critical," she defended. "I hardly ever drink, either. Maybe an occasional glass of wine with dinner. And I've always admired you for being a practical nerd." *The world's hottest nerd, but I won't say that.*

"Nerd? Is that what you were going to say? Or were you planning to call me a coward?" He threw his wadded napkin on the table.

"Why on earth would I call you a coward?" If Bran hadn't looked so furious, she would've laughed out loud. "You're not afraid of anything. You face the world every single day without the benefit of sight, and look what you've accomplished. No one can call you a coward."

"Stop it! Stop saying what you think I want to hear." He pushed back from the table and stood up. He pivoted behind his chair, his knuckles white as he gripped the back. "You don't have to lie. I'm not going to fire you, Stephanie. I couldn't, even if I wanted to."

She flinched at his wrath, wondering what she'd done to rile him up. For two years he'd been as steady as a rock, seldom displaying any emotion at all. She had no idea how to act around this new Branson. "I'm sorry," she mumbled.

"Do you know why?" he bellowed. "Do you know why I can't fire you?"

"No," she croaked, barely holding her emotions in check.

"Because I made a mistake with you. A huge mistake. I let myself..." He stopped, covering his face with his hands. "I can't believe I'm telling you this."

What was he trying to say? A seed of hope sprouted in her heart. Had he developed feelings for her, after all? Did he regret proposing to Carina?

"What is it? You can tell me," she encouraged, her voice barely above a whisper.

"I'm weak, and I despise weakness." He let his hands fall to his side, as if surrendering to his emotions. "I let myself become dependent on you. So dependent, I can't function without you anymore."

Her heart sank like a lead weight, a surge of revulsion shooting up. "That's it? That's what you're agonizing over? You need me? So I'm like a... like a shoehorn or something? Useful to perform certain tasks? And you're so tough, you can't stand needing a little help?"

"Don't you see?" His face turned red, blood vessels bulging at his temples. "I have to be able to rely on myself and no one else."

"Why?" She was on her feet and in his face. "What's so terrible about needing someone else? We all need each other. That's what life's all about."

"*You* don't," he insisted, though he took a step back. "Your husband left you, and you got a job and took care of yourself and Ellie. You proved you didn't need anyone."

"No." She stomped her foot so hard it stung. "All I proved was I didn't need Jeff. But my life would be a wreck without

Laurie. And if you hadn't given me this job, I don't know what I would've done. I need people now, more than ever."

"But—"

"So stop feeling sorry for yourself. It's…" She struggled to find the appropriate word. "It's unattractive."

For a fleeting second, she thought she saw a smile on his face. "Unattractive? Shouldn't you use a term I'd understand better? What does a blind man know about attraction?"

This was a recurring joke, whenever she used terms associated with sight, which happened all the time. But Steph wasn't ready to let go of her irritation. "Okay, how about this? It's ridiculous."

"Ridiculous? Not sure I like that one better."

"It fits, though."

His hand lifted, rubbing his temples. "I apologize again. I don't know what's wrong with me, lately. I don't usually—"

"Lose control," she finished the sentence for him. "I know. I was thinking the same thing. It's not like you."

He tapped his foot on the floor, squinting like he was deep in thought. "I want you to go with me to Las Vegas."

"What? I can't. I can't leave Ellie for an entire weekend."

"It's one night. We leave on Saturday, come back on Sunday. Laurie will be here with her. And I'll give you an extra week of vacation, anytime you want."

"Seven days? Any time I want them?"

"Yes."

"Just to be clear—those are twenty-four-hour days we're talking about?"

His smile crooked to the left, the way it always did when she caught him off guard. He lifted his hands in surrender. "I'll put it in writing, if you don't trust me."

"What about Carina? I doubt your fiancée will want me to tag along."

For a moment, his expression clouded. Then his grin was back, infectious as ever, dimples flashing. "It'll be fine. Finn decided to fly out with us. I'll say he invited you. I'm sure he'll go along with it. You'll be Finn's date, of sorts. You can dress up and go everywhere with us."

"Wait a minute. This can't possibly work." Stephanie's head swirled. "I'll stand out like a sore thumb with you and your friends. Why do you even want me to go?"

In a blink, his grin was gone. "You can't tell a soul."

"I won't. You know I'd never tell anyone."

His face paled and he reached out to grip the chair again. "I haven't gone anywhere in a while. I get these panic attacks when I leave the property, and you…" He swallowed hard, his Adam's apple bobbing. "You make me feel secure."

Her heart melted like warm butter. After two years, he finally trusted her enough to be vulnerable. In her heart, she'd always known he could never love her. If she could never be more to him than a security blanket, she'd take what she could get.

"Okay. I'll go to Vegas." She saw his tense countenance relax, and added, "But Branson…"

"Yeah?"

"Don't come asking for my help if you're nervous on your wedding night."

~

THE LONGER STEPHANIE was in the room, the more Bran's coiled muscles relaxed. Since she'd promised to go with him to Vegas, his stomach had stopped churning. Though he broke out in a cold sweat when he imagined being inside the casino, he could handle it with Steph close by.

He was feeling so cheery with the turn of events, he offered to let her go an hour earlier than usual.

She hadn't been gone long when someone buzzed the entrance monitor outside his office door.

"Who is it?" he asked, hoping it wasn't Carina.

"It's me."

Dad. His blood pressure shot up.

Reluctantly, Branson pushed a button to open the door. He leaned back in his chair, trying to appear relaxed.

"Good morning, *son*."

His dad had perfected the art of speaking that word in a demeaning tone.

"Father." He used an equally mocking inflection. "Or would you rather I called you Martin, so no one knows we're related?"

"I see you haven't changed. You're as disrespectful as you've always been. And you wonder why we never got along?"

"What do you want?" Bran had no intention of rehashing this argument.

"Why do you think I want something? Can't a father visit his son?"

"A *father* could, but *you* can't."

He could hear his father breathing hard and felt his fury lurking below the surface.

"I came to congratulate you on your engagement. Is that so bad?"

"How do you know about it?"

"You're joking, right? Horace Parker announced it to the world. He probably took out an ad in the New York Times." Martin's disdain was obvious. "The man's a low-life sycophant."

Bran didn't care much for Carina's father, but felt compelled to defend him. "He's no worse than anyone else in your circle of friends."

"Horace isn't in the circle. He's new money. That's why he wants the Knight name."

"Interesting. And I was considering having mine changed to be rid of it."

In the cold silence that followed, his father's breathing grew louder, still.

"Though you take joy in spitting in my face, I've come to offer a wedding present." His father's voice came closer, leaning across the desk.

"Thanks, Dad. I'm sure Carina will make a list."

"I plan to set up a trust fund for your first child…"

Martin left the sentence hanging, as if he had more to say, but decided not to share. Though Bran was curious, he refused to take the bait.

"How do you know my first child isn't already walking around somewhere?"

"Let me clarify—your first *legitimate* child."

"Offer what you want. I'm not planning my life around your desires."

"I do have a few conditions."

"Why am I not surprised?" Under his desk, his hands clenched and unclenched.

"I'm willing to offer a substantial trust fund if you produce a child within the next two years."

"No thanks."

"You don't know how much I'm offering."

"It doesn't matter, Dad. You have to know the value of Escapade's stocks has skyrocketed. I don't need your money, and I don't want it, either." He almost mentioned that his dad's company was currently floundering, but thought better of it.

"You'd turn your nose up at my money? Even 250 million?"

He fought to keep from gasping aloud. "You'd give my son or daughter a quarter of a billion dollars?" Bran couldn't figure out his dad's game. *Could it be I've finally earned his respect? Is this his way of offering an olive branch?*

"It's a trust fund." Martin sounded earnest, at first. "But you'll be the trustee until the child inherits at age eighteen. It has to be a blood-child, of course, not adopted. Your firstborn sighted child."

"*Sighted* child?" Bran's blood boiled, throbbing so loudly in his ears that his father's voice sounded far away.

"Don't worry, complete blindness is really rare."

"Get. Out." He ground the words on his molars.

"Think about it… the ultimate slap in my face, to take my money. Is it so bad to ask for a legitimate grandchild?"

Branson slammed his hands on his desk and stood up, aiming his angry face at his dad. "*Get out!*"

"I'm leaving." Martin's voice receded, but he paused to have the last word before shutting the door behind him. "Think about it."

Bran collapsed into his chair, knowing he would obey his father's last order, no matter how hard he tried not to.

CHAPTER 6

"Mom?" Ellie's voice, scratchy from sleep, floated from her bedroom door, where she stood watching as Stephanie attempted to zip her overflowing suitcase. "Aren't you going to kiss me goodbye?"

Stephanie sighed, abandoning her futile task. She sat on the couch and opened her arms, nodding at Ellie, who immediately ran to her mom. The impact pushed Stephanie backwards and she rolled, with Ellie in her grip, laughing at their game. "I kissed you goodbye last night." She sat up, bringing Ellie with her, and kissed her daughter's forehead. "It's early. Why are you awake?"

"I needed one more kiss." With big brown eyes, soft blond hair in curly disarray, and her lower lip protruding, Ellie's angelic face would've softened the hardest of hearts. "I don't want you to go, Mom. My tummy hurts."

"Probably hurts because you ate too much dessert at dinner last night." Steph kissed the top of her head. "I'll be back tomorrow night. Laurie's going to keep you so busy, you won't even miss me. You get to tour the mansion."

"The whole thing?"

"Yep."

"I thought I couldn't go past the kitchen. What about all those people who don't like kids?"

"It's only two people—Mr. Knight and Ms. Parker—but both of them will be gone, so Mr. Fordham promised to give you a private, guided tour. Wait until you see the library. You're going to love it."

Stephanie glanced at the time—a quarter 'til five. She needed to hurry. "Laurie will give you your breathing treatments, and you have to do them without complaining."

"Do I have to?" she whined. "Can't I skip one since you're going to be gone?"

"Nope, not even one. But if you're good and don't give Laurie a hard time, I'll bring you a present from Las Vegas."

"A Bridgette doll?"

Ellie had asked for the popular doll last Christmas, but Stephanie couldn't spare that kind of money for something frivolous, especially with Ellie's medical costs.

"Not a Bridgette doll, but something really cool. Something you can only get in Las Vegas." Hopefully she'd be able to find something besides a pair of fuzzy pink dice. Maybe an autograph from an Elvis impersonator. Ellie loved to watch the old Elvis movies and sang his songs all the time. She rubbed Ellie's head, ruffling her soft curls. "Now, go to bed. I'll be back before you know it."

As Ellie trudged back to her room, Steph attacked her bulging suitcase with vigor, sitting on it until she wrenched the zipper around the final bend. She was determined to pack every single item that had come in Thursday's surprise delivery. Branson's personal shopper arrived with a rack of clothes and shoes, all with designer labels. Her anxiety about blending in with his wealthy friends overcame her initial guilt about accepting the expensive clothes. In her excitement, she forgot to ask how he knew her sizes.

Relishing the feel of the flowing emerald green, silk blouse she'd paired with leggings and leather boots, she slipped on her new trench coat and hurried out, rolling her suitcase behind her. She navigated the maze of hallways to the rear entry room, where they were supposed to meet.

With only a solitary suitcase waiting beside the door, she breathed a sigh of relief. If Carina had beaten her here, she would've gained more ammunition for criticism, a pastime which seemed to provide her endless pleasure the past three days. Carina hadn't even committed to making the trip to Vegas until she discovered Stephanie was going.

Outside, a driver stood next to a black Suburban, ready to transport them to the airfield. Steph debated whether to wait inside or out, but opted to park herself inside on the marble bench beside the suitcase, which undoubtedly belonged to Bran. No one else would've been awake early enough to have come and gone.

Nervous, she retrieved her laptop and started working her way through Bran's latest business emails. More than twenty messages had arrived during the night, a common occurrence due to business connections across the Atlantic.

"Don't you ever stop working?"

She startled at the voice by her shoulder. "Oh! You scared me, Mr. Anderson."

"Better call me Finn, since you're supposed to be my

date for the weekend." He winked then glanced behind him, like he'd forgotten their conversation might've been overheard.

"Don't worry—she's not here yet." Steph stifled a yawn as she tucked her laptop away. "I honestly can't believe Carina agreed to get up this early."

Finn answered with a yawn of his own as he slumped onto the bench beside her. "I can't believe *I* agreed."

"I'm actually used to it. For the past two years, I've been waking up at five so I can get to work by six thirty. Honestly, I don't mind, though. Most days, he lets me off at four, so I'm home by five and get more time with Ellie."

"Now that you live here, you'll get to sleep in, right?"

"You know Bran better than that." Steph rolled her eyes. "Since I don't have to drive across town, he decided we could start work at 6:00 a.m."

"Of course he did." Finn shook his head. "How do you like the east wing? I bet the view of the rose garden almost makes up for the fact Carina's nearby."

"Carina banished us to the west wing. But we're more than happy there. I don't really want Ellie to come in contact with Carina, for a number of reasons."

"I bet Branson was ticked when he heard about it."

"I hope not. The west wing is still ten times better than where we lived before. I'm doing my best to be supportive, hoping I won't lose my job when he gets married."

"I'd hire you in an instant. You're way more loyal than Bran deserves."

Finn shifted and his hand came to rest on her knee. Steph went rigid and stared at it, as if it was a tarantula, waiting to bite her.

"Uhmm, Bran didn't tell Carina we'd been going out, so we don't have to be physical or anything."

"I know. I came up with the idea to say we hit it off because I found out Ellie has CF. Still, I figure we should at least be at the handholding stage."

She continued to stare at the offending hand on her knee. "That's not my hand you're holding."

He snorted a laugh and removed his hand. "Am I that repulsive?"

"Do all you handsome billionaires fish for compliments?" she retorted, shaking her head. "I'm here to help Bran, and that's all."

"I'm not planning to jump your bones, Stephanie, but you'll have a hard time convincing Carina we're together when you're that stiff around me."

She groaned, knowing he was right. "I can do better. Give me a second." With her eyes squeezed closed, she jutted her hand toward him and focused on relaxing.

"Seriously?"

She looked up to find his wide blue eyes crinkled with humor, her orphaned hand left hanging in the air. "What's the matter? I thought you wanted to hold hands."

"That expression you made—looked like you were about to swallow cough syrup."

"It's not my fault. I haven't held hands since... Well, I don't remember the last time I held hands with Jeff, and we split up five years ago."

"You haven't even been on a date since then?"

"I haven't had the time. Or the energy. And Ellie's constantly in the back of my mind. You get it, right?"

"Yeah, I do," he whispered, sympathy glistening in his eyes

as his arm went around her shoulder. This time his touch didn't feel awkward, and she found herself leaning into him. An ache formed in her chest, and she realized how much she missed the comfort of a man's embrace.

The rumble of wheeled luggage interrupted the moment, and they sprang apart.

"Well, well, well…" Carina's sarcastic voice rent the tranquil air. "Seems the lovebirds are getting an early start."

"Lovebirds?" Branson's thick brows knitted over bright blue eyes that seemed to sear Steph's skin. She couldn't help feeling guilty, as if she'd somehow betrayed him.

"We had to do something to pass the time." Finn met Carina's sarcasm with an equal dose, his arm returning to Steph's shoulder. "We've been waiting a while, since the two of you were late."

"Only one of us was late," Bran retorted, as Carina's face reddened. "I was here early but, as I suspected, Carina overslept. If I hadn't banged on her door, she'd still be in bed."

"Like any reasonable person," Carina snapped. "You didn't even give me time to finish getting ready." Her hand snaked up to her blond tresses, which were pulled back in a sleek ponytail instead of her normal, perfect array of beach waves. Stephanie thought she looked better—less artificial—but doubted Carina would appreciate hearing her opinion.

"We don't have to go," Bran growled. "In fact, let's call the whole thing off. Finn can go by himself."

"Fine by me," Finn retorted, much to Stephanie's surprise. Hadn't he been the one who organized the whole trip in an effort to get Bran out into the world again? Finn stood, grabbing the handle of his bag and offering a hand to help

Stephanie up. "Steph and I can take my jet. I'll bring her back tomorrow."

"*No.*" The blood vessels on Bran's face bulged like his head was about to explode. "Stephanie and I have work to do."

"You already promised she could go to Vegas with me," said Finn, not bothering to hide his grin. "So, if you want to get any work done, you'll have to come along and do it on the plane." His fingers gripped Steph's elbow, propelling her, stumbling in confusion, toward the door.

"We're going in *my* jet," Branson pronounced, striding past them. Without pausing he spoke over his shoulder. "Carina, you can come if you want or stay here. It makes no difference to me."

"Branson, wait." She trotted after him, dragging her huge rolling suitcase behind her. "I'm coming."

Finn whispered in Steph's ear, "Have you ever noticed Carina talks through her nose?"

Steph muffled a laugh with her hand. "No. But it's going to drive me crazy now that you've mentioned it."

※

STEPHANIE HARDLY HAD time to enjoy the experience of flying on a private jet, since Branson kept her so busy working. At first Carina flirted with Finn, laughing loudly and complimenting everything from his accent to his muscles. When Bran not only didn't respond with jealousy, but appeared not to notice, Carina flounced over to a seat in the back and sulked. Once Carina abandoned her efforts, Finn reclined his chair and went to sleep.

"Bran?" Steph spoke in a lowered tone, glancing over her shoulder at Carina, whose slack mouth produced soft snores.

"Yes?" He took off his headphones.

"I've never been to Vegas. I don't even know what to do. So, I'm thinking, since I won't fit in anyway, I might just watch from the side."

"No worries." He waved his hand. "It's a high-roller, charity event. Each participant pays a ridiculous entry fee that comes with a certain number of dollar credits. Yours is already paid. Everyone plays games anywhere on the floor until their credits are gone."

"All the money goes to charity?"

"Not hardly," he scoffed. "But a percentage does. At the end of the night, whoever has the most money is declared the winner, and a million goes to the charity of their choice."

"You've done this before, I guess. Have you ever won?"

"I did, once. But Finn's won multiple times. He's the king of blackjack. But the big money comes from the craps table. Everyone will be there by the end of the night."

"Maybe you should try to get your entry fee back for me, since I can't play. I'll be staying with you to calm your nerves. Isn't that the whole reason I came?"

He tilted his head closer, though Carina was too far away to hear, even if she'd been conscious. "Yes, it is. But I only need you for the first hour or so. I plan to lose my money early and escape to my room. Then you'll be free to try your hand at anything you choose."

"I don't think that's going to make Finn very happy." She glanced at Finn, his feet propped up and a cap pulled down over his eyes. Something told her he wouldn't let Branson get away that easily.

"Maybe..." Bran drummed his fingers on his legs, twisting his mouth to the side. "I expect Finn'll be having too much fun with Cole and Jarrett to care if I slip away early. It's enough that I came. They won't be expecting me to be with them the entire time."

"Ah. That's a good thing. Carina will be less suspicious if I spend most of my time hanging out with Finn and the guys instead of you."

His fingers froze. "Yeah. About that." He shifted in his seat like he had a sudden knot in his back. "You don't have to spend the whole time with Finn after I'm gone. Carina can't be jealous when I'm not around. You can play any game you like—slots, roulette, poker, craps, whatever."

"Oh, I don't mind being with Finn. He's actually fun."

"Great." Bran's lips stretched into a weird, flat smile. "I'm glad you like him."

～

The jet landed, and a stretch limo picked them up, whisking them off toward the heart of Las Vegas. Steph had seen the strip on TV, but never in person.

"Wow," she remarked to no one in particular. "I can't believe there are so many people on the streets on a Saturday morning. I would've thought they'd all be in bed, sleeping off a Friday night hangover.

"They are," Finn confirmed. "Tonight, there will be twice this many people."

"You've honestly never been to Vegas before?" Carina's question might've been a polite inquiry, had her tone not been dripping with disdain.

"I've never had a desire to go." Stephanie lifted her chin. "I don't gamble. But the hotels are pretty amazing."

"The shows are spectacular," said Carina. "Too bad you won't get to see any. Bran doesn't like them, of course."

"I don't mind if I don't see a show on this trip," Steph hurried to assert. "Maybe some other time."

"I can take you to see a play in New York, instead." Finn's hand slipped over to rest on her knee. "How about weekend after next?"

Steph fumbled for a polite response. "I... uh... I guess it depends if I can get enough time off."

"We should go today," Bran blurted out. "We could hit a matinee. There's plenty of time. Our tournament doesn't start until seven p.m." Three sets of eyes stared at him in surprise. "What?" he asked, into the awkward silence.

"You told me you hate going to shows." Carina narrowed her eyes, her hands balled into tight fists.

"He does hate them." Finn clicked his tongue in disapproval. "He's probably planning to send the rest of us to a show and hide out in his room. It won't work, Bran."

"I wasn't planning to hide out," Bran objected, looking miserable.

Steph's heart clenched in her chest, seeing Bran so out of his comfort zone. She knew he probably wanted to be able to sit and listen to someone sing for a few hours, rather than have hundreds of voices in his ears, coming from every direction. She hadn't been to a casino, but she knew from television they were noisy and distracting. Bran didn't know, but she'd brought something special along, a surprise she hoped would make the whole experience better.

"I think it's an awesome idea." Steph shook her finger in

Finn's face. "You have no business giving Bran a hard time. He heard his fiancée wanted to see a show and decided to take her. What's wrong with that? Aren't there some famous singers who perform in Vegas? Bran could enjoy that as much as any of us."

"Fine." Finn pulled out his cell. "I'll text Jarrett and tell him to get us six tickets to a matinee."

Stephanie wasn't sure what was going on. Instead of a repentant expression, Finn looked so smug she wanted to slap him. *If he keeps this up, I might do it.*

CHAPTER 7

The limousine pulled to a stop, and the door flung open. "Welcome to the Grand Laurencia, where good times are had by all," said an irritatingly jovial hotel employee.

As everyone piled out of the limo, Bran stayed behind, trying to slow his racing heart. He felt someone slide beside him on the seat.

"You don't fool me," Finn said. "Not in the slightest."

"I don't know what you mean." Bran found his cane and checked to be sure his sunglasses were sitting straight on his nose.

"We've come out here together at least twenty times, and you refused to go to a single show. Not even when we got complimentary front row tickets to hear Donovan Ray sing."

"So what?" Bran scooted toward the exit, but a hand on his shoulder held him back.

"So, isn't it funny that you suddenly insist on squeezing in a show right after I invited Stephanie to New York. And don't try to tell me this has anything to do with Carina."

"You're trying to steal the best PA I've ever had." Bran gripped his cane so hard his hand hurt.

"I was only asking her on a date, not stealing her."

"Same difference," Bran shook off his grasp and climbed outside, but Finn caught him and spoke in his ear.

"Weren't you the one who said I should start dating?"

"Not *Stephanie*," Bran mumbled from the side of his mouth. "So, back off."

"I'll be happy to back off," said Finn, "as soon as you admit you're in love with Stephanie."

"I'm not in love with her." He didn't love Stephanie. He *needed* her. Like his body needed air and water. He couldn't survive without her. Finn would never understand the difference.

"Just tell her you love her and see what she says. What's the worst that could happen?"

He didn't want to dream about something that could never happen. "It won't work. We've been over this. I'm marrying Carina. End of story."

Bran grabbed the elbow Finn bumped against him and walked beside him. His cane found the curb, and as he stepped up, Finn whispered in his ear, "Okay. But if you're not in love with her, she's fair game."

Before Bran could blast him with a furious retort, Finn was gone.

"Bran! You made it." Cole wrapped him in a hug, and Bran squirmed, trying to get away. Cole laughed. "Nobody thinks it's weird for me to hug you, Bran. No one's even paying attention."

"You know I don't do hugs. Has nothing to do with what anyone thinks."

Nevertheless, the arm remained around his shoulder, ushering him through the doorway onto the plush carpet. Inside, Bran's heart rate kicked up another notch, as the noises of the casino in the back mixed with voices from every direction. *Why did I agree to come? I can't do this.*

"Hi, Cole." Stephanie's voice came from his left, and he felt her arm wrap around his. "I'm going to steal Mr. Knight away for a minute. One of his managers has a crisis situation. You know how it is." She tugged Branson to the side. "They've already checked us in, so we can go straight to the elevator. But I have a present for you." She slid something into his hand.

"What's this?" He probed the small plastic piece.

"It's my dictation earpiece. I've got the microphone attached to my scarf—a beautiful designer scarf, thanks to you. And the transmitter is in my new purse, which, by the way, is worth more than one of the smaller states."

As her plan became clear, a smile fought its way onto his lips. He placed the discreet receiver in his ear. "If this works, I'll buy one you could trade for Alaska."

Her gentle chuckle played clearly in his ear, drowning out the other sounds. "You might have to get your three cohorts to help purchase that purse."

With the earpiece in place, the room sounds were muffled in that ear, and he found he could put that noise in the background.

"Is it okay?" Steph sounded anxious. "You can toggle it until it's not too loud or too soft. If anyone notices, you can say you're wearing an earplug in that ear."

"No, it's good. I think it's going to help."

"Great." Her breath whooshed out. "I had my fingers crossed."

A band tightened around his chest. He didn't deserve someone so good. "I owe you, big time. I think my blood pressure's already dropped."

Her hand squeezed his arm. "You're going to be fine. It's like riding a bike. You need to get out and have fun with your friends again. And with Carina. This way, no one will know I'm helping you."

"What about you? Are you still nervous about gambling?"

"I'm only nervous about fitting in," she said, from the corner of her mouth.

"Branson! Jarrett's here." Carina's call cut through the ambient noise. "We're all waiting on you and Stephanie." Something about her voice was already getting on his nerves. It was going to be a long twenty-four hours. And a long three years after the wedding.

∽

Since she hadn't muted her microphone, Branson got to hear Stephanie's exclamation when she opened the door to her suite. Of course, she shouted so loudly, the other four heard it as well. "Jiminy Cricket! This place is amazing! There's a swimming pool in my living room."

Carina made a sarcastic remark about her lack of sophistication, but it didn't dampen Steph's enthusiasm.

Branson's room was sandwiched between Stephanie and Finn. Carina had made a point of demanding her own room, which was fine with Bran. In fact, he had no plans to share a bedroom or bathroom with Carina, even after marriage. Certain things had to remain private, and those things would be impossible to hide in close quarters. In particular, he hadn't let anyone see him without his prosthetic eyes since his teen years. Carina would undoubtedly run screaming at the sight, and the marriage plans would disintegrate, along with his opportunity to control Parker-Aston Pharmaceuticals.

Inside his room, Bran made a methodical examination, to learn the location of the furniture and fixtures in the living area and bedroom. He normally had excellent spatial recall, though he was somewhat out of practice. In his early-to-mid twenties, when he traveled frequently, he could navigate a room flawlessly after a sixty-second inspection. Now, he had to circle the room twice and backtrack, as well, before he felt comfortable.

Lunch time had been moved up, thanks to his suggestion that they attend a matinee. *What was I thinking?* But he knew the answer. He didn't want Steph to visit Finn in New York. No matter how much devotion Stephanie displayed, Bran knew she could be enticed away from him, especially by someone like Finn. Not that Finn would ever do such a thing on purpose. But Finn had everything Bran had—money—and all the things he didn't—good looks, confidence, charm, and quick wit, in addition to sight. What's more, Branson could never stand in the way of their happiness if they were to fall in love. That's why he had to prevent it from happening.

Unpacking his suitcase, he ran his fingers across the small Braille labels Stephanie had used to organize his pants and shirts so he could dress without her aid. He'd have preferred having her come in and lay out his clothes, as she did at home, but she insisted Carina wouldn't be pleased to discover them in his room together.

He'd changed clothes and splashed some water on his face, when Finn rapped on his door. "Hurry up, Bran. We've got a lunch reservation in ten minutes."

He took a deep breath and opened the door. "I don't hear anyone else out here."

"Cole and Jarrett went down to arrange a limo. We don't have time to walk to the restaurant."

"What about Steph?"

He heard the sound of a door opening as Steph's voice sounded in his ear. "I'm ready. Do I look okay?"

Finn whistled. "You look amazing, with a capital A."

Bran fumed, wishing he could compliment her, as well.

"Bran bought this dress for me," said Steph. "In fact, he bought every outfit I packed in my suitcase."

"It's not the dress that looks amazing. It's what's in it." Finn's voice grew louder in Bran's receiver, as if his mouth was close to Steph's microphone. *Is he planning to kiss her? Right here in front of me?*

A door rattled across the hallway. "I hate being rushed," Carina announced. "I barely had time to change clothes, much less fix my makeup. I look atrocious."

"I think you look amazing," Bran said, adding a wink to show he was teasing. "With a capital A."

Carina gave a haughty laugh. "Bran, your opinion isn't worth anything. What do you think, Finn?"

Bran felt like he'd been slapped in the face. He and Carina often jested in this manner, despite his lack of vision. He usually complimented her on the scent she was wearing or the softness of her skin, while throwing in a quip about how he'd never seen a more gorgeous woman. She'd never been so insulting in the past.

With a knot in his stomach, he realized their relationship was going to require a lot of work to make it last for three years. Though they agreed to marry for business reasons, they had to at least get along, or she would leave him anyway. Up until now, she'd always acted as if she were attracted to him, despite his appearance. But perhaps her attitude had been merely that… an act. He couldn't fault her for it, since he was guilty of the same.

Finn responded with what Bran recognized as a sidestepping accolade. "You've seen yourself in the mirror, Carina. You don't need me to tell you how beautiful you are."

Carina cooed a thank you, apparently unaware of the slight.

"Let's go. They're waiting for us." Finn moved down the hallway in the direction Branson remembered the elevator being. Bran counted his steps so he could easily find his room on his own if he returned by himself. On the ride down, Stephanie chatted about how nice her room was and the incredible view from her balcony, thanking Bran profusely.

"I'm glad you like it." Bran basked in her appreciation.

"Of course, Finn paid for Stephanie's room," Carina sniped. "No reason you should be taking credit, Branson."

It happened to be a true statement, though Branson intended to rectify the situation.

"I'm sorry, Finn." Anxiety flooded Steph's tone as she apologized. "I assumed Branson had paid, you know, since we worked the whole time we were on the plane. I should've realized—"

"No worries, Steph. Branson and I would never quibble over a few thousand dollars." Finn followed up his declaration with a noisy kissing smack, so loud he undoubtedly wanted Bran to hear it. "We reserve our battles for more important matters."

The gesture apparently rendered Stephanie speechless for the rest of the ride down, but Bran was so irritated he didn't need her voice to allay his nerves. As the elevator doors opened to the boisterous lobby, Bran could only think he needed a moment to pull Finn aside and finish their earlier conversation.

Though people customarily gave him a wide berth when he was using his white cane, he didn't attempt to navigate the bustling crowd alone. He hated hanging onto someone's arm, but noise from every direction bombarded his ears, making it difficult to walk alongside a person and maintain a steady distance, utilizing only the sound of their voice.

Fortunately, Stephanie came to the rescue, murmuring directions through the receiver in his ear. "Wanna walk with me?" She tugged on his elbow, but released his arm as they started to move. "You're doing great, Bran. Straight ahead. We're probably twenty feet from the lobby exit. There. Did you hear the doors open ahead of us? Traffic outside?"

"Got it. Thanks." He walked with more confidence.

"Are you going to wear sunglasses the whole time we're here? Even inside the show and the casino?" she asked.

"That's the plan. Strangers are more comfortable when I wear them." He stepped outside, his eardrums battered by the din of car motors and horns, while the acrid exhaust fumes assaulted his nose.

"You shouldn't wear them."

"What?" he asked.

Resentment bubbled out in her words. "The sunglasses. You shouldn't wear them. I like seeing your eyes."

Her remark left him slack-jawed. "Why would you say that about these fake eyes?"

"Because it doesn't matter what other people think. Cole's wearing a bright green mechanical hand today. It looks like something from a science fiction movie. A few people stare, but most don't even notice. Jarrett can't hide his limp, but he doesn't seem to care."

"I'm not hiding my blindness," he argued. "I'm wearing dark glasses and carrying a white cane. I'm sure plenty of people are staring."

"I think you're hiding *behind* your blindness. You use that cane and those glasses like a wall, to keep yourself from having to interact with sighted people. I'm pretty sure, if you didn't have those dark glasses on, no one would even realize you're blind."

"But I *am* blind. That's why I'm more comfortable at home, around things I'm familiar with."

Their argument was interrupted when Jarrett tapped his elbow. "Hey, that's our limo across the circle. There were too many cars for it to get any closer."

"We're coming," Steph answered and grabbed Bran's arm, walking him ahead. "I guess I should've let Carina do this. She's waiting at the car, giving me the stink-eye."

"I don't think Carina cares about me one iota. She seems

to want Finn's attention, not mine." He thought the same of Stephanie, though he didn't say it.

"No. Carina's in a huff because you ignored her on the plane. You need to be nice and give her some attention. I think she's insecure, though I can't imagine why. She's got a perfect body. Perfect hair. Perfect teeth. Perfect everything."

"I'm sure she's no more beautiful than you."

"I'll take that as a compliment, though my body is far from perfect." *Of course Branson has no idea what I look like.* "But you need to be saying those sweet things to your fiancée instead of me. I know you can't pick up body language cues. Let me tell you, hers are screaming she feels neglected."

"I didn't realize she was going to be high maintenance," he mumbled.

"Don't give me that," Stephanie snapped, her voice loud enough to make him flinch. "Requiring an occasional kind word and caring touch hardly qualifies as high maintenance."

Hadn't he done that for Carina? Had he been so caught up with anxiety he'd been thoughtless and rude to his fiancée? He wasn't in love with her, but he hadn't meant to treat her badly.

"The door's open," said Cole as they arrived. "Crawl in the back."

Bran felt for the overhead opening and ducked inside. "Where's Carina?"

"I'm back here, with Jarrett and Finn," she replied.

"Well someone better move over and make room for me," Bran edged his way toward her voice. "I'm sitting by my fiancée."

Carina giggled. "Sorry, guys. One of you has to give up your seat."

"Well done." Stephanie murmured encouragement in his ear.

He settled beside Carina and reached over to hold her hand, receiving an affectionate squeeze in return. "You smell nice today. What perfume are you wearing?"

"Monet." She practically purred. "It's your favorite. Remember? From L'eau du Paris?"

So Stephanie had been correct. Her twenty-second counseling might've saved his relationship with Carina. It also confirmed what he'd told Finn. Stephanie had no romantic feelings toward him. She was simply a loyal employee, doing her job.

CHAPTER 8

Stephanie thought Branson seemed more relaxed as lunch progressed. He'd certainly taken her advice to heart, dousing Carina with affection and hanging on every word she said. Perhaps Steph's counsel had been too effective. The green monster of jealousy was clawing at her insides.

She slipped her hand in the outside pocket of her purse to turn off the transmitter. No need for it in the quiet booth in the rear of the restaurant. Besides, Bran didn't appear anxious at all. Fumbling for the transmitter controls, she fought against a sudden bout of stress. Without a sense of purpose, and isolated at the end of the booth, she felt awkward and out of her element. *Why did I come? I don't belong with these people.*

"Whatcha got there?" Finn's voice made her jump out of her seat.

"Nothing." Her hands trembled as she tucked her purse to her side.

Finn's eyes narrowed and his hand gripped her arm. He bent close and murmured in her ear. "I'm disappointed, Stephanie. I like you, but I can't let you get away with spying on one of my closest friends."

"I'm not a spy," she whispered, frantic to make him understand. "I would never do that to Branson."

"Then why do you have a recording device in your purse? You can't lie to me. I saw you turn it on when you came out of the hotel room."

"Keep your voice down," Steph begged in a desperate whisper. "Follow me to the restrooms, and I'll explain." She scooted out of the booth with a remark about freshening up, but the others didn't even pause their conversation.

Finn caught up with her as she rounded the corner. "Okay, I'm listening. You've got sixty seconds to explain."

"It's not a recorder. It's a transmitter." Steph spread open her purse pocket to expose the device. "Bran has a receiver in his ear. The microphone is right here." She used her finger to point at the mic, hidden discretely in the folds of her scarf. "But no one knows. Please don't say anything."

Finn's eyes widened, and he rested his shoulder against the wall. "A microphone? You don't say. What for?"

"So he can hear my voice over the crowd. To keep him calm when the noise makes him crazy."

"Hmm." Finn tilted his head. "Branson's idea?"

"No. Mine. Someone had to look out for him." She glared at Finn as adrenaline shot through her system, turning her anxiety into fury. She tapped her finger against his chest. "*You.*"

"What?" He staggered back a step and lifted his palms toward her.

"*You're* supposed to be his best friend, but you pushed him to make this trip. It's way beyond his comfort zone, and you know it. You should've started with a ski vacation or rock climbing—something outside and physical. Instead, you bring him to a place where a thousand people are talking at once and a million bells are ringing from every direction. Don't you know how awful that is for a blind person?"

Finn had the good grace to grimace with shame. "We didn't force him to come. He could've said no."

"Not if he wanted to keep his pride with the only people he cares about in the world. You gave him no choice but to come. I'm only trying to keep him from having a panic attack. If that happens, he'll probably go back and hole up inside his mansion and brick the doors closed."

"I think I understand." Finn's mouth widened in a slow grin, as if her whole lecture was a comedy routine.

"I don't think you do," she retorted, hands on hips. "If you understood, you'd be shaking in your boots and watching your back. Because if this trip goes badly and you screw him up for the rest of his life, *you're* going to answer to *me*."

～

STEPHANIE AVOIDED Finn as much as possible for the rest of lunch, claiming to feel a draft and persuading Cole to trade places with her. She didn't join in the conversation on the way to the matinee show, keeping to herself in the front corner of the stretch limo. While Carina prattled on about the upcoming concert with Bran's rapt attention, the other three put their heads together and conspired, with frequent glances toward Steph. At the concert, Jarrett spoiled her plan to sit by herself on the end of the row.

"Hello, Stephanie." He slipped into her spot so quickly she almost sat in his lap. He patted the seat beside him. "We haven't had much time to get to know each other."

"That's not going to work, Jarrett."

"Why not? Is it because I have a limp?" His deep brown eyes twinkled with humor.

"I don't know what Finn said about me, but I'm basically done with all three of you."

"Won't Carina be suspicious? You're supposed to be Finn's date."

"She didn't think I was good enough for Finn, anyway. As long as I stay away from her man, she won't care." Stephanie made a grand show of opening her playbill and studying the inside, though the words didn't register in her brain.

"If it makes any difference, I wanted to take Bran skiing, instead."

She glanced from the corner of her eye, without turning her head. "Why didn't you?"

His shoulders shrugged. "I got outvoted. Slopes are always crowded in March. Spring Break, you know? Then Finn got wind of this charity event, and the rest is history."

"I think it's a bad idea," she insisted, pushing her jaw so far forward it ached.

"I promise it won't be that bad inside the casino. Finn told me about your cool microphone setup to help Bran with the jitters. But there's something you don't know about Bran."

"What?" Steph eyed him with suspicion. After spending

almost every day with Branson Knight for the past two years, she'd wager it was actually the other way around.

"When Bran comes to Vegas, he always has a few drinks."

"*N-o. Wa-y.*" She pronounced each of the words with two syllables. "Bran doesn't drink alcohol."

"I guess you didn't notice he had a piece of pie at lunch."

"Jiminy Cricket!" She exclaimed so loud the lady in front of her turned her head to look. "You're right. Why would he do that? He's so careful with everything he puts in his body."

"It was always his way of saying *what happens in Vegas stays in Vegas.*"

"Can't believe Bran gets drunk."

"Not drunk," Jarrett clarified. "Not Bran. He never loses control. His limit is two drinks. Any more than that, and he'd probably be dancing on the tables. He's got low tolerance, that's for sure."

"So what if Branson has a drink or two? What's the big deal?"

"A couple of drinks, and he'll be completely relaxed. You won't have to worry about a panic attack."

"I'll believe it when I see it." Steph gave him her best, you're-lying-through-your-teeth glare. "I don't see him purposefully using alcohol to relax. He could've taken a prescription anti-anxiety med, and he refused. He doesn't like drugs of any kind. Says they don't like him, either."

As Jarrett chuckled at her comment, Cole dropped into the seat on her other side. "Hey. I've come to plead for your forgiveness."

"What did you do?" Steph whipped around, suddenly realizing her boss hadn't taken his seat yet. "Where's Branson? Have you done something to him?"

"Hold on, little lady," Cole drawled in an exaggerated Texas accent. "Bran's fine. He's waiting for Carina to come out of the ladies' room."

She sagged in her seat. "Okay. Then what are you apologizing for?"

"Not *what*, but *who*. I'm apologizing for Finn."

"If Finn wants forgiveness, why isn't he asking for it, himself?"

Jarrett chuckled. "Finn's a coward. He's making Cole do his dirty work."

"That's true. He's afraid of you," Cole agreed, "because you threatened to tear him to little pieces and feed him to the dogs." His grin was contagious, and Stephanie fought to remain stern.

"I meant what I said, but my threat was tied to whether Finn and you guys push Branson into a full-blown panic attack. My job is to protect my boss. If that means I have to turn someone into dog food, that's what I'll do." She bobbed her chin to punctuate her words, hoping the matter was settled.

"Your commitment runs a bit beyond your job description. You're so passionate... it's almost as if you have feelings for him." Cole lowered his voice as Bran and Carina made their way down the row of seats. "Wouldn't you say?"

"No, I would *not*," she spewed between her gritted teeth as her cheeks grew red hot.

"Whatever." He waggled his eyebrows, still sporting that irritating grin. "Finn says he's sorry he accused you of spying."

Right on cue, Finn appeared at the far end of the row, wearing a sad puppy face, hands folded together in supplication under his chin. Stephanie covered her smile with her hand, and turned her head. "Fine," she mumbled from the side of her mouth. "Tell Finn he's forgiven, for now. But he's on probation, and so are the two of you. One wrong move and..." She stretched her mouth and used her finger to mime slicing her neck, sending Cole and Jarrett into fits of laughter that had the surrounding audience members turning their heads.

Jarrett was the first to control his mirth. "Bran will be fine. We're on the same side, you know. We all want what's best for him."

"Okay." Her tension melted as she realized, for all their teasing, the guys truly cared about Bran. Surely they wouldn't push him so far that he got hurt.

"And sometimes," Cole leaned in to whisper, "we know what's best for him, better than he does."

The lights dimmed and the music began to play before Stephanie got a chance to ask him to explain that cryptic statement.

CHAPTER 9

Branson tapped the device in his ear. He hadn't heard a peep out of Steph since sometime during lunch. Either it quit working, or she'd turned it off. Whatever the reason, he was irritated. Not that he needed her voice to prevent a panic attack. Truth be told, his anxiety had faded as the day progressed.

He enjoyed the show more than he expected, and was laughing and joking with his buddies as they returned to the limousine. Everyone seemed surprised when Bran suggested stopping at the Bellagio so Carina could watch the famous fountains.

As Bran leaned on the railing, listening to the classical music that accompanied the beginning of the water show, Finn edged beside him. "Stephanie seems captivated by the fountains."

"Ah. Glad she likes it." Bran kept his expression neutral, though Steph had been his major motivation for suggesting the show. "I assume Carina's enjoying herself?"

"Ha! You can't fool me, Bran. You could care less whether Carina likes it or not. However, I believe you can congratulate yourself for the rapturous expression on Stephanie's face."

"Humph," he grunted, wishing he could see her face for himself. He'd read books describing rapture. Were her lips parted? Were her eyes glazed? Were her pupils dilated?

"I'm thinking you could find *other ways* to make her look rapturous, and it might be a lot more fun for both of you."

As Finn let out a hearty chuckle, Bran swung his fist toward his stomach, but only caught the edge of his shirt. His missed punch only prodded Finn to laugh harder. Bran would find a way to get even, eventually. He smiled, remembering the practical jokes he and his buddies had exchanged over the years. Feeling comfortable and relaxed, he considered his friends might've been right about the ill effects of shutting himself off from the world.

Bran was even beginning to look forward to the casino event, though he didn't relish the head-splitting battery of sounds that came with it. He'd tried ear plugs in the past, but then he was totally out of any conversations that took place inside the casino. Hopefully, Stephanie's microphone trick would be the answer to that dilemma, especially if she stuck close and repeated the bits of dialogue that were drowned out by the commotion.

Though Bran had thought to blow his tournament money quickly and escape upstairs to his suite, a persistent inner voice now enticed him to stay and compete until the bitter end. And part of him wanted Stephanie to see him win.

THE LIMO MADE slow progress down the strip, in stop-and-go traffic, while Carina's high-pitched chatter continued, grating on his nerves. Some movie star had married some rock singer, and now they were getting a divorce. Blah, blah, blah.

Fortunately, his fiancée had never been a night owl. He fully expected she'd be asleep by midnight at the latest. Between the lulling vibration of the limousine and sheer boredom at Carina's monologue, Bran had to fight against sleep, even on the short drive back to the hotel.

"Hey, Bran. Can you hear me?"

At last, Stephanie's microphone was back on. He smiled and pointed upward with his left thumb in a motion he hoped was discreet enough to escape notice by the others. Steph was sitting somewhere on the opposite side.

"You seem to be fine without my help," her soft voice continued. "Do you want the microphone off or on when we go into the casino tonight?"

He frowned and gave a thumbs down.

"You want it off?"

He shook his head and mouthed the word *on*.

"You want it on?"

He reversed his thumb, lifting it up in the air to be certain she understood.

"What are you doing, Bran?" Carina's elbow jabbed in his ribs. "You're not even paying attention, are you?"

"Yes, yes. I'm listening." He quickly folded his hands in his lap.

"Then what was I talking about?" she challenged.

Bran thought hard, in an effort to recall a single word she'd spoken.

"Cancer," he declared, triumphantly. "You were talking about tumors."

"Not tumors. Turmeric. It's supposed to be really good for you."

"It is," he confirmed. "It's anti-inflammatory. Good for your heart. I have it every morning in my eggs."

"You never listen to me!" Her voice went shrill and all the other conversations inside the limo paused in the wake of her outburst. "That's exactly what I said, and you ignored me. I have a master's degree in finance, but you treat me like a child."

"I know you're smart, Carina—"

"You always talk down to me," she snapped. "And you keep secrets. You'd rather talk to your hick secretary about your business than ask my opinion. How do you think that makes me feel?"

"I thought it would make you feel like my fiancée instead of my personal assistant." Bran's jaws clenched with such strength he could barely force the words between his lips. He knew everyone in the limo was listening, but he was beyond caring. After the all-day effort he'd made to give Carina his undivided attention, this is how she repaid him? She was a leech. She demanded so much she sucked all the energy out of him. How had he ever thought their relationship would be a mutually-beneficial business deal?

The limo stopped and the door opened. "Welcome to the Grand Laurencia, where good times are had by all."

"Speak for yourself," Bran said, under his breath.

"When will we eat dinner?" Stephanie asked no one in particular, as the group, minus Bran and Carina, rode the elevator back downstairs. She'd had enough time to freshen up and change into a backless cocktail dress. She was prepared to return to her room and change clothes if she had to, though Finn assured her she wouldn't be overdressed for the event. As if to make a point, the three men were wearing tuxedos, though Cole wore his with cowboy boots. In a moment of jealousy, she wished she had on comfortable boots instead of teetering on five-inch heels, no matter how beautiful her designer sandals were.

"I don't know what the schedule is," Cole replied. "Carina kind of threw a wrench in our plans with her conniption fit. If you ask me, Bran should've let her stay in her room and pout."

"Will Branson miss the tournament?" Steph asked.

"No chance," said Finn. "It lasts until one a.m. and the casino throws a party for us, after that. He'll merely miss the opening bell, thanks to Carina."

"A party?" Steph's already frayed nerves started sparking. She felt like a fraud. She'd never make it through a party with all these ultra-rich people. "I might go to bed by then and let you guys take care of Branson."

"No way," Cole piped in. "The ratio of single men to single women is way too high to lose a potential dance partner."

"Maybe Branson will share Carina with you." Steph smirked.

"I'd pass on that offer even if Oscar liked dancing," Jarrett scoffed.

"Oscar?" Steph asked.

"My leg. That's his name. I also have Flash Gordon, but that's my sports leg. I call him Gordie."

"Einstein loves to dance." Cole lifted his bright green prosthetic arm. "Have to watch him. He sometimes slides down a little too low from the waist. Says it's because he has no nerve sensation, but I think he's trying to cop a feel."

Stephanie suppressed a snort, when Finn jumped in the discussion. "I'll dance with Stephanie. Cole can have Carina."

"I don't want her," Cole said, in a gruff tone. "I don't know why Bran wants to marry her, anyway. She's too controlling, if you ask me."

Finn started forward as the elevator doors opened, but Cole grabbed his arm and hauled him backwards. "Ladies first."

Finn offered an elbow instead, and Steph accepted, hoping to steady her rickety feet on their precariously high perches.

"Bran's got his reasons." Finn guided her out, turning left, toward the casino.

"Good reasons?" Jarrett asked.

"Unfortunately, yes. But I'm working on a way around it." Finn's cryptic reply piqued her curiosity, but she didn't dare ask.

"Care to share?" Cole inquired.

"It'll have to wait."

Steph got the distinct impression she was the reason Finn was waiting.

"I wish they wouldn't fight." Steph was being honest. She was a peacemaker at heart and couldn't stand being around people who were quarreling. "I'm going to do my best to help them work things out. That's one of the reasons I came. I wanted to convince her I'm not a threat."

"Personally, I'm glad Carina's in a snit," said Finn. "She's playing right into my hand. If everything goes as planned, Branson's going to back out of this relationship, soon."

Steph ought to object, but secretly wanted Finn's plan to work. She kept her mouth shut.

"You've got a plan to break off the engagement?" Cole's eyes lit up.

"I do. We all have a part to play." Finn's lips curved in a special grin, one Steph was beginning to recognize, indicating he had something up his sleeve.

"I'm in." Cole raised his voice to compete with the casino noise as they drew closer.

"Me, too," Jarrett confirmed.

"Stephanie has a special role," Finn added.

She stopped in her tracks. "No way. I don't want any part in this. I'm here to back my boss. I'm not risking my job to help with your little scheme."

"Surely you don't believe Carina's good for him, do you?" Finn's hand nestled on her bare skin on the small of her back, nudging her onward.

"My opinion doesn't matter." She marched faster, escaping from the unwanted intimacy of his touch, a feat made difficult by her gangly heels. "It's what Branson wants."

Finn passed her up, blocking her path, and the other two caught up and flanked him. "What if I told you she's trying to steal from him?"

"Carina's stealing from Branson?" Steph felt a sudden impulse to slam her fist into Miss Snobby's perfect teeth. "Why haven't you told him?"

"It's a hunch. I don't have any proof. That's where you come in. When you get back, you have to spy on Carina… see what she's up to."

Her dampening armpits made her want to flap her arms like a chicken. "I can't. She hates me, already. If she catches me nosing around, she'll get me fired."

Finn's special grin returned. "Don't worry about that. If my idea works, it'll be impossible for him to terminate you."

Her curiosity overcame her better sense. "What's your idea?"

"Come on. You wouldn't want me to spoil the surprise, would you?" Finn scrunched one eye shut in an exaggerated wink. Cole and Jarrett shuffled their feet, as if they didn't want to confront her.

She crossed her arms and gave all three men a scorching, angry-mom look that would've made the average man tremble in his shoes, even if he wore fancy boots like Cole's. "I don't like surprises."

"You'll find out soon enough," said Finn. He hooked an imprisoning arm around her shoulder and towed her onward. "This way to check in."

With all the fees prepaid, a quick ID inspection produced four tournament tags, and four small pouches with twenty chips each.

"Only twenty poker chips?" she wondered aloud. "That won't last long."

"Each one of those chips is worth a thousand dollars. Plus, you have twenty thousand more banked on that ID tag," Cole explained as the group wandered inside.

Frustrated she hadn't discovered the price of her tournament entry, Steph tried to wheedle the information from Finn, while thanking him, once again, for fronting her entry fee.

"Branson insists he's paying me back," Finn replied. "Seems he can't stand the idea you might be obligated to me in any way. Guess if you want to know the buy-in amount, you'll have to ask your jealous boyfriend."

So much blood rushed to her face, she needed to fan herself. "Don't say things like that. If Carina gets wind of it, she'll use it against me. Branson Knight is my boss and nothing more. Not my boyfriend. There's nothing romantic between us, and there never will be."

Finn's enigmatic smile never faltered as his arm slid around her waist. "That's good to hear. I'll give you a chance to prove that tonight. Will you be my date, for real?"

The heat in her face spread down her neck. She searched for a way to escape him without hurting his feelings. "Honestly, I don't even know how to date, it's been so long."

"I doubt that," he replied in a throaty voice, dipping so close she could smell the spicy musk of his aftershave. It was nice, but sweeter than the one Branson wore.

She tried to sidestep away from him, but his arm held firm, pulling her toward one of the slot machines. He herded her into the chair in front of the machine with flashing lights and a sign that read, "$10,000,000 Payout." His hands rested on her bare shoulders and feathered a stroke on her neck, sending a rippling shudder down her back.

Great. Now he'll think I'm attracted to him. Better nip that in the bud.

"I should've brought a sweater. I'm going to run upstairs." She wriggled free of his hold and slid out of the chair. "Be right back," she threw over her shoulder.

Ignoring his protests, she walked as fast as her towering sandals would allow, belatedly realizing her stride made her hips move in exaggerated form. When she got on the elevator, she joined a couple dressed in elegant fashion, the woman with a diamond-studded necklace. Of course, Steph had no idea if the jewels were real or fake. The only diamond she'd ever owned was the modest solitaire in her old engagement ring.

"You look beautiful," Steph complimented. "Does everyone dress up like this to gamble?"

"To gamble? No." The woman shook her head, with a puzzled smile. "You can wear anything you like to play in the casino. The dress you have on is gorgeous."

"Thanks." Stephanie lifted one of her feet and pointed to the five-inch heels. "Thinking about changing into something more comfortable."

"Whatever you want will be fine," she confirmed. "Anything goes in Vegas. From blue-jeans to formal wear. Most people are dressed somewhere in between."

"I just wear whatever my boss tells me to wear." Her husband nudged her arm with his hand.

The wife rolled her eyes. "He's color blind. He'd look ridiculous if I didn't lay out his clothes for him."

"I know what you mean," Steph agreed. "I do the same thing for..."

She halted as she realized, with a pang, that aspect of her job would soon be ending. It was part of her almost daily routine she enjoyed more than she was willing to admit.

The elevator stopped and the couple exited. "Have a nice evening," the husband said, in parting.

In her room, Stephanie opted to add a lightweight cape

made entirely of delicate lace. It was surprisingly warm, despite the holes. But her strappy heels had already started to rub a blister where they went across her little toe. She chose a beautiful pair of sandals with a more modest heel of three inches. A few trial steps proved the soft straps didn't rub like the other pair, though her heel slid from side to side when she walked. Her only other choice was a cheap pair of comfy flats she'd intended for wearing around the hotel room.

I'll be fine, as long as I'm careful.

She opened her door just as Branson stepped out of Carina's room, jaw-droppingly handsome in his tuxedo.

"Hi." Her voice squeaked like a nervous schoolgirl.

"Stephanie? I thought you went down with the guys." His hair was a bit messy on top, and Steph wanted to smooth it, as was her custom. She stopped herself just in time. Carina appeared, her upper lip twitching on one side when she spotted Stephanie.

"Bran-son." Carina said his name in a stretched-out singsong, like a flirty come-hither. "Will you zip me up?"

Carina turned, revealing the back of her gold satin evening dress, gaping open to expose a red lace thong.

"Seriously, Carina?" Bran muttered, as he tucked his cane under his arm to use both hands for the task.

Stephanie's empty stomach churned. Some naïve part of her had thought, since they had separate rooms at the house and the hotel, they weren't sleeping together. Evidently that wasn't the case. From the self-satisfied expression on Carina's face, she was thrilled to rub Stephanie's face in it.

Steph pivoted toward the elevator, to avoid watching the intimate moment. "I'm heading down. See you guys in the casino."

With long strides, she was pleased to make more rapid progress, thanks to her slightly more practical and much more comfortable shoes. She punched the elevator button multiple times, praying the doors would open quickly and allow her to escape the awkwardness. But evidently her guardian angel was taking a restroom break, because Carina and Branson arrived at the same time as the elevator.

On the ride down, she ventured a glance at Branson, whose expression was unreadable, as usual. Carina caught her looking, her mouth stretched into a perfect imitation of the Wicked Witch of the West.

Why not *kill 'em with kindness*?

"Carina, your dress is beautiful." Compliments were easy. Carina always looked perfect.

"Thank you. I'll get rid of it after tonight, of course. Never wear a dress more than once."

"Really? Seems like an awful waste."

Carina was such a sharp contrast to Branson, who never expressed a squandering attitude, despite his wealth.

"I always donate them to the resale shop, so it helps someone less fortunate." Carina lifted her pointy chin, seeming more like the witch with every passing moment. "I'd offer it to you, but of course it would be way too small."

In her stunned silence, Steph struggled to appear unaffected by the jibe. She swallowed the rock inside her throat and turned her head. Carina already had Branson. Why did she have to rub Steph's face in all her inadequacies?

"*Carina.*" Branson's tone was filled with pent-up rage, clearly expressed on his face. "I've had enough of your insults."

"What?" Carina's voice was full of innocence and her eyes

rounded in exaggeration. "I didn't say she was fat. I was insulting myself for being too thin."

Bran didn't answer immediately, but his expression said he wasn't buying it. Did Carina think he was that stupid? Or did she even care?

"You've changed, Carina," Branson growled. "I've never seen this side of you."

Carina's hands went up to her slim hips. "What's that supposed to mean?"

The elevator doors opened on the tournament floor, and Steph hurried out, escaping while she could, their raised voices following behind her. She felt a sense of dread, recognizing how much Carina detested her. Flashing her badge at the doorway attendant, she slipped inside the casino, which was already filling up with players. Even in her designer gown Steph felt out of place, like a child dressing up in a costume. These people all had money to burn or they wouldn't be in a charity tournament. Each had probably paid more for one entry ticket than she made in a year. Somehow, Branson had always made her feel his equal, even though he was her boss. But here, she felt everyone could see through her façade and was sneering at her, like Carina. She kept her head ducked downward as she wove through the aisles, looking for Finn and the guys, but could feel curious gazes following her. Her pulse was pounding a rapid beat in her ears.

I wish I was in jeans. I can't even wipe the sweat off my palms.

She jumped at a hand on her shoulder.

"Hey, Stephanie," said Jarrett. "Over here. Finn and Cole are playing blackjack."

He offered his elbow, and she tucked her hand in the

crook of his arm. Her heart rate slowed, which only made her angry at herself. *I don't need a guy to make me feel confident.*

"You're turning a lot of heads, tonight," Jarrett bent to murmur in her ear as he guided her toward the back of the casino.

"I felt them staring at me. They know I'm a fake."

"Are you crazy? They're staring because you look absolutely beautiful. Too bad Branson can't see you."

"Thanks," she said, though she knew he was being polite. But his words reminded her why she was here. To help Branson, and no other reason. Why was she worried about something superficial, like her appearance or being accepted by these affluent people who meant nothing to her? She had to focus.

"Branson and Carina rode the elevator down with me. I need to find him, in case the crowd noise is bothering him."

She tapped her ear, to indicate Bran's receiver, and Jarrett nodded, making a sharp left turn. "He'll go straight to the craps tables."

He wound his way through the milling crowds, and pointed as they rounded another bend. "There they are."

On the opposite side of a table where people were yelling and clapping and throwing dice stood Branson and Carina. Bran's fingers were gripping the edge of the table with white knuckles, his face strained. Though Carina hung on his elbow, she was talking to the man beside her. She threw her head back, laughing at something the man said.

Jarrett led them around the table, edging in on Bran's right side, where the tiny receiver was barely visible, especially with sunglasses camouflaging the receiver wire. "Hey, buddy. Glad you made it down. Want a drink?"

Bran shook his head. "No, thanks."

Something exciting happened on the table, and the crowd cheered. Stephanie had never seen craps played, so she had no idea what was happening. One person rolled the dice and everyone else seemed very excited each time he threw them.

"No drink?" Jarrett raised his voice to be heard over the commotion. "Remember... *what happens in Vegas stays in Vegas.* You always have a drink or two while you're here."

"Not this time."

"Why not? You need to relax a little."

"You know I don't believe in using alcohol to relax. That's for alcoholics."

"Give me a break." Jarrett flung an annoyed hand, though Bran couldn't see it. "You can't become an alcoholic by having a drink once every two years."

"I'm not in the mood."

Bran's probably upset because Carina's flirting. Or maybe the noise in here is making him tense. Steph slid her hand into her purse and turned on the transmitter.

"Hey Bran," she talked quietly, her chin dipped toward the microphone. "Do you want this on or not?"

He gave a sharp nod. Out loud, he asked, "Hey, Jarrett? Where's Stephanie?"

"I'm here," she spoke up. "I'm on the other side of Jarrett. Wish one of you guys would explain what's going on with this game."

Jarrett and Bran both talked at once, using words like "come-out roll" and "pass line" and "field," along with a bunch of random dice combination numbers that seemed to be significant.

"Got it?" asked Jarrett.

"Sure." Steph huffed a chuckle. "Why don't you guys play, and I'll learn by watching?"

Both men traded thousand dollar chips for smaller denominations and placed bets on the table as a new person started rolling the dice—a woman who looked to be in her fifties, dripping in diamonds that sparkled almost as much as her eyes. The dice tumbled and stopped with a pair of twos showing, and the onlookers cheered.

"Four, the hard way!" called a man with a long crooked stick, as he raked the dice back to the roller.

"That person with the dice is called the shooter," Jarrett explained. "And that woman is the stickman."

"Who's that other woman?" Steph asked. "The one who's frowning, at the end of the table."

"That's the boxman. She's in charge of the whole table. Has to watch everything like a hawk."

Chips were added and taken away and moved around, and the sparkling shooter threw the dice again.

The crowd clapped when the dice stopped with a six and a four.

Bran mumbled something about "don't pass" and handed a stack of chips to Jarrett, who placed them on the table and added some chips of his own. The shooter tossed the dice against the far side of the table again, and they stopped with a three and a four showing.

Everyone shouted, and someone gave both Bran and Jarrett a bunch of chips. Stephanie was more confused than ever.

"New shooter!" announced the man with the stick.

"Why aren't any of these people upset?" Steph asked. "Some of them lost a bunch of chips."

"Because it's only a game," Branson explained. "Everyone paid to play and no one is taking any money home tonight, not even the grand-prize winner."

"Cole and Finn found a less crowded table," said Jarrett, looking at a text on his phone. "Let's go find them."

"Finn usually plays blackjack the first three or four hours." Bran's brows furrowed, his voice full of suspicion. Steph hoped Finn wasn't planning to make another move on her. She couldn't watch out for Bran and fend off Finn's advances at the same time.

Jarrett led the way, with Carina and Branson following and Steph trailing behind. She took the opportunity to enjoy Bran's form from the rear. So handsome in the well-cut tuxedo, his broad shoulders tapering to narrow hips. She knew exactly how his muscles rippled as he walked, having observed his workouts a multitude of times. She never tired of watching him.

Carina walked beside him, moving with easy grace on her stilettos. *Something else for me to be jealous of.* Steph had to admit the two made a striking couple. Carina appeared to belong with this crowd, while Stephanie would never blend in.

Reality sunk in and churned in her belly. She didn't care for Carina, but had to find some kind of common ground with her. She couldn't count on Finn breaking up the relationship, especially since she had no intention of helping him with his scheme. And she had to remember MawMaw's advice and find out Carina's sad secret. Maybe she could help her get past it. Maybe Carina needed a real friend.

Somewhere nearby, one of the slot machines got really excited, bells clanging long and loud like a railroad crossing.

Passing another craps table, the circling crowd cheered and yelled encouragement. The noise bothered Stephanie, so she knew Branson must hate it. "We're almost there," she murmured in his earpiece. "Finn found a table in the far back corner, so maybe it will be a little quieter."

With Carina clutching one arm and his cane in the other, Branson couldn't wave to indicate he'd heard her remark, but Steph saw his head nodding, and decided now would be a good time to give a running monologue, as she customarily did during their workday lunches. She'd discovered, quite by accident, if she kept him distracted by telling stories, he'd linger at the table and eat more slowly. MawMaw had always insisted it was bad for you to wolf your food down. Though Branson had ridiculed her advice, Steph was convinced she'd made him healthier.

"It's been a beautiful day, so far." She lowered her chin toward the microphone in her scarf. "I want you to know I really appreciate this trip. I've never done anything like this before. It's so special. I loved it all." *That's not quite true. I hated seeing you and Carina fight. And I didn't enjoy her calling me fat, even by implication. But, the rest was wonderful.* "Everything. The private jet. The fancy room. The show. The clothes. The food. And I appreciate whatever ridiculous fee was paid for my tournament entry. The fountain was the best part. Wish I could come back and show it to Ellie. She'd love it. One more thing to put on her bucket list. I hope Ellie gets to see it someday…"

CHAPTER 10

As Branson tuned into Steph's monologue, the noise of the casino seemed to recede. Not only did the sound of Steph's voice soothe Bran's nerves, but her words of gratitude reminded him of his own good fortune. It was hard to be selfish with someone like Stephanie around.

Then she said something that shook him to the core. "One more thing to put on her bucket list. I hope Ellie gets to see it someday."

Though he was certain Steph hadn't intended it to happen, Bran thought of how short Ellie's life was likely to be, especially if she couldn't get the very best medicine available to battle her cystic fibrosis.

"This is better," Steph's voice broke into his reverie. "We're in the very back, and there aren't any slot machines around."

Her assessment was correct. As Bran expected, Finn found an area with less noise. He'd always been sensitive to Bran's needs. Even as a teenager at camp, Finn would arrange their group so Bran always had a friend on either side. He was thoughtful like that. Though he claimed he was having a bad run at blackjack, he probably switched to craps so he could take care of Bran. Finn would make a good husband, but he had to agree to date someone first. Bran's chest went tight. *But not Stephanie.*

"Hey, Bran?" Steph's voice came back in his ear as his hands touched the edge of the table. He couldn't tell where she was standing—she was too far away to hear her voice in the other ear. "Couldn't I give you my money and let you gamble that, too? I really don't understand this game, but I like watching you play."

Bran shook his head, wishing they could talk alone.

Carina's long nails bit into his arm, and he stiffened, turning toward her. Had she spoken to him? He'd been paying attention to Steph. "I'm sorry, Carina. Did you say something? The noise in here is distracting."

"I think it's too quiet back here. Hardly anyone around." Her whiny toned made it clear she preferred being the center of attention. "And you're ignoring me."

"I'm listening, now. What did you say?"

"I asked what you told Stephanie about us. Does she know about... *everything?*"

"I didn't tell her about the stock deal, if that's what you're asking. I guess she thinks we're in love."

"You know, Bran, there used to be more between us... a lot more than stocks." Her voice went sultry as she wedged her body against his arm. "There could be, again. Why not let me move into your suite? You're not going to make me stay in the east wing after we're married, are you?"

His body refused to respond to her efforts. He bent

toward her until her hair brushed his chin and muttered, "We're not going to sleep together, Carina. Not now. And not after we're married. How could I ever be with you again, when you made it clear you're repulsed by me?"

"Not by *you*." A hand slid inside his coat, caressing his chest through his shirt. "You have an amazing body. I told you, I'm only creeped out by those fake eyes, imagining they could pop out at any time. As long as I keep my eyes closed, I'm fine."

"That was a one-time mistake we both regretted." He seized her roaming hand and pushed it away, straining to keep his voice low. "I'm perfectly happy with our nonphysical relationship."

"Even after we're married? Three years is a long time to abstain. What if I never mention the fake-eye thing again?"

"No." His gut roiled at the thought of sleeping with her, knowing how she felt. Maybe it would be different if he weren't blind. He'd read somewhere men were most turned on by sight, and supposedly Carina was stunning.

"I bet you'll change your mind." She cleared her throat and announced in a loud voice, "I'm off to hit the slots for a while."

Yes. Perfect.

Carina continued, "Stephanie? Want to come with me?"

Not perfect. His hands gripped the side of the table.

Steph's voice quavered. "Well... I thought Bran might need—"

"Bran's fine. He's with his friends," Carina insisted. "Let's go."

Bran wanted to scream, to beg her not to go, but Finn clapped him on the shoulder. "Hey, buddy. Ready to play?"

In his ear, he heard Steph speak to Carina, presumably as they walked away. "How can you walk so smoothly in five-inch heels? I tried some earlier, but I had to go upstairs and swap them out for these. Three inches, and I'm barely stable."

Bran heard the thin notes of Carina's response, but couldn't distinguish any words.

"Bran? You okay?" Finn's hand squeezed his shoulder.

"Yeah."

Steph spoke again. "Don't worry. I'm well-aware this isn't my world."

He should've stopped them from leaving. No doubt Carina would say something to hurt Stephanie. He strained, trying to hear Carina's reply.

"Me and Finn?" Steph answered with a question in her voice. "No, I'm not expecting that relationship will go anywhere. Not that I don't think he's handsome."

Finn demanded Branson's attention. "Come on, Bran. Lay your bet. Cole's the shooter."

Bran grabbed a handful of chips. "Put them on Don't Pass. Cole's an awful shooter."

"You want to bet against him?" Finn asked. "Rather insulting."

"Absolutely," Bran confirmed. "He has dreadful luck. Cole even bets against himself."

He heard Steph in his ear again. "I promise, you have nothing to worry about from me, Carina. Branson's my boss, and nothing more. I work hard to make him happy because I need my job."

It hurt to hear the words from her lips, though it wasn't the first time. He had no false illusions about her feelings.

"Snake eyes—shooter dies," yelled someone, likely the stickman.

"Ha! That was fast." Finn chuckled.

Branson had won, but he was more interested in Steph's conversation.

Stephanie spoke. "I admire your drive. Had to put my career on the back burner once Ellie was diagnosed with cystic fibrosis."

"New shooter." The stickman's voice intruded.

"Leave it all on Don't Pass," Bran said, pushing his chips forward.

"Are you sure?" Finn asked.

"I'm sure," Bran said, impatiently, trying to hear Steph's conversation.

"Oh, no! That's terrible," Steph exclaimed. "No, I won't tell a soul." Then her voice dipped low. "Forgot this was on. So sorry."

His receiver went quiet.

"Yes!" Finn shouted, his fist pounding Bran's arm. "We won again. You're hot, tonight, Branson. Think I'll just copy your bets."

"Your loss. I'll bet Pass." Bran strained to hear Stephanie again, but his ears rang with silence.

"Where did the women go?" he asked Finn.

"Uhmm," Finn's voice undulated, apparently a result of his head turning as he scanned the massive room. "I don't see 'em. But they were headed toward the front, where all the slot machines are. Do you want me to fetch Carina for you?"

What could he say? If he mentioned wanting Stephanie back, Finn would tease him without mercy.

A new shooter rolled a four on the come-out.

"No, I don't need her. Fifty thousand on the odds," said Branson.

"Are you crazy?" Finn's voice went up an octave. "Are you trying to lose everything early, so you can go upstairs? It's not happening, buddy. This trip is about spending time together, so you're staying to the end."

Finn had hit the nail on the head, but Bran only grunted in reply. No use arguing or trying to explain his sudden discontent.

The crowd around the table exploded with excitement.

"Four the hard way," shouted the stickman.

"You *lucky* dog." Finn's voice split his eardrum as a hand gripped his arm and shook him like a rag doll. "Can't believe it."

Jarrett and Cole let out congratulatory whoops and pounded him on the back. A huge stack of chips slid into Bran's waiting fingers, and he grinned, the old thrill of winning rushing back like an avalanche. *Maybe I'll hang around and play, after all.*

～

As Branson's stack of chips grew, so did his sense of ease in the noisy surroundings, even without the comfort of Steph's voice. Yet he wished she'd return to watch him play. Besides, he was worried that she'd spent too much time alone with Carina. Bran was wary enough to handle her, but Stephanie was often naively trusting.

After a particularly lucrative round, Cole suggested they take a break. So the four moved to a table in the bar. His friends were feasting on nachos, but Bran was in the mood for something healthy. Unfortunately, nothing nutritious was available in the bar. Finn seemed particularly insistent that Bran should have an alcoholic beverage, but Branson resisted.

"I'll stick to water, for now. I don't want to mess up my concentration while I'm winning."

"You're winning," Cole lamented, "and I'm losing everything but the shirt off my back."

"How do I know you haven't lost that as well," Bran teased. "I'm blind. For all I know, you're sitting here naked as the day you were born."

Cole shot back, "Because if I'd lost any of my clothes, we'd be surrounded by women right now."

Bran's laugh sent him into a coughing fit.

"Big ego, much?" Jarrett asked Cole.

"You know how it is," Cole answered, drolly. "I'm from Texas, where *everything* is big."

Bran didn't need eyes to guess what gesture Cole made to accompany his claim. This time, Bran laughed without spilling his water. Finn's answering groan carried across the table.

"I don't know about that, Cole," Jarrett quipped. "You seem to be running *short*... very short in fact. Short on *luck*."

Cole scooted close and wrapped an arm around Branson's shoulder. "I'm hoping some of Bran's luck will rub off on me."

His friend's deliberate attempt to make him uncomfortable was working, but Branson knew one sure way to make him stop. He turned toward Cole and threw both his arms around his neck, pulling his face close and planting a loud smacking kiss on his cheek.

"*Aaaak!*" Cole disentangled himself and pushed away from Branson, chuckling. "Come on, man. You're going to ruin my chances with the ladies."

"Give up, Cole," said Finn. "These ladies will take one look at that neon hand and go running."

Interesting that Cole had chosen the less socially-acceptable prosthetic for the tournament. But Branson wasn't completely surprised. Cole had always been a bit of a rebel.

"Forget the glowing hand," said Jarrett. "It's those cowboy boots that look out of place."

"You're just jealous," Cole asserted. "Should we get you a boot-leg? Oh, wait… Would that be illegal?"

"Very punny," Finn added.

"It ought to be illegal to wear cowboy boots with a tux," Jarrett avowed. "That look would scare away any decent woman."

"Who said I wanted a *decent* woman?"

Bran knew better. Cole was the kind of guy who threw his coat across a puddle so a woman wouldn't get her shoes dirty.

"Bran's getting all the single female attention, right now," Jarrett complained. "No one's interested in a loser."

"Female attention?" Bran thought he must be joking.

"Of course you don't know they're all hanging around the craps table watching you play. It's a good thing you can't see it. You'd have an even bigger head."

Bran figured his buddy was kidding, so he ignored him. "There's plenty of time for you guys to make a comeback before one a.m."

"Carina's on her way over here, by herself. Wonder what happened to Stephanie."

His concern for Stephanie peaked. He'd had enough of bowing to Carina's wishes, merely to get his hands on that pharmaceutical company. He could afford to provide Ellie with the drug for the rest of her life, rather than attempting to make it readily available to all in need. His gut churned. That option felt too selfish. He clenched his fists in frustration. Perhaps he could simply delay the wedding as long as possible while he pursued a backup plan.

"Branson, darling," Carina's strident voice gushed, as her hand slid across the back of his neck and onto his shoulder. He felt her breath on the side of his face, while an overwhelming floral scent threatened to gag him. He'd tried to explain to her how sensitive he was to heavy perfumes. "I need to talk to you alone. It's urgent," she rasped in his ear.

"Why?" he whispered back.

"Gotta call from Dad. We need to get married. Pronto."

BRANSON LET Carina lead him out of the bar to speak in private, though he suspected he would share the conversation with Finn, if not all three of his friends. He hadn't a clue as to why Carina would want to rush the marriage. They walked on soft carpet, voices fading in the background. His cane hit something hard. A piece of furniture.

"There's a couch here," she explained.

He wanted to get this conversation over with quickly and return to check on Stephanie.

"What's this all about, Carina?"

"Sit down. I'll explain everything. A lot happened since I left."

He perched on the edge of the seat, too tense to sit back against the cushions. She sat down so close their legs were touching from the hips to the knees, but he was too impatient to enjoy the contact. "I'm listening. Make it fast."

"We need to get married right away. Tonight would be best."

"No way. It's not happening."

He leaned forward, preparing to stand, but her hand gripped his sleeve and tugged him down.

"Wait. Hear me out."

As he sank back to the couch, he twisted to face her, aiming his gaze in a way he knew agitated his fiancée.

"Ughh! Please don't stare at me like that. It gives me the creeps."

With deliberately slow movements, he took his sunglasses from his inside coat pocket and slid them on. "You've got two minutes."

She let out a huff of air. "Fine. Dad called to tell me someone's been buying up the individual shares of Parker-Aston. It started months ago, but picked up pace this week. Dad's worried about a hostile takeover."

Branson shook his head. "I don't see how that could happen. There aren't enough individual shares available. I already acquired most of them."

"That's not the worst. Today, Dad found out the Astons' son-in-law sold off their shares. It was almost half their total stock holdings."

"At what price? I offered them almost double market

value and they turned me down, cold." Branson fumed. If he could've gotten his hands on those stocks, a marriage to Carina wouldn't have been necessary.

"You did? When? Trying to make a deal behind our backs?"

"Before we started dating. I've been upfront. Have you?"

"Yeah. Sure." Bran was excellent at interpreting intonations, and hers had the hesitancy of a lie. No surprise. He knew better than to trust her. "Dad's furious about the stocks. He's so mad, he'd sell you some of the family shares outright, if he could. He's had his lawyer on it all day. They think we can get around the family restrictions on the Parker shares, even if the marriage only lasts ninety days."

"This is ridiculous, Carina. I'm not rushing into a marriage without a signed prenup, no matter what."

"I e-signed it thirty minutes ago. Call your attorney and verify it." Her flat tone gave nothing away. "No changes to the contract. Ten percent of Escapade Resorts to me. You get eleven percent of Parker-Aston."

It was a good deal. The shark inside him wanted to pounce on it, despite his misgivings. Ninety days. He could handle being married to Carina for ninety days. But something about the whole thing made his skin crawl.

"I need to think about it. Talk to my lawyer." He tightened his grip on his cane, the information swirling in his head. It wasn't in his nature to make a hasty decision.

"Every day we wait adds to the risk. We need to call an emergency board meeting on Monday. We're here in Las Vegas. We could get married tonight or in the morning."

"Too fast. I don't rush into things. Not doing anything until we get back to Chicago."

"If we wait and get a license in Illinois on Monday, the earliest we could get married is Tuesday. Anything could happen in forty-eight hours."

Branson was already shaking his head. It felt like someone was pushing him toward the edge of a cliff. "No. The answer is no."

"Why can't we at least keep our options open while you call and talk to your attorney? You've got nothing to lose. Come with me to get a marriage license before the office closes. Dad's people researched everything. It only takes five minutes to get one in Las Vegas, and they're open 'til midnight."

"No use. I'm not getting married here."

"Don't say no until you talk to your people and confirm what I'm saying. If you still don't want to get married in Vegas, we can throw the license away. But you might change your mind. If we get it, at least we'll have the option. The chapels are open twenty-four hours a day."

"I don't want to miss the tournament."

"We'll be there and back in fifteen minutes. Finn can come. Please. Do this much for me. Talk to your people, and you can mull it over while you're at the craps table. I promise I won't be upset if you still insist on waiting."

He checked his tactile watch. *Nine twenty-two.* "Okay. It's a waste of time, but I'll go."

"Thank you." Her hand slid across the back of his neck. A swell of the nauseating perfume preceded the kiss she planted on his cheek. "Wait here. I'll grab Finn."

"Carina! Wait!"

"Be right back," called her receding voice.

His rib muscles contracted, refusing to allow his lungs to

expand. *Abandoned. Strange surroundings.* He couldn't even find a restroom without the help of a stranger. He gripped the arm of the couch and fought back the threatening panic, blood pounding in his ears. *I'm not alone. My friends will be here any minute.* Fumbling in his jacket he found his cell phone.

"Call Stephanie," he rasped from his dry throat. *Why did I call her instead of Finn? Or Jarrett? Or Cole?* He ought to hang up and call one of the guys, but it was Stephanie's voice he wanted to hear.

It rang so many times, he thought it would go to voicemail. At last, her sweet voice answered. "Branson?"

"Steph. I... can you find me?"

"Branson? What happened? Where are you?" Her voice shook.

"I don't know. I can't remember which way we turned when we came out of the bar." *Why hadn't he paid attention? That wasn't like him.*

"I don't know how to find you." Her words were shrill and panicky, with a catch at the end.

Branson felt like a jerk for scaring her. Why couldn't he have sat quietly and waited for Carina to come back? It's not like he was going to be attacked by wolves while sitting in the lobby of a hotel in Vegas.

"Don't worry, Steph. I'm fine." He took long, deep breaths, attempting to slow his racing heart. "Carina said she'd be right back. I shouldn't have called."

"Carina?" She said the word like it tasted bad. "Carina left you alone somewhere?"

Oh, no. I've heard that tone before. She's peeved. Gotta fix this before she starts a fight. "Yes, but she's coming right back. I'm fine. Really. I felt like I was suffocating, but now I'm breathing fine. It's nothing. Just out of practice. Probably missed hearing your voice in my ear."

"I'm taking care of that right now. I'm turning the mic back on."

"But we're talking on the phone."

"I'm hanging up, so you can't stop me from doing what I'm about to do." Stephanie had that grim, forced tone she only used when she was extremely angry.

"What are you going to do?" He was almost afraid to ask.

"Something that might get me fired. But I don't care." The phone went dead. After a few seconds, her voice spoke in his ear. "I'm going to give Carina Parker a long-overdue piece of my mind."

CHAPTER 11

Stephanie's hands were shaking with barely controlled rage, and every bit of it was targeted on Carina. An hour ago, the woman had kindled her sympathies, playing her like a fool, with the tearful confession that she couldn't have children because she had a rare heart condition.

"I don't really hate children," she'd confessed. "I didn't want to admit it, but every time I see you, I'm reminded I'll never be a mother."

Following MawMaw's advice, Steph was convinced she'd discovered her adversary's sad secret. In an instant she'd forgiven Carina's insults and rude remarks about Ellie. "I'm so sorry. I'm sure that must be awful."

Carina sniffed. "I felt lucky when Bran and I started dating. I love him so much. Since I can't have children, I'm going to devote myself to taking care of him. Bran will get a hundred percent of my attention."

Good point. My attention will always be divided. Ellie has to be my main focus. "I'm so glad you told me this, Carina. I worry about him. Feels good to know you care so much."

"Willing to give me some advice?" Carina looked from the corner of her eye, appearing nervous, but sincere.

"Guess so. Don't know why you'd want advice from me."

"You see, Bran and I get along great in the bedroom—fireworks, every time."

Carina paused, as if she expected Stephanie to respond, but the thought of Branson sleeping with Carina made her feel like she'd swallowed a pint of castor oil. Struggling to appear unaffected and hoping Carina didn't intend to share more details, she kept her mouth shut and stared at her feet while they threaded their way through the aisles of slot machines and tables until they were within sight of the entry doors.

Carina stopped at one machine that looked the same as all the others and proclaimed, "This is my favorite." She slid onto the swiveling chair, patting the empty one beside her, before continuing her uncomfortable speech. "Even though we're obviously compatible, Bran and I have been fighting a lot. It's like he's been in a bad mood ever since we got here. He criticizes everything I do."

"Of course he's in a bad mood. He doesn't like unfamiliar surroundings. And it's noisy, to boot."

Carina punched a button on the machine, producing a series of ringing bells and flashing lights. "He's got his friends with him. What's the big deal?"

"Are you kidding me?" Steph snapped, before tamping down her unruly temper and continuing with what she hoped was detachment in her tone. "Branson hates being dependent on anyone for anything. When he's home, he can handle stuff without any help. In the casino, he can't hear well and can't find his way around."

"I still think he's trying to get attention." Carina's gaze never left the slot machine as she continued to punch the button, producing a cacophony of sounds that was beginning to grate on Steph's nerves. "I guess it doesn't matter if we fight, anyway. The makeup sex is great."

"You could make an effort to be sensitive about it," Steph suggested.

"Branson needs to put on his big-boy pants and grow up. He's being a baby."

"No, he's not," Steph defended, barely keeping her voice civil. "He's trying hard, and he's not even complaining, because he wants his friends to have a good time. I think he's doing an amazing job of adapting and keeping his cool."

Carina paused her play and rotated until she faced Steph, sporting a smile with a hint of scorn. Her huge almond-shaped blue eyes blinked slowly, examining Steph like a lab specimen. "I suppose that's how we're different, Stephanie. You're an employee, paid to be loyal no matter what your boss does. Whereas, I'm not afraid to point out Bran's faults. Frankly, I'm good for him. With my help, he'll change a lot... for the good."

"The difference between you and me is you want to change Bran, and I lo—" She choked and coughed, cutting off her word. She'd almost blurted out *I love him like he is.* "I don't think Branson needs to change."

"How sweet." A sneer marred her flawless face. "Spoken like a naïve fan club president. You wouldn't think he was so perfect if you knew him the way I do—up close and *personal.*" Carina purred the last word like a bad actress in a B movie.

"I didn't say he was perfect—"

Carina silenced her with a raised palm. "Hold on. My phone's ringing." She withdrew her cell from her purse and answered it. "Wait a second," she told the caller. "Let me move somewhere more private."

Steph's angry retort had died on her lips. She'd sat in stunned silence as Carina strode away with her phone to her ear, down the aisle and out the doorway. Too angry to rejoin the men at the craps table, she'd turned woodenly to the slot machine in front of her. Again and again, she'd stabbed at the bright red button on the machine, while her mind boiled, replaying the conversation in her head.

Now, having had plenty of time to fume and learning Carina had abandoned Branson, she was about ready to explode. She stood and faced the approaching woman, her arms crossed so tight she could barely breathe. Her mind rehearsed a scathing monologue, designed to point out all the ways Carina had misjudged and mistreated Branson and why she didn't deserve to marry him.

Unsuspecting, Carina drew closer, chatting on her cell phone with a serious expression, her gaze scanning the casino in every direction. With Carina almost in range, Steph sucked in a deep breath, ready to blast the woman to smithereens, but her opponent took a sharp turn to the left.

"No... No, no, no. Come back here, you witch." Steph took off after her. She made the left turn, only to find Carina was nowhere in sight. *Where did she go? Must be heading back to the craps tables.*

Retracing her steps as best she could remember, Steph wound her way toward the back of the casino, but she saw no sign of the guys. There were way too many men in black tuxedos—they all looked alike from a distance. At last, she spotted Carina and rotated toward her, her right heel catching and twisting as she turned.

"*Dang*, that hurt." Attempting to ignore the pain, she continued toward her adversary, albeit at a slower pace. Carina and Finn appeared to exchange heated words as Carina tugged him away from the craps table. Before Steph could reach the table, the pair left, with Cole and Jarrett trailing behind them.

She picked up her pace, wincing each time her right foot came down. "Jarrett!" she called. "Wait up!"

Jarrett stopped, his eyes widening when he spotted Steph. Moving back, he fell in stride beside her, offering his arm. "You're limping worse than me. What happened?"

"Nothing," she claimed, though she accepted his arm with gratitude, giving some relief to her ankle. "Where's everyone going?"

"I have no idea," Jarrett admitted. "Cole told me to come. He said something about Bran getting married."

"Now? A quickie Las Vegas wedding?" What little she had put in her stomach threatened to reappear. "I have to stop them. She's not in love with him. I don't think she's capable of loving anyone except herself."

"I happen to agree with you." Jarrett's eye's crinkled in the corners as he flashed her a grin. "But I'm not worried. Finn'll find some way to stop it."

"Hope you're right," she mumbled, suddenly determined to help Finn with whatever diabolical plan he might have.

"Hey." Jarrett waved his hand at her, then put a finger to his lips. He spoke in a hoarse whisper, pointing to his ear. "Is that thing on?"

The mic! She'd forgotten to turn it off. What had Branson heard? She replayed the last few minutes in her mind, and sighed with relief. She hadn't said much, other than criticizing Carina. And she'd already decided it was worth risking her job to prevent the marriage. Fumbling inside her purse with her left hand, she murmured, "Bran, we're on the way," before flipping the switch.

On her next step, the toe of her sandal somehow caught on the carpet, wrenching her already-throbbing ankle. The next thing she knew, she was hopping around on her left foot, gripping the sleeve of Jarrett's tux for dear life. "Ow. Ow. Ow. Ow."

"Steph. You've got to see a doctor."

"No. Please. It's just a sprained ankle. Nothing serious. Right now, I have to get to Branson so I can talk him out of this marriage."

The room tipped, as Jarrett swept her into his arms. "I'll get you there, but then you're seeing a doctor."

She almost commented she was too heavy for him, but he might've taken the statement as a remark about his prosthetic leg. In fact, he carried her with seeming ease, no strain evident on his face. Except for his slightly uneven gait, she would never have known he didn't have two normal legs.

"Thank you, Mr. Alvarez. You're my knight in shining armor."

"More like your Zorro." His deep brown eyes sparkled. "Happy to rescue a damsel in distress." He smiled, displaying perfect white teeth. She studied his face—strong and masculine. He was certainly handsome, but there was no thrill at his touch. *How am I ever going to get over Bran if I'm not even attracted to a guy this hot?*

At last, they caught up with the others, and she spied Bran, bowed in private conversation with Finn. Carina's sins momentarily forgotten, she searched his face for signs of panic. Finding him composed, she breathed relief.

"What's this?" Carina's strident voice startled her. She whipped her head toward her adversary, who clapped her hands with delight. "Didn't know you were such a slut, Stephanie. You came with Finn, and now you're with Jarrett?"

"Shut up, Carina." Steph wanted to say so much more. To tell the woman exactly what she thought of her. To scream at her for pretending to love Branson. To let her know exactly how selfish she was. But all that would have to wait until Steph could get Carina alone. She couldn't make a scene now and embarrass Branson.

Bran's brows creased as his head turned toward her, glaring as if he could see her ensconced in Jarrett's embrace. She wriggled, trying to free herself.

"You can put me down, now," Steph whispered to Jarrett.

He complied, lowering her feet to the floor, but his arm still supported her weight. A tentative step revealed the ankle more tender than before, so she gave in and leaned against him.

Carina's face contorted in a sneer, and Steph knew she wasn't going to let it go. "Maybe you and Jarrett should get a marriage license, too. Is that what you're after, Steph? Trying to land a *different* billionaire husband, since I took Branson away?"

"Carina, don't be a—" Finn froze in mid-sentence, his furrowed brows lifting, while his downturned lips curled up at the corners. In two long steps he reached Jarrett and

Steph, though he continued his address with his back to Carina. "Actually, Carina, that's a great idea. Stephanie *should* get married while she's here..." Finn put a silencing finger to his lips and winked, before he dropped to one knee. "She should marry *me*."

Steph knew the invitation was a joke, designed to make Branson jealous. It wouldn't work. She'd already explained Bran wasn't attracted to her in a romantic way. Why didn't Finn believe her?

"No one's getting married," Branson declared as he moved closer. "I get your point, Finn. It was a stupid idea."

"No." Finn stood and faced Branson again. "I'm with Carina on this. You should get a marriage license tonight."

Carina's eyes widened, as she gaped at Finn. "You agree with me?"

"Sure. What does it hurt to get a license, Branson? Keep your options open until you talk to your lawyer tomorrow."

What does Bran's attorney have to do with this? Guess Carina still hasn't signed a prenup agreement.

"Fine. We'll get a license." Branson replied, his nostrils flaring, "But stop joking about marrying Steph."

Was Bran actually jealous? Did he care about her, after all? Steph's heart caught in her throat.

"I'm not joking." Finn turned his head to Stephanie and caught her gaze. "I'm still waiting for your answer."

"We've already talked about this." Bran's deep voice rumbled, as dangerous as his dark expression. "You're not stealing my personal assistant."

Steph's heart plummeted into her gut, landing with a sickening thud. She turned her head, blinking back sudden tears. Why couldn't she get it through her thick head? He didn't love her. He *needed* her. Stephanie forced a lump of air down her constricted throat.

"Finn..." She extended her hand toward him. "I accept."

"No." Branson's face was blood-red, heavy jaw muscles bulging. "I won't allow it."

"Finn isn't being serious, Branson," Carina interjected, one brow arched high on her forehead and fingers tapping out a tense rhythm on her crossed arms. "But, Branson... I want to know why you're so concerned about Stephanie?"

"Carina's got a point," said Finn. "You're marrying her, so you don't need Steph anymore." Finn covered his mouth with his hand and coughed, a gesture Steph suspected was covering a chuckle, though it didn't seem funny to her.

Finn's hilarity was short-lived, as Branson shot forward, grasping his collar in a balled fist and pushing him stumbling backwards into the path of passersby who yelled and scattered out of the way.

Steph gasped, thinking they would both end up in a pile on the floor, but Finn managed to stay upright and shake free of his grasp. Bran had succeeded in moving them beyond earshot, but it was obvious the two were exchanging angry words.

"We should do something." Steph feared Finn had gone too far, this time.

"They'll be fine." Jarrett yawned.

How can he be so relaxed at a time like this?

"Don't you care?" Steph punched his arm to get his attention and pointed toward Bran and Finn. "This could be the end of their friendship."

"Nah." Cole appeared on her other side. "They're like an old married couple. They've been fighting like this for fifteen-plus years. Finn knows just how much he can push Bran's buttons without sending him over the edge."

Branson's hands flailed like a madman as he vented his wrath on Finn.

Steph mumbled, "Hope you're right."

CHAPTER 12

"I've had enough, Finn." Branson seriously considered taking a swing in the general direction of Finn's jaw. He might've done it, if they hadn't been in a public place.

Finn shook out of his grasp. "Hold on, buddy. I know you're riled up right now, but later on, you're going to thank me."

"For stealing my personal assistant? I'm supposed to be grateful?"

"Ignore that part for a second, and listen to me. You don't want to marry Carina this weekend, do you?"

"I've already told her I won't marry her, but she wouldn't take no for an answer. I only agreed to get a marriage license to put her off."

"So, you need me there, to make sure things don't get out of hand." Finn's hand came to rest on his arm, as if he thought all was forgiven.

Bran flung his hand away, fostering his fury. "Marrying Stephanie is your way of doing that?"

Finn huffed in exasperation. "In the fifteen years we've know each other, have I ever stabbed you in the back?"

Bran hesitated, though he knew the answer, loathe to admit his anger was unfounded. "There was that time at camp when you put my hand in warm water while I was sleeping, trying to make me wet the bed."

"As I recall, that was in retaliation for when you put Kool-Aid powder in the shower head," Finn said, wryly. "And if that's the worst you can think of—"

"Okay. You're right." Bran took a deep breath and held it, willing his heart rate to slow. "But why are you doing this? Why involve Stephanie?"

"I think Carina's pulling a stunt of some kind, and I'm trying to get to the bottom of it. I can only think of one reason she'd insist on getting a marriage license tonight, when you've already sworn you won't marry her in Vegas. She's planning to trick you into getting married here."

"What?" Bran's mind raced. "Is there some kind of crazy law in Nevada where she can get us married without my participation?"

"She might think she can get you drunk and talk you into it. Or maybe she's underhanded enough to get someone to fake the wedding official's signature."

"All the more reason not to get a license tonight."

"You really believe she'll accept that answer?"

Branson caught a whiff of steak cooking and his stomach did a flip. An hour ago he'd been starving, but now he had no desire to eat. "I think she'll hound me all night if I don't agree to go. But I still don't see how it helps for you and Stephanie to get a marriage license."

"Mostly, it's an excuse for all of us to come along." Finn's voice faded for a second, and Bran assumed he was checking over his shoulder. "We'll be getting two marriage licenses at the same time, and I'll be helping you sign yours. I'll get the guys to distract Carina, and I'll mess things up—put the women on one license and you and me on the other."

"Like Carina won't notice? I mean, I'll admit I'd be happy if she and I didn't end up with a legitimate license, but she's not stupid."

"I'll keep it away from her, somehow."

Branson mulled the idea over in his head. "I could insist you hold onto it for safekeeping until I hear back from my attorney."

"It might work. I like it. We have one other problem, though." Finn's voice grew closer and quieter. "You don't want Steph to know the real reason you're marrying Carina, do you? She's got to be suspicious, after all this."

"No one knows the truth but you. Correction—you and Fordham. Nothing gets by him." Bran used his left hand to rub his temples, while gripping his cane like a lifeline. "This is turning into a nightmare."

"We need to think fast. Everyone's waiting." Finn came closer and lowered his voice. "Evidently, Steph has a hurt foot or ankle. I'll come up with a plausible explanation when I take her to get it treated."

"Steph's hurt? What happened?"

Panic threatening once again, he turned and headed to find Stephanie. If she was injured, she needed him. A hand grabbed his arm and jerked him to a stop.

"Hang on, Bran. That's the wrong direction."

"I have to get to her." Overwhelmed by a lack of control, Branson felt like he was being buried alive. "I've had enough of Vegas. Forget the tournament. Forget the marriage license. Let's fly home, now."

"Calm down, man. Steph's okay. I've been watching her. She just limped over to the couch without any help, so it can't be too bad."

"Need to go home," Bran demanded, his head swimming.

"Listen to me." Hands gripped Bran's shoulders, and Finn spoke in his face. "It's our fault you're panicking—me and the guys. I should've realized what was happening two years ago. I never should've let you hole up inside that mansion all this time. I hope we didn't wait too long to force you back into the real world. Good thing Fordham finally called us."

That got his attention, but his heart still sprinted. "Fordham called you?"

"He said he was worried. He claims you won't listen to him."

"He shouldn't have called. It's not your responsibility." Bran wanted to crawl in a hole. He'd always prided himself in his ability to govern every aspect of his body—physical, mental, emotional. When had his control started unraveling? He forced his body to relax, one muscle fiber at a time. "You can let go. I'm not leaving."

"Sure you're okay?" The hands released their vise-like grip.

"Maybe a little mortified I can't seem to regulate my reactions. But yes, I'm okay. I don't know why my head's so messed up."

"I don't either. It's so not like you. But I might know the solution."

"I'm all ears." Might as well listen—Bran was fresh out of ideas.

"The old Branson—the one who traveled the world and spit in the face of fear—that Branson laughed all the time. No matter what."

"I'm older now. I've got more responsibilities. And more common sense."

"I don't think so. I think you're suppressing everything because you decided to become *proper*."

"Proper?" Branson started to object. Then he recalled something that might explain a lot. "I wonder… Remember about two years ago, when I had that huge fight with my dad?"

"You two are always arguing."

"This was worse. He discounted everything I'd ever done. Phantom Enterprises didn't impress him one iota. I was so furious. I hadn't thought of it 'til now, but ever since then, I've been trying to prove myself to him. I'm not trying to be proper, exactly. It's more like trying to show I could beat him at his own game. That's why I started Escapade Resorts—to compete with his Good Knight Resorts chain."

"And in two years, Escapade has grown twice as big as Good Knight," Finn remarked. "But I'm betting he's still not impressed."

"Nope." Bran popped the *P*. "Says it grew too fast. The value's inflated. It's set up to fail."

"Does it still bother you? His opinion? Can't you just forget him?"

"He had the audacity to inform me he's set up a trust fund. Not for me, but for my first child."

"So? One day your kid will get your old man's money. Sounds good to me."

"He had stipulations. A blood child—not adopted, not blind."

Finn let out a string of curses.

"I know. Just confirmed my plan to never have children."

"Could that be why Carina wants to get married?"

"No way. I haven't told a soul. Not even Fordham. Besides, the kid has to be eighteen to inherit." Branson balled his fists until his fingernails bit into his palm. When he spoke again, his voice was croaky. "How can he hate me so much?"

A hand squeezed his shoulder. "I'm sorry, Branson. Your dad sucks. If it makes you feel any better, my parents like you better than me."

The corner of his mouth twitched, threatening a smile. "I can't blame them."

He anticipated the shove that knocked him off balance.

"You're such a jerk," Finn said playfully. Then he gripped Bran's arm. "There was this guy I used to know... His name was Branson Knight. He was always up for an adventure. Nothing he wouldn't try. He didn't give a flip what anybody thought, least of all his *pretentious* father."

"Sounds like a fun guy." Bran grinned, somehow feeling lighter than he had in a long time.

"There was nothing he'd like better than pulling a fast one on a fiancée who's bound to have something up her sleeve."

Yes. Why hadn't he seen it before? Carina *had* to be hiding something. Two could play that game. In a flash, Bran was a college freshman, planning a prank on the hall bully, with the help of his three roommates. Those had been the happiest days of his life, before he got bogged down in responsibilities.

"What did you have in mind?" Bran asked.

"It depends. First... about Carina... It seems like you'd reject any woman your father might like. How determined are you to marry her and complete your business deal?"

"Less by the minute. It seemed like a good idea at the time. I have to find some other way to get control of that CF drug. I'm still ticked someone got the Astons to sell their shares."

"Are you sure she's telling the truth about that?" asked Finn.

"No, I guess not. I'll message Fordham. Maybe he can find out the real reason Carina wants to rush this marriage."

"How far are you willing to go to beat Carina at her own game—whatever that is?" Finn's slight English lilt grew heavier as he got more excited. "Ready to get a marriage license with me?"

"I'm in," Bran swore. "I'll do whatever you say. But Finn, I'm warning you..."

"About what?"

"If you and I end up married, you better not try to kiss me on the lips."

Bran heard garbled laughter. Then a hand grasped his and shook it with so much vigor his shoulder almost came out of joint.

"Branson Knight," Finn said his name with a chuckle. "Glad to have you back again."

With a text on the way to Fordham, Branson joined the rowdy group on the trek to the clerk's office. Carina pulled him to the back of the limo and plastered herself to his side. He wanted to push her away, but he needed to soothe her suspicions if he was going to uncover the truth.

As her fingertips slid up his thigh, he clamped his hand on top of hers to stop its progress.

"What's the matter, Branson?" Her silvery voice, meant to entice, set his teeth on edge like fingernails scraping on a chalkboard. "Are you mad at me?"

"Of course not. I'm just tense." He listened to the other conversations inside the limousine, relieved to hear everyone laughing and chatting. No one seemed to be paying any attention to them. He lifted her hand and placed it on her knee, covering it with his own to hold it in place.

"I'm sure I could help you with that tension."

Her suggestion made him shudder. "Not now, Carina. But I'd like to know how your father found out about the buyer. If the Astons told him, he must know who it is."

"Dad didn't have time to explain the details. Only said they expect a hostile takeover attempt any day."

"It could affect the company's stock prices, too."

"I'm sure it won't," she answered a little too quickly. "Dad said Aston-Parker is extremely stable right now. Shouldn't affect us at all."

Why would she deny the obvious possibility?

"But a takeover—especially a hostile one—would probably send prices plummeting."

"We won't let that happen. That's why we should get married tomorrow, while we're here, and sign the contract for my shares. Monday could be too late."

"Right now, I want to get this license thing over with and get back to the tournament."

"You're not being very romantic," she whined. "Aren't you even a little bit excited? We're on our way to get our *marriage* license."

"For a marriage that will last a few months," Branson added. "I have to say, I'm surprised you'd consider getting married in a Las Vegas wedding chapel. Figured you'd want a big to-do with a long white dress and a fancy dinner."

"I'm planning on it. We'll have a proper wedding when we get home."

"I'm not interested in an elaborate wedding." *Not interested in any wedding. Maybe a bachelor's party, though.*

"What are you smiling about?" She leaned into him, nuzzling at the base of his neck. "Thinking about the wedding night?"

"Carina, we've talked about this. There's not going to be a wedding night."

"You could change your mind." Her words almost sounded like baby-talk, probably because her lower lip was protruding.

"I'm not changing my mind." Remaining calm was becoming more of a challenge.

"Shhh... Don't raise your voice. The others might hear."

What would the old Branson Knight do? Maybe goad her a little?

"I'm thinking of adding a clause to the prenuptial agreement." Bran lowered his voice, but tilted his head closer to Carina. "I might throw in a cheating clause. If either of us engages in sex with someone other than our spouse while we're legally married, the stocks revert back to the original owner."

A small gasp. Then silence. Branson enjoyed imagining her expression. Was her mouth hanging open?

"You can't do that," she rasped. "If you want to be celibate, that's your business, but you can't expect me to go along with it."

"I can. I'm thinking about it." He was proud of how even he kept his tone, without a hint of the laughter he was hiding.

"Too late. I've already signed the other one." Her voice was cold and hard. *The real Carina.*

"It's not valid until we're married. And your reaction tells me I *need* that clause added."

"Remember, it goes both ways." She hissed her warning like a snake. "So you can't sleep with Stephanie anymore."

The hair bristled on the back of his neck. "I've never slept with my personal assistant. Stephanie's not that kind of woman."

"That explains a lot." Carina sounded as if she could barely condescend to speak about her. "Pretending to be some innocent virgin, as if she hadn't been married and popped out a kid. How did she manage to pull the wool over your eyes? She's even fooled Finn, conning him into getting a marriage license. Maybe she puts out some hormone designed to make billionaires' brains quit functioning. Or maybe your brains are in your pants."

"Stop it—"

"You know, she's not what you think. My people have been digging and found something that might give you a whole new perspective on your PA, Miss Polly Perfect. Bet she told you her husband was a villain who deserted his blameless wife and sick kid."

"Shut. Up."

Though he'd never hit a woman in his life, Branson's muscles trembled with the desire to slap Carina for the insult.

She must not have sensed the danger, because she continued, undaunted. "The truth is, her ex is a really nice guy whose wife cheated on him. Did you know she refused to do a paternity test on the girl?"

"That's *enough*." He raised his volume enough that the other conversations halted for few seconds.

"I'm sorry, Bran. I didn't mean to upset you." Her voice went sugary-sweet, like an overripe melon. "I shouldn't have mentioned it. What's in the past is in the past. I promise I'll never bring it up again."

The limo pulled to a stop and someone opened the door.

"We're here." Finn followed his announcement with an off-tune hummed version of *Here Comes the Bride*.

"Believe me, you've made the wise choice," Carina whispered in his ear. "I'm not perfect. But then again, I don't pretend to be." She brushed a kiss on his cheek before scooting out of the limo.

Though Carina's accusations didn't sound like the Stephanie he knew, her words lingered in his mind like stale cigarette smoke.

CHAPTER 13

Stephanie was having second thoughts. In fact, she was having third and fourth thoughts. What had she been thinking when she'd blurted out an acceptance to Finn's outrageous marriage proposal? She looked like a hapless idiot. Or worse, a gold-digger. What must Branson think of her?

Even when Finn had informed her of his planned prank, to switch the names on the marriage licenses, she still felt miserable. And Branson, though he'd been laughing and joking when he returned from his tête-à-tête with Finn, appeared distraught as well. She was tempted to turn on her microphone and speak a few calming words, but he'd brushed past her when he came into the building with Finn, giving off a hostile aura.

Better get used to the cold shoulder. I'll probably get a lot of them once he and Carina are married... if I'm still around.

Stephanie needed to face the facts. Even if Finn spoiled Carina's plans for a Las Vegas wedding, the two would get married eventually. Steph had thought to warn Branson against Carina, but should she? Branson wasn't stupid. He knew exactly what he was getting from Carina. The witch might be spoiled and selfish and hateful, but she was also poised, beautiful, and born into high society. Branson had made his choice with his eyes open, so to speak.

Though Steph's job was guaranteed in writing for the next twelve months, she realized she couldn't stay. She could hardly bear seeing the two of them together now—it would be ten times worse after the marriage.

Too bad she couldn't convince herself to fall in love with Finn. Not that she believed for a minute his proposal was serious, but it would help her get over Branson. Finn was a fun guy, and he'd certainly understand Ellie's struggles with cystic fibrosis. As charming and handsome as he was, though, her heart was fastened to Branson like a wet tongue on a frozen metal pole.

Stupid. Stupid. Stupid. Why do I do this to myself? She'd only been in love twice in her life, and both were impossible relationships.

Her first love had been Jeff. When they were dating, she'd thought his possessiveness was cute. Immediately after marriage, however, that possessiveness morphed to insane jealousy, as he cut her off from all her friends and family. Convinced she was cheating on him, he refused to believe Ellie was his child until she proved it with a blood test. And when Ellie was diagnosed with cystic fibrosis, he presented that as infallible evidence of her unfaithfulness. He left her and immediately hooked up with an old girlfriend, with whom he'd been having an affair the entire time. Too preoccupied with saving Ellie's life to argue with him, Steph had been almost relieved to see him go. Except for the financial strain, life was easier without him.

She was fine with being single and gave all her attention to Ellie, swearing off men forever. That worked for a few years, until she met Branson. Yet another impossible relationship. She was drawn to him like a magnet to steel, a gentle soul hidden behind a gruff exterior. Steph was convinced she alone saw his true inner beauty, not to lessen the impact of his amazing muscles and drop-dead gorgeous face.

Why can't I control my feelings?

"Can't believe they stay open this late," Jarrett remarked as they exited the elevator and made their way into the clerk's office.

"That's Vegas, baby," said Cole.

Steph limped along, with Finn's help, carrying her shoes instead of wearing them.

They arrived to find two other couples already waiting in line. The clerk must've been remarkably efficient, checking both out in less than five minutes. With a tired smile and worn-off makeup, the middle-aged clerk looked up. "How can I help you?"

"Good evening," Finn greeted her with a flourish of his hand and a deep bow. "We need two marriage licenses, please."

"Have you filled out your applications online?"

Though she was pleasant in her delivery, Steph could tell she'd probably asked the same question a thousand times every day for years.

Finn cocked his head. "No. We didn't know we could."

The woman leaned to the side and craned her head to

check out the boisterous group, which now included Cole at the back, attempting to link arms with a mortified Jarrett.

"Those two with your group?" the clerk asked.

Finn rolled his eyes. "Yes, but they're not getting married. Only four of us."

"As long as no one else is in line behind you, you can just fill out your forms right here." She slid some papers forward. "Print and sign at the bottom. Include your social security number. I'll need to see picture ID—a driver's license or passport."

"Carina, you go first," said Finn. "Then I'll help Branson."

Carina moved up beside Finn and quickly finished her part, flashing her driver's license, which included an image worthy of a magazine cover.

Who looks that good on their driver's license? Steph decided to keep hers in her purse until the last minute, lest anyone see her disastrous picture. The lady at the DPS office had attempted three previous shots, each one capturing Steph's eyes closed. In the final attempt, Stephanie had held her eyes open so wide she looked like someone had punched her in the stomach. Over her objections, the DPS agent had pronounced it perfect. Steph had often considered misplacing her license rather than being stuck with the bug-eyed image for eight years.

Cole and Jarrett were laughing at a video on one of their cell phones, and they called Carina back, clearing the way for Finn to work his prank, putting her and Carina together on the marriage license.

"Stephanie, you can go next. Okay, sweetheart?" Finn gave her a wink.

The pen slipped in her sweaty fingers as she attempted to

write her information down. She whispered, "No offense, Finn, but I'm nervous filling this out. You sure you can pull this off? And when are you going to tell her? What if she doesn't think it's funny?"

"No doubt, she won't see the humor in it. But the rest of us will have a great laugh." His elbow nudged her, and she glanced up to find him staring with unrepentant merriment in his eyes. "Stop worrying. She'll be angry with me, not you. And I could care less."

"If you say so." She passed her driver's license to the clerk, who gave it a summary inspection, compared it to her paperwork, and slid it back to her, face up. She sucked in a surprised breath and slapped her hand over it. *Not quite fast enough.*

"You take that picture at gunpoint?" Finn attempted to pry it from her fingers, then tickled her ribs and succeeded in snatching it away.

"You cheated," she hissed, giggling. "Give that back."

"Sorry, sweetheart." He guffawed, holding it out of reach and ogling her fish-eyed expression. "I can't pass this up. It's a perfect distraction. Hey, Jarrett! Catch!"

To her complete horror, he tossed her license to the back of the room, into Jarrett's waiting hands.

"Nooooooo!" She scrambled after him as he held the license high, displaying it to Cole and Carina. "Give me that!"

"Stephanie," Cole cackled as Jarrett passed him the license in a cruel game of keep-away. "Back in Texas, we'd say you look like you got stuck with a cattle prod."

"So not funny," Stephanie replied, though she couldn't help laughing. "Be nice. I'm injured."

"I think you look cute," Jarrett argued. "Kind of like a baby owl."

Carina opened her mouth to comment, but Stephanie sent her the murderous look she'd used for years on Ellie when she'd been misbehaving. Carina bit her lips, instead. *Wise move.*

"Okay," Finn announced. "We're all done."

"I'll take ours." Carina waltzed up to Finn, her hand outstretched.

"I have it, safe and sound, and I'm keeping it." Branson's grim expression brooked no argument as he patted the chest of his tuxedo.

Steph wondered if Carina would find a way to steal it.

"Let's get back to the tournament," said Cole as he handed Steph's license back. "Hey, Stephanie. Don't be upset. Shock and awe looks good on you."

"Cole, you are walking on thin ice," Jarrett replied. "Did you see the look Steph gave you? She's about to put you in time-out."

"Time-out, I can handle." Cole held up his palms in mock terror. "I was afraid she might stick that license where the sun doesn't shine."

∽

BRANSON HAD a concierge doctor waiting in the lobby when they returned to the hotel. He insisted on remaining behind with Stephanie, since he needed to authorize his employer insurance, but sent the others back to the tournament. Carina hesitated, giving Steph a dirty look, but Cole propelled her forward, whispering something hilarious in her ear, her strident laughter echoing off the high ceilings.

Though the baby-faced guy wore a white coat with M.D. emblazoned on the pocket, Steph could hardly believe he was a doctor. With wide eyes and sparse beard, he could've been high school aged. As he poked and prodded her ankle, Steph bit her lip to keep from crying out. Breaking out in a cold sweat, she quickly shed her wrap and gripped the arms of the chair.

This innocent-looking kid is a sadist.

She hissed in pain as he twisted it one direction and back the other.

"You sprained your ankle," he said.

Duh. Thanks for nothing.

"How did it happen?" he asked.

"Walking in those." She pointed to the abandoned heels beside her chair. "It's a good thing I changed shoes earlier tonight. The other pair had even taller heels. I'm obviously meant to wear flats."

"Are you sure her ankle's not broken?" Branson asked. "Should we go to the emergency room?"

"I don't think it's broken," he explained as he placed a boot on her foot. "But if it doesn't seem to be improving in a few days, you should go see an orthopedist. Rest it. Ice it. Elevate it. You should be fine."

"Can you give her something for the pain?" Bran asked.

"It's not that bad," Steph interrupted before the doc could answer. "I'll just take some ibuprofen."

The doc nodded. "Good idea. Anti-inflammatories like ibuprofen or aspirin or naprosyn sodium, around the clock. Elevate to reduce swelling. Use these crutches for at least the first twenty-four hours to keep the weight off your foot. This air cast ought to keep you from twisting it while it's healing."

"I'll be sure she uses the crutches," Branson assured the doctor, as he completed some sort of online transaction via his accessible cell phone.

With a few forms signed and final instructions given, the doctor was on his way. The entire appointment took less than fifteen minutes. Bran stood and offered his hand to Stephanie. She accepted his help, irritated that his touch still sent tingles up her spine.

She had to get over him. He belonged to Carina, now. She resolved to forget all about him. She willed the tingles away. *I need to concentrate on something else. Okay, I'm at the dentist, and she's about to drill on my tooth.* It worked... right up until the moment Branson spoke.

"Stephanie, I can't stand that you're hurting." His brows were knit in anguish. "I wish it was me, instead."

Melting. She was literally melting. Her resolve turned to mush. Carina didn't deserve him. Yet, she had to accept that Bran had chosen her, whatever his reasons.

Bran passed her the crutches, and she attempted to balance on one foot while holding a crutch and a shoe in each hand, her purse strap slung over her shoulder.

"*Woops*," she exclaimed, as she wobbled.

Bran's steadying hand grasped her arm, holding her firmly until she was stable. Then his fingers slid across to the bare skin of her back, eliciting a new set of quivers, more intense than the first.

"You're shivering." The tender concern in his voice almost broke her heart, as he dropped his cane and used both hands to rub her arms, warming them with the friction.

Thank goodness that's all he did. If he'd chosen to share his heat by pulling her against him, she would've dissolved in a puddle, right there on the lobby floor.

Her back shouldn't have been bare. She spied her lace wrap, still on the chair.

"I didn't pick up my cape. Don't think I can reach it without dropping something."

Before she finished her sentence, Branson was groping for the wrap. He retrieved it and draped it over her shoulders, smoothing it in place with gentle hands. "Is that better? It feels really lightweight. You could wear my tux coat."

"I'll be fine."

"Guess we need to get you changed out of that sexy dress." His husky intonation sent blood rushing to her face.

"That's my plan. I'll help you find the others and then head upstairs and hit the sack. I'll be in my warm PJs in ten minutes."

"I'd rather have you with me. I've been missing your voice in my head."

"Branson, I think it's time we faced reality. You told me you're dependent on me, but that needs to change. Once you're married, Carina won't want me around. She can't stand me."

His laughter startled her. "I don't care if she *hates* you. She has no say about my employees."

"So this is some sort of power play between the two of you?" Fury bubbled to the surface. "What am I? Some sort of pawn in your game? Stuck in the middle?"

"No. That's not it at all." He pushed his fingers through his hair, mussing it up in that charming way that tugged at her heart strings. *He probably does it on purpose, to torture me.*

"I can't take it anymore, *Mr. Knight*. I'm sorry. I love my job, but I think I need to quit." She had no idea how she could afford to take care of Ellie if she quit her job, but she couldn't worry about that right now. She had to escape, or she would go insane. What good was a crazy mother to Ellie?

"Hold on." Branson lifted an open hand and tilted his head to the side as if he were listening to their surroundings. "Let's go upstairs to your room where we'll have some privacy. You can change clothes, and I'll… I'll explain some things."

Steph blew a stray strand of hair out of her face. "This better be good."

CHAPTER 14

The elevator ride was silent, but for the mechanical noises. Though they were the only two occupants, Bran didn't want to begin his explanation, only to be interrupted if someone joined them on another floor. Besides, it gave him time to consider his approach.

No telling what Stephanie was thinking. She probably wished she'd never met him. What a mess he'd made of things. He'd planned to bring Carina in as a wife in name only, a business deal with mutual benefits. He'd thought she wouldn't want to interact much, perhaps spending most of her time in Europe. She'd caught him off guard with her efforts to rush the marriage. And he hadn't anticipated her ability to hurt Stephanie. In fact, his main purpose in the marriage had been for Stephanie and Ellie's benefit, though he didn't want to reveal that to her. Now she was threatening to quit her job, and he wasn't sure he could live without her. He was certain he didn't *want* to.

When they reached Stephanie's door, she stuffed a pair of

shoes into his chest. "Here. Hold these, please." After a bit of rustling noise and some frustrated mumbling, she added a purse. "This, too. I can't do anything with these stupid crutches."

"How did you carry all this stuff with your crutches? Why didn't you let me help you?"

"Didn't figure you'd want people to see you carrying high heels and a purse."

"Really? Did you forget I'm blind?"

"I had no idea," she said, with heated sarcasm.

The hinge creaked, and Bran heard the rhythmic clack of her crutches passing through the doorway. He followed her inside, still holding her things.

"I mean, I don't care if people stare. I'm already walking around with a cane and these scary eyes. Didn't you notice I haven't been wearing my sunglasses?"

"Cut it out, Branson. Why do you put yourself down?"

He shrugged. She probably thought, when he mentioned the chilling effect of his prosthetic eyes, he was fishing for affirmation. In fact, he admired Steph, who acted unperturbed by his appearance, as his Phantom Enterprise partners had since the day they met at camp. He didn't want or need false flattery.

"That wasn't my intent. I was simply offering to carry your purse or heels or ribbon or bows. I don't care what people think. I'm not even embarrassed to be seen holding feminine hygiene products."

"I'll keep that in mind if I ever buy one so large that it's beyond my power to lift by myself." The purse was jerked from his grasp, followed shortly by both shoes. He followed the sound of the clicking crutches.

"You can't come in here," she said, in a squeaky voice. "I'm changing clothes."

"So? It's not like I can see anything. I can explain things while you're getting dressed."

She mumbled something he didn't understand.

"What did you say?"

"Nothing. Just... I can't..." The crutches clacked closer. "Turn around."

"What? Why?"

"It feels like you're looking right at me." A hand gripped his arm and pushed. "Please, do it. Okay?"

Chuckling, he rotated obediently, until his back was toward her, and gathered his thoughts before beginning his explanation. Now more than ever, he regretted his lack of sight. Not because he couldn't spy on her as she changed clothes. But because he wanted to gauge her reaction as he revealed how the wedding plans had developed with Carina. What if she despised him for it? He might lose her anyway. The one thing he couldn't do was tell her he was doing it to gain control of the breakthrough CF drug Ellie needed. He wanted her to stay, but not because she felt obligated.

He heard clothing rustling behind him.

"Go ahead. I'm listening."

"I've dated Carina a few times, starting about a year ago."

"I remember. I made the initial appointment. She came to the estate, supposedly to talk about an investment opportunity. I was surprised when you actually went on a few dates. I was happy for you."

"You were?"

"Of course I was. I wanted you to date and get married

and have a normal, happy life. But I have to tell you, Carina's not good enough for you. She doesn't love you."

He could tell by her stiff speech she was getting riled up. He had to keep her calm.

"I know that. I don't love her either."

"Then why are you getting married?" she shouted.

So much for keeping her calm. "I—"

"It's hard enough to make a marriage work when two people love each other."

"It only has to work for a short time. We're only getting married to exchange stocks in our companies. Then we'll get divorced."

Silence. Then the bed springs creaked with weight, and the sound of Velcro ripping free rent the air. Still, she didn't reply. Was she shocked? Disgusted? He started to rotate toward her.

"*Stop.* Turn back around. I'm not finished changing."

"But… what are you thinking?"

"I haven't decided yet." Her words were terse. The creaking of the bed was followed by the rustle of clothing. "Why do you have to get married at all? Why isn't it strictly monetary, like all your other deals?"

"Because her dad put a clause in her stock ownership to keep them in the family. My attorney looked at the contract, so I know she's not lying about it."

The bed creaked again, more Velcro sounds, and her voice came from a standing position. "If you're getting a divorce, the stocks aren't staying in the family. Makes no sense."

"Originally, the stock ownership was provisional until

we'd been married for three years. I guess he hoped, by then, the marriage would last."

"Originally?"

"Carina got a call from her father tonight. Someone appears to be attempting a hostile takeover, so he's desperate enough to change the provisional period to three months. Guess he prefers me in charge to an unknown, even if I'm not in the family."

"Something's fishy. Too convenient. A sudden need to rush the marriage when we *happen* to be in Las Vegas." The crutches clinked and her voice shifted. "You're not usually that trusting, so I think you have more feelings for Carina than you're admitting."

"I don't trust her either. We did the marriage license thing just to put her off while we check out her story." He pulled the folded license from his pocket and held it out toward her, giving it a shake to attract her attention. "Finn told you about this, right? That he put the guys' names on one license and you and Carina on the other?" *What if she didn't know about Finn's plan? Maybe she wants to marry Finn.*

"Yeah, he told me. But I don't get it, Bran. If you aren't in love with her and you don't trust her, why marry her? No stocks could be worth that much. And I don't want to hurt your feelings, but I can tell you she doesn't love you either." Soft thuds of the crutches on the carpet were followed by the sound of a drawer opening.

"I'm not. I'm not marrying Carina. So you don't need to resign." He stuffed the paper back in his pocket. Finn had probably shown it to her while they were at the clerk's office.

"No, no, no. Don't put this on me." The drawer slammed

shut. "I didn't mean to give you an ultimatum, like *it's her or me.*"

"I'd already made the decision before you threatened to quit. Now, I'm playing along with her, trying to figure out her game."

Silence again. Then a huge sigh. "I'll be glad when this drama is all over. I've been so frazzled I forgot about finding a present for Ellie."

"What does she want?"

"Besides a Bridgette doll?" Steph chuckled. "I've already told her she's not getting one of those."

"What's Bridgette doll?"

"Nothing. I was making a joke. Believe it or not, I wanted to get her a picture of one of those Elvis impersonators with a personalized autograph. I thought those guys would be all over Vegas, but I haven't seen one yet."

"Isn't she a little young to be an Elvis fan?"

"It started when she was in the hospital with a lung infection. She must've watched a solid week's worth of those old Elvis movies. She knows every song he's ever sung, by heart."

Suddenly, nothing was more important than getting an autographed Elvis picture for Ellie. "We'll go find one of those guys, right now."

"No, it's almost eleven o'clock. You need to get back to the tournament. Carina's going to be spittin' mad we've been away this long. By the way, you can turn back around now."

As always, Steph was placing his needs first. It was high time someone started doing the same for her.

"I don't give a flip what Carina thinks."

"Yes, you do. You need to keep her happy until you figure out why she's rushing you into this marriage."

He pulled out his cell phone. "I'm calling Finn. He'll keep Carina occupied. The hotel concierge can find an Elvis for us. And when we get back, I'll still have at least an hour to play. Meanwhile, I've got my people checking out her story."

"You sure you don't mind?" Her words came out breathy and excited, and he felt warm all over. He'd give anything to see the smile he'd put on her face. Maybe more to see the one on Ellie's face when she got her present.

"Not at all."

∾

"I called every place I know, but only one answered the phone. Like I said, it's a little late." The concierge spoke in a medium-pitched, staccato tone, louder than Branson preferred.

"Did you find an Elvis for me or not?" Bran lowered his voice, hoping the concierge would do the same. He didn't want Stephanie to overhear the extent he'd gone to in order to locate an Elvis.

"They closed at eleven, but they agreed to stay open if you get there by eleven fifteen and purchase the super bonus package that includes three songs, pictures and a video." The loud-mouthed man didn't take the hint.

"Branson, I don't want a package," Stephanie tugged on his sleeve. "I just want a single signed photograph. I was thinking fifteen or twenty dollars. If it's more than that, I'll get her some pink furry dice. She's six years old. She'll like anything I bring her."

"Ellie likes Elvis. That's what she's getting. I'm paying for it." He aimed his face toward her and lowered his brows, duplicating the intense expression that always disturbed Carina.

"Stop doing that," Steph complained, in a stern tone.

He maintained his severe expression. "You were really excited about it five minutes ago. Nothing has changed. Consider it overtime pay for the weekend. Or hazard pay for spending time with Carina."

At that, she laughed. "Fine. You win. I think I actually deserve that hazard pay. I was chasing after her so I could chew her out when I sprained my ankle." She let out another awkward chuckle. "Just stop looking at me like that."

"You finally admit it bothers you?" Glad to have won the contest of wills, an event that was rare with Stephanie, it still hurt for her to reveal her aversion to his prosthetic eyes. She'd refused to concede the fact the past two years, probably one of the reasons he'd felt so secure around her.

"Yes, it bothers me. I don't know how you do it, but it makes me feel…" Her voice trailed off.

"What? Creepy? Frightened?" He tried to laugh it off and sound unoffended.

"Naked," she whispered.

"*Naked?*" He must've repeated the word a little too loudly, because she punched his arm.

"Shhh!" She tugged him away from the concierge desk. "Yes, *naked*. Like you can look inside my soul. Like I can't hide anything from you. Like you know all my thoughts. All my emotions. Makes me feel out of control. Surely you get that, don't you?"

He tried to swallow, but his dry tongue stuck to the roof

of his mouth. "You don't feel terrified when my eyes seem to be focused on you? Or grossed out? Knowing they aren't real?"

"What a stupid question! Is this some kind of joke?"

"Mr. Knight, your limousine is here." The concierge spoke in the flattering tone used by people courting a hefty tip. "Your driver will wait and bring you back to the charity tournament as soon as you're done. I hope you have a marvelous time with Elvis."

Bran slid a hundred from his wallet. The bill zipped from his hand so fast he might've gotten a paper cut.

Inside the limousine, Stephanie chatted with her usual unbridled excitement. "I can't believe it. We're going to get a video recording with three songs. Plus pictures. Ellie's going to be out-of-this-world thrilled. She may forget all about the Bridgette doll. Really, I don't know how I'm going to top this."

"Uhmm," he mumbled, as his thoughts scrambled about like mice in a maze. If Stephanie didn't mind his eyes, could she possibly care about him more than she admitted? And what about his own feelings toward Stephanie? He'd never let himself consider the possibility of a romantic relationship. The same way he beat his body into submission with exercise and diet, he'd honed his emotions where Steph was concerned. Yet he'd failed, allowing himself to become *dependent* on her. Were there deeper feelings lurking beneath the surface? Was he in love with Stephanie, as Finn had suggested? Was he capable of love? And even if he admitted to being in love with her, didn't she deserve better than a broken man?

"We're here! I think *I'm all shook up*." Steph sang the last phrase in a poor imitation of Elvis, chuckling at her own joke. "Let's go."

The door opened and Stephanie exited, her crutches clanking together as she dragged them out behind her. Branson followed her, using one hand to locate the top of the opening and his cane to find the curb. He stood up, waiting for Stephanie's hand to guide him.

"Steph?" he called.

"Oh no! Branson, get back in the limo." From a few feet away, her voice altered as if she'd been facing away and then swiveled toward him. Her crutches clomped back, and she grabbed his arm, clamping down so hard his adrenaline kicked into overdrive.

"What's wrong? Did someone try to hurt you?" He attempted to shuffle in front of her, wishing he knew where the threat originated.

"No, but this place… it won't work."

"Why not? Is it a bad neighborhood? Are there drug dealers? Hookers? What is it?"

"It's a *wedding chapel*."

CHAPTER 15

Stephanie stared at the lettering on the glass door —*Hunka Hunka Burning Love Wedding Chapel.*

"Go on," Branson urged. "What can it hurt?"

"We won't actually be getting married, right?"

"We can't. We don't have a marriage license. The only person I can marry tonight is Finn."

"Yes, but we won't have to do the whole, *I-do* thing, will we?" *If we have to go all the way through a fake ceremony, I might start crying. He'll find out I'm in love with him. It'll ruin everything.*

"Would it be so hard to pretend we were in love?"

No. The hard part is pretending I'm pretending.

"I'm not much of an actress. It'd be better if we could skip the ceremony."

"But Ellie would probably get a kick out of seeing her mom get married by Elvis on the video."

"And how would I explain to her that you and I aren't really married? Did you think of that?"

"You can tell her we made a movie together, like all those Elvis movies she watched."

Yeah, but how will I explain it to my heart?

With a huge breath to bolster her courage, she pushed the door open and hobbled inside.

"Mr. Knight! We're glad you made it." A gray-haired man in a fifties-style suit—definitely not an Elvis look-alike—greeted them as they entered. "And this must be your lovely bride."

She started to correct him. "We're just here to—"

"That's right," Branson interjected. "This is Stephanie and I'm Branson."

"I'm George. I'm the wedding director here." He jotted down their names. "Mr. Sampson told me to take special care of you two. I understand you want the super bonus wedding package, right?"

"Whatever it takes to get signed pictures and a video with Elvis."

She grabbed his hand and squeezed, her fingernails biting into his skin. "What're you doing?" she muttered from the side of her mouth.

"Don't worry. I'll handle it," he muttered back.

"Let's take care of the financial details first," George said, with a bright smile. "And if you'll give me your marriage license now, I'll be sure it gets signed. If we wait 'til the end, couples sometimes forget. It's not legal unless Priscilla signs it."

"Priscilla? As in Elvis' wife?" Branson asked.

"That's right," he said, as he swiped Branson's credit card and handed it back. "Our wedding official is really named Priscilla. Only her last name is Parsons. She's considered getting it legally changed to Presley. Wouldn't that be cool? To have your marriage certificate signed by Priscilla Presley?"

"We aren't getting Elvis?" Stephanie asked.

"You get Elvis, for sure. In the super deluxe bonus package, Elvis will sing you three love songs. Plus, you get digital images, an autographed print, and a video recording of the ceremony." He frowned. "I don't have your marriage license."

"We don't have one," Steph replied. "And Branson's in a pretty big hurry to get back to the hotel."

George smiled, revealing a jagged broken front tooth. "I understand, man. Raring to get back for the honeymoon, right?" He doubled over, cackling with laughter until he started choking. Meanwhile, Stephanie searched the room for a hole to crawl into and hide until her face stopped burning. Her only solace was Branson appeared equally uncomfortable.

"Sorry," he whispered, giving her hand a squeeze.

When did we put our hands together? Did I do that?

When George caught his breath, he coughed a few times, low and hoarse, like an old smoker. "Well then... no license? We'll skip that part. We do it all the time." George walked to a set of ornate doors and waved for them to follow. "Lots of people get married in Vegas without a license and have a legal ceremony later."

"Can we skip the ceremony and just get the pictures and the video?" Steph asked, tottering behind him with Branson.

An incredulous voice behind them inquired, "You don't want to get married?" The owner of the voice was woman, approximately the size and shape of a linebacker, sporting a low-cut blue-velvet dress and a mass of Orphan-Annie curls on her head. She stared for a long time, her round eyes, accented with thick black liner, taking in every detail of their appearance, and then burst out with a peal of laughter. "You're teasing, aren't you?" She stuck out a proportionately-sized hand. "I'm Priscilla. I'll be doing the ceremony."

For the first time, Stephanie realized how they looked—Branson in a sleek black tuxedo and her in a flowing, floor-length, designer gown that happened to be white, with tiny strands of embroidered coral flowers—exactly like a couple getting married. Would Priscilla believe Branson was wearing a tux for a charity tournament, while Steph had chosen her dress because it had a matching bolero jacket to keep her warm and a long skirt to hide the boot on her foot?

"We're mostly here to get pictures with Elvis," Steph explained.

The doors burst open and there stood a twenty-something Elvis in all his tight-white-panted, shiny-sequined glory. "Hello, darlin'," he said, with a charming southern Elvis accent.

"Hi." Steph couldn't help the nervous giggle that escaped. She felt so silly, she was embarrassed to discover a video camera trained her direction.

Strains of music poured from overhead speakers and Elvis began to croon, "Love me, tender..." As he sang, his eyes zeroed in on Stephanie, his upper lip twitching, his body gyrating. He moved closer and closer, until he edged Branson out of the way. Her cheeks couldn't have been any hotter if someone had lit a fire around her neck. When he finished the song on one knee, holding her hand and swearing that he loved her and he always would, George and Priscilla clapped and cheered.

He rose to his feet. "Thank you, very much," he said, Elvis style.

"Can we get on with the ceremony?" Branson seemed irritated, probably because he wasn't able to see the performance.

"You must be the blind groom." Elvis turned and grabbed his hand, giving it a shake. "I'm Elvis. You're a lucky man, marrying this beauty. Do you need help getting inside the chapel? There's some steps at the front—might be kind of hard."

Steph cringed. Branson hated it when people assumed he couldn't do anything without help, simply because he was blind.

"Shut up, Billy," said Priscilla. "Pardon my son, Mr. Knight. He inherited my musical talent, but none of my social graces. Must've gotten those from his no-good, worthless daddy."

"He's your son?" Steph looked back and forth between the odd pair.

"I know." Priscilla gave a conspiratorial wink. "He didn't inherit my good looks either."

"Sorry if I said something wrong." Elvis apologized, his expression truly befuddled.

"It's okay," said Branson. "I'm not offended."

"Well, you should be," Priscilla insisted. "Billy, Mr. Knight here has more brains in the tip of his little finger than you do in your entire head. I believe he can navigate a set of steps without your help. Do you know who he is?"

"No." Elvis scratched his head, staring at Branson as if he were an abstract painting.

"He owns Phantom Enterprises."

"Oh geez!" Elvis snatched Branson's hand again, and shook it even harder. "I'm your biggest fan. I own every video game you ever created."

"That's great," said Branson in a tone that pleaded for interference.

Steph took pity and rescued him from his admirer. "I'm afraid I need my fiancé's hand back, Elvis. And you might be surprised to know video games are only a small part of Phantom Enterprises."

"Could I maybe get your autograph after the wedding, Mr. Knight? I could trade you for an extra Elvis print."

"That's enough, Billy." Priscilla wagged a finger at him. "We need to start the wedding. Mr. Knight, come with me. We'll wait in the front while Elvis walks your bride down the aisle."

Elvis offered his elbow, and Steph placed her hand in the crook, eyeing him with suspicion. "How old are you, anyway?"

"I'm old enough, sugar."

She doubted it.

Crutches in hand, she stepped into the room, and there stood Branson, waiting at the front of the chapel, with George beside him, like a weird best man. The music began, and Elvis started singing *I Can't Help Falling in Love with You* as they walked. Except it only took about half a verse to get to the front. The rest of Elvis' song came while she and Branson stood awkwardly facing one another, once again holding hands. Her heart was beating so fast, she thought she would die any second. No doubt her drumming heart drowned out Elvis' song. Yet Bran didn't act as if he noticed.

His thumbs began to trace slow circles on the backs of her hands, calming her rapid breaths, but causing an ache in her chest. Each time she glanced up at him, his blue eyes were stripping her bare. *He must know I'm in love with him. He can probably sense it through his fingers. Or feel it in his bones.*

"Do you, Branson, take Stephanie, to be your lawfully wedded wife?" Priscilla asked in a sweet tone that belied her massive size. Stephanie thought no one would dare answer no, or Priscilla might beat them up. "To have and to hold from this day forward, for better or worse, in sickness or in health, in poverty or wealth, forsaking all others until death do you part?"

After the question, the room fell deathly quiet. Trembling from head to toe, Stephanie stared at their joined hands, living out a silent nightmare. The fake ceremony was a mockery of her love. A tear dripped from her eye and trickled down her cheek, and for once, she was glad Branson couldn't see. His hands squeezed her fingers, and she glanced at his face, shocked to find it wet with his own tears. His lips moved.

"I do."

His answer was barely audible, but it rang in her ears and echoed inside her head, throwing her world into confusion. Was he acting? Or was it real? Surely he didn't mean it. In two years, he'd never hinted he had feelings for her. If he loved her, why would he even consider marrying Carina?

His hand slipped inside his coat and emerged with a handkerchief to dab his eyes, as a piece of paper fluttered to the floor.

"I'll get that." George snatched it up, lest it mar the perfect photos of a wedding that was wrong on every level.

Priscilla repeated the same question to Stephanie. She said, "I do" before she lost her nerve, praying the rest of the ceremony would be quick, so she could escape this torture.

"Do you have rings?" Priscilla asked.

"No." Steph sent her a pleading look. "Let's skip that part."

"I'm always prepared," said George, as he retrieved a black cloth pouch from his vest pocket. "We have these solid gold rings available, just for you. They're not included in the package, so they would cost an extra—"

"That's okay," Steph interrupted. "We don't need—"

"We'll take them." At Bran's reply, George flashed a smug smile. Tonight must've been a lucrative event for the little chapel.

Priscilla selected two bands. "These will do for the ceremony. We can trade them out after, if they don't fit. Now Branson, take this ring and place it on Stephanie's finger and repeat after me."

Bran slid the thin band onto her ring finger and spoke in a strangled voice. His words of love and commitment had no more significance than the ones Elvis had sung to her. That it fit perfectly only sharpened the sting. She stared at the wedding ring on her hand, the image wobbling in her tear-filled eyes, and her heart ached at the perversion of meaning. It wasn't real. It should've been made of cheap plastic, rather than gold.

Priscilla tapped her shoulder. "Your turn, dear."

Moving as if she were swimming in a fog as thick as honey, Steph placed the ring on Branson's finger and repeated Priscilla's words. "With this ring, I thee wed, and promise to love, honor, and cherish you, with all that I have, and all that I am, as long as we both shall live."

"By the authority vested in me by the state of Nevada, I now pronounce you husband and wife. You may kiss your bride."

Would he complete the farce, sealing it with an empty kiss? For two years, she'd fantasized about this moment, never believing it would happen. He was everything she'd ever wanted. Every muscle coiled in anticipation, though she attempted to tamp down her expectations. It wasn't like a single kiss from the lips of Branson Knight could wipe away the pain and humiliation of the sham wedding ceremony.

Branson's hands rose in slow motion, cradling the sides of her face, tilting her chin up. Blood drummed in her ears, as his eyes closed and his mouth moved toward hers. His lips brushed against her own, only for a second, sparking a thousand nerve endings. Those lips returned, soft and tentative, a gentle caress that left her wanting more. Then his mouth slanted across hers. Colors erupted inside her head. Her hands locked around the back of his neck, to pull him closer. His demanding lips took possession of her mouth, as he stole her breath and stopped her heart in its tracks. She responded with a force born of years of unfulfilled desire. When his mouth wrenched away, he left her panting for air.

It was everything she'd dreamed it would be, and more. It was also an illusion. A mirage, taunting her with false promises. Fresh tears stung her eyes. Her insides hurt like salt on raw blisters. Even in a haze of pain, she recognized the weakness she'd exposed and hated herself for it. She was so hopelessly devoted to Branson Knight that she would replay the entire agonizing ceremony for another taste of his lips.

I'm such a fool. Like a wounded soldier who'd lost a battle, she limped outside, leaving Branson to collect the package that would become Ellie's gift. Maybe she would throw away every mocking reminder and buy a pair of furry dice instead.

Five minutes later, she was back inside the limo with a solemn Branson. As they motored back to the hotel, he handed her an envelope. Inside was a flash drive and two signed photographs.

"Stephanie?"

"Branson, don't. I can't talk about it."

"For what it's worth, I'm sorry. I thought maybe you..." He didn't complete the sentence. Perhaps he sensed the feeble wall she'd erected around her emotions.

He was sorry. He regretted the ceremony as much as she did. He probably regretted the kiss as well. Everything was ruined. How would she be able to work for him, after this?

He knows. Steph balled her hands into fists, her nails biting into her palms. *He knows I love him, but he doesn't love me. He only needs me.*

"I know you're upset." His voice broke into her thoughts. "But here's something to make you laugh. George found that marriage license on the floor, and guess what... Priscilla signed it." He pulled the license out and passed it to her. "So I think this means Finn and I are legally married."

He snickered, shaking his head, and she clapped a hand over her mouth to stifle a laugh. When it burst from between her fingers, the dam broke. Stephanie laughed with Branson until they were both in tears and gasping for air.

"I'm just glad I didn't have to kiss him," Branson quipped. "I warned him about that."

His comment sobered her as she, once again, relived their own shared kiss. No doubt, he hadn't wanted the intimate contact, yet he pretended enough enthusiasm during the moment. Perhaps, with his experience and skill, a kiss felt no more personal than driving a car. More likely, her thrill at finally kissing the man she loved had simply blinded her to his reticence.

She was glad when the limo stopped at the hotel. With any luck, she could escape upstairs and leave Branson under the watch-care of his friends. Her pounding head would welcome the respite from the lights and noise of the casino.

The car door opened. "Welcome to the Grand Laurencia, where good times are had by all."

Good times. Ha! Not even close. Steph's eyes fell on the paper resting on her lap. All at once, the world tilted on end.

"Branson." Her hand grappled toward him, clenching a wad of his tux coat, while she tried not to hyperventilate.

"Steph. What's wrong?"

"This isn't you and Finn." Cold sweat broke out on her neck. "It's you and *me*."

CHAPTER 16

Branson sat on the couch in his suite, his fingers toying with his wedding band, as Stephanie paced in front of him. She hadn't stopped moving for the past ten minutes, broadcasting from one side of the room, gradually coming closer, then moving to the other side of the room and back again, like a huge fuming pendulum.

"What're we going to do? This is a disaster."

Bran wasn't really listening. He was still reeling from that kiss. From the moment his hands touched her face, his heart had turned inside out. The feel of her skin beneath his fingers. The electric charge building in his gut. Her lips... so soft, so responsive. It took every bit of his power to maintain an appearance of control, while desire raged inside him. Not simply to possess her physically, but to meld with her for eternity. The emotions he'd been denying for the past two years had come rushing in like flood waters from a broken dam. He knew the truth, without a doubt.

I love her.

His soul already belonged to her, and he yearned to have hers. When he spoke those wedding vows, he'd never meant any words more in his life. While Stephanie had been shocked and horrified to discover what Finn had done to the marriage license, Bran had fought an impulse to shout for joy and kiss her senseless. At the moment, he couldn't even drum up an ounce of anxiety about Carina and losing his opportunity to gain a controlling share of the stocks.

Her tirade continued. "I'll lose my job. You're going to hate me. Divorces are ugly, you know. Not that I would ever want anything from you. I just want out, that's all. I know you want out, too. What're we going to do?"

She wants out. Could she be afraid of commitment? Carina had intimated the divorce was her fault, rather than her husband's desertion. No, he refused to believe something like that about Steph.

Why didn't she want to be married? She'd freely admitted she wasn't repulsed by his prosthetic eyes, and she'd responded to his lips. He'd felt her tremble at his touch, heard the soft moans when he kissed her. Yet she seemed terrified of the idea that they would remain married. He couldn't force her into a relationship she didn't want.

"Stephanie?" he interrupted her ongoing speech.

"What?" She spewed the word out with a burst of air, like a relief valve on a pressure cooker.

"I don't hear your crutches. Are you walking on your sprained ankle?" He kept his voice low and even, hoping to soothe her frazzled emotions.

"We have bigger problems on our plate than a stupid sprained ankle. Who cares about my foot at a time like this?"

"I do." He rose to his feet, leaving his cane behind. He

reached her in four strides and placed a hand on her shoulder.

She flinched. "What are you doing?"

"I'm doing this." He bent to sweep his left arm behind her knees, scooping her off her feet and cradling her against his chest. She let out a squeal. She felt good in his arms—as if she belonged there. A fresh scent wafted from her hair.

"Are you using a new shampoo?" he asked, hoping to distract her, but truly curious.

"As a matter of fact, I am. It's strawberry and—"

"Wait, don't tell me." He buried his nose in her hair and filled his lungs with air. He was tempted to go further and test the tender skin of her neck with his lips. Instead, he pulled away. "It's really faint. Strawberry and *mango*?"

"That's it," she exclaimed with wonder. "You never miss."

"Nope, I don't."

"Hey." Her outraged tone was back, and she squirmed indignantly in his firm grasp. "Put me down."

"You didn't mind when Jarrett carried you." He marched from the living area to his bedroom. "Why would you object when your *husband* does it?"

"How can you joke about this? It's a disaster. You have to do something."

"I *am* doing something. I'm making my *wife* follow the doctor's orders." Branson smiled. He liked the way the word *wife* rolled off his lips.

"We can't stay married, Branson."

Best not to mention the fact he wasn't the least bit upset to find they were legally married. She obviously had different feelings on the matter.

"It doesn't do any good to panic." His knees found the

side of the mattress and he set her gently on the bed. "Stay," he commanded.

"I'm not a dog, Bran. You can't order me around."

He dropped to one knee and lifted her hand, eliciting a gasp of surprise. "Stephanie? Will you please stay off your foot, like the doctor asked? As your temporary husband and caretaker, I'd be immensely grateful."

"Fine. I'll stay." He could hear the grin in her voice and knew he had the upper hand.

He sat on the edge of the bed beside her. "Now let's talk about this logically. What are the facts?"

"Fact one—we're married. Fact two—we can't be married. Fact three—we need to do something about it, like go back to that wedding chapel and have them un-marry us before it's too late."

"No… fact three—there's no such thing as getting un-married. It's called a divorce, and it takes a while, like months."

"What about an annulment?"

"Maybe." Branson had hoped she wouldn't think about an annulment. He'd done enough research with his upcoming marriage to Carina to know an annulment was quick and immediate, but each state had specific specifications to qualify. Maybe he'd luck out, and they wouldn't meet the legal requirements for annulment in Nevada. "We can look it up, I suppose."

"Hand me my purse, so I can get my phone," she directed. "It's on this end of the couch. I'll research it right now. Maybe we can get an annulment tonight."

"Do I look like your personal servant?" he bantered, though he followed her instructions.

"No, you look like my personal captor, who won't let me off the bed."

"Hmm... interesting idea," he said, as he returned with her purse. "Your personal captor, who keeps you in bed? I like the sound of that."

"Branson! Don't be disgusting!"

"It was your idea. And we're married, so we could give it a try. I never thought about that sort of thing, but if you're into it..." He should've shown a bit of mercy, adding a wink or a laugh to assure her he was teasing. But her sputtering objections and shocked inhalations were too fun to pass up.

"I'm ignoring you," she announced. "I'm looking up annulments in Nevada. Let's see. Grounds for annulment. Number one—lack of parental or guardian consent. Nope. Number Two—insanity or lack of understanding. Does it count that I'm going crazy right now?"

"Compared to whom? You're in Las Vegas, remember?"

"Okay, number two's out. Three—fraud by one spouse, inducing the other to marry. Don't think so. Four—illegal marriage due to close relations. You think we might be long-lost cousins?"

"Doubtful. I'm sure my father would've told me, since he can't keep his nose out of my business. My family tree has been plotted back to the Mayflower. You see, my relatives wouldn't enter into marriage without meticulous research of the genetic line. It's like breeding a thoroughbred. Of course, I'm living proof that meticulous planning can still produce a botch."

"A botch. Yeah, right," she responded, though it was obvious her mind was on other matters. "The fifth one is that one spouse was married to another person at the time of the marriage. But my divorce has been final for years. So, I'm thinking the one about fraud is our best shot. What if Finn committed fraud when he put our names on that marriage license without our knowledge. Do you think that would work?"

"Didn't it say one spouse had to commit fraud on the other spouse?"

"Yes, it does. Rats! I think we're stuck."

He pulled his lips down, in an effort to appear disappointed, though every bone in his body wanted to lift her into the air and laugh and celebrate. Or maybe, celebrate with their lips together.

"It's no big deal, Stephanie. No one knows about it but you and me. We can keep it a secret until the divorce is final, even if it takes a few months."

His attorney could find ways to delay the process. And maybe by then, he could prove himself worthy of her love.

"But I'm not good at telling lies."

"You won't have to. It's not like anyone's going to say, 'Hey—are you guys married?' No one's going to suspect. All you have to do is not mention it."

"I guess you're right." Her tone wasn't as confident as her words. "But what about Carina? She thinks you're getting married right away. She's hoping to get married before you leave here."

Carina. No doubt, she'd find a way to destroy the marriage if she discovered it.

"I kind of forgot about her. Guess we'll have to keep it a secret, especially from Carina. I don't know what she's up to yet, but we can't let her use this as ammunition."

"Ohhhhh. We're doomed. I'm a terrible secret keeper. I

don't have trouble keeping things like your business details confidential, but when I'm upset about my personal life, I blabber like a drunk man."

He sat on the edge of the bed and found her hand. "I'll help you. It won't be so bad." He touched her fingers, soft and slender. Then he noticed the smooth thin band and murmured, "You still have your ring on."

"So do you," came her throaty reply.

Was it possible? Could she have feelings for him?

His pulse galloped as he worked up the courage to speak his heart. "I like the way this ring feels on your finger."

"What do you mean?" she whispered.

"I wondered if we might stay married instead of getting a divorce."

He heard a gasp. "No. You can't marry someone just because it happened by accident. A marriage has to be based on love and commitment."

His mouth was so dry his lips stuck to his teeth. "I agree. And I'm going to be honest with you… and honest with myself. I love you, Stephanie. I'm sure of it. I've tried to deny it for a long time, but I was lying to myself."

"Bran—" She started to respond, but he held up a finger.

"Wait, let me finish. I'm not trying to pressure you. I know I'm springing this on you all at once. And I know you had a bad experience with your first husband. But, what if we keep this marriage under our hats and don't pursue a divorce right away? Give me some time—say three months—to convince you to stay married. If it doesn't work, we'll end it, with no hard feelings."

"I… I don't know…"

He moved one hand and laid it on the side of her face.

"May I?" He swallowed the thick emotion that bubbled from inside. "May I touch your face? I want to see you... really see you."

She gave silent assent with a nod, and he moved his other hand to her face. His fingers gently traced the lines of her jaw. He let his hands move across her cheeks and felt her brows, her eyelids, her delicate nose. Then his fingers trailed across her quivering lips and down her chin to her neck. Her pulse throbbed under his fingertips.

"Beautiful," he rasped, a rapturous feeling swelling until his chest felt it might burst open. "You're even more lovely than I thought."

He bent to capture her lips with his. Though he tried to hold back, he felt like a starving man. Never had he wanted a woman the way he craved her. As he deepened the kiss, she responded, her breaths coming faster.

Thud, thud, thud, thud. A deafening pounding on the front door made both of them jump. Bran sprang to his feet, his face burning hot, as if he'd been caught doing something wrong.

"Branson what's going on?" *Cole's muffled voice came through the door.* "Carina's getting suspicious. Finn sent me to find you."

"Coming!" Bran answered, counting the twenty-three steps to the front door before he flung it open. "Why didn't Finn call me?"

Cole stepped inside. "Said he tried to call, but you didn't answer. He's on a roll at the craps table. He didn't want to stop, so I volunteered to come."

"How did I miss his call?" Branson retrieved his cell from his pocket and discovered the phone was set to silent. A quick check of his call record revealed several missed calls, one of them from Fordham. "Thought I had it on vibrate."

"Where's Stephanie?" Cole asked.

"She's in the bedroom."

"Maybe I should come back some other time." With a humorous lilt, Cole raised his voice for Steph to hear. "I'll leave you two alone so you can finish... *whatever* it was you were doing."

"I'm on top of the covers," Steph shouted. "*Fully clothed.*"

"That's enough, Cole," Branson growled, trying to listen to Fordham's message.

"We weren't doing anything. See?" Steph's voice came from the bedroom door, and Branson heard the soft thumping of Steph hopping across the carpet. At least she wasn't putting weight on her bad ankle.

Cole let out a long whistle. "You look gorgeous, Stephanie."

Bran hung up, having found it impossible to concentrate on Fordham's voice. He'd have to listen later.

"Thank you, Cole," she said. "Sweet of you to say that. I have to admit, with Carina around, I can't help feeling frumpy, especially when I'm limping around with this stupid cast on my foot."

"Trust me," Cole replied. "No one will be looking at your feet. That dress is stunning on you."

Branson felt an insane impulse to punch his so-called friend in the gut. A friendly punch, just hard enough to make him double over and wish he'd never flirted with his wife. Never mind that Cole didn't know they were married. And forget that Stephanie hadn't agreed to stay that way. For the moment, she belonged to him, even if it was a secret.

"I think she's stunning all the time." Bran let his indignation show. "She's just as beautiful *without* the fancy dress on."

He realized his mistake the moment the words left his mouth.

"Too much information, my friend." Cole pounded him on the back, guffawing so loud he sounded like he was dying of the whooping cough. "I won't even ask how you know."

"That's not what I meant," Bran mumbled.

"Cole, did you say Carina's upset?" Steph piped in, changing the uncomfortable subject. "We should probably hurry and get down there."

"Want me to bring you these crutches?" Cole's voice came from the wall beside the front door, where Steph had leaned them when she came inside.

"I'll take them to her," Bran snapped, striding to Cole and holding out his hands. He not only wanted to keep Cole away from Stephanie, but he also needed a chance to speak to her. To settle things.

"Here you go." Cole handed Bran the crutches, but added in a low tone, for Bran's ears only. "Be careful. You're giving off protective vibes, my friend. Might be confusing to Stephanie. I'd hate to see her feelings hurt any more than they already are."

Bran responded with a grunt, snatched the crutches, and marched back to Stephanie. What did Cole know about her feelings?

"I'll go catch the elevator." Cole called from the hallway as the door slammed shut behind him.

Bran cleared his throat. "Are you okay?"

"Yeah," she said, in a tremulous tone.

"You think you can handle going downstairs?"

"I don't have much choice, do I?"

He knew she didn't like feeling out of control. If she felt trapped into the marriage, she would reject him before he had a chance to make her fall in love with him—before he could prove he was worthy of it.

"You have a choice, Stephanie. We'll do whatever you want. If you don't want to be married, I won't force you."

"Before we left, you were furious that you *needed* me. Now you say you're in love with me. How am I supposed to believe that?"

"I think I've been in love with you for a long time. But I never allowed myself to consider the possibility of the two of us being together."

"Because we're from different worlds?" Her tone was tight. "I've got news for you. Nothing has changed. I'm still a nobody, and you're still a successful, wealthy businessman."

"You're putting words in my mouth. That's not what I was thinking."

"You're fooling yourself, Branson." Her voice cracked. "Carina is from a prominent family. She's beautiful and rich and educated. She probably went to Harvard."

"Oxford."

"Of course! Oxford." She exhaled an exasperated huff. "Don't you see? You're trying to convince yourself otherwise, but the truth is you'd never be satisfied with someone like me."

He cringed at the hurt in her voice. He had to tell her the whole truth, no matter how humiliating. Nothing less would ease her pain. He reached to sandwich her hands between his.

"Listen to me." He swallowed a lump the size of his fist. "I thought no one could ever really love me. People show me deference because of my wealth and power, but even Carina can barely stand to look closely at me. But something you said made me think…" He paused, turning to face her squarely. "You didn't seem repulsed. And the way you responded… I thought you might actually be able to love me."

"Oh, Branson." Her voice cracked. "I'm so sorry you've felt that way all your life. But I don't—"

He lifted his finger to her lips. He couldn't bear to hear it. "Please. Don't say anything yet. All I'm asking for is a little time. Please give me a chance to change your mind. Maybe you don't have to love me. I think I could be happy with whatever you can give me."

He withdrew his finger slowly, holding his breath.

She responded in a small voice. "I'm afraid, Bran. Really afraid."

He wilted. She'd rejected him. He couldn't make her feel something that wasn't there. "I understand."

She spoke again, so quiet he barely heard her. "But I'll think about it."

CHAPTER 17

Steph's mind spun in dizzying circles. She'd almost recovered from the initial shock as they sat in his hotel room, calmly discussing how to end the accidental marriage.

An inkling of hope had sprouted during the ceremony. As Branson spoke his vows, all the air seemed to vanish from the room. The sincere expression on his face... the fervent timber of his voice... She almost believed him. Yet she knew it was an act. The vows were merely the means to an end. At the time, like her, he had no idea the fake wedding would result in a legal marriage. It hurt. It hurt a lot. But she was accustomed to tamping down her dreams.

Then he said the three little words she never thought she'd hear from his lips.

"I love you."

If only it were true. Just a week ago, he'd announced his engagement to Carina with cool detachment. And hadn't she seen the couple emerging from her hotel room with Carina in a state of undress? As much as Steph wanted to believe he'd kissed her and suddenly fallen head-over-heels in love, even she wasn't that naive. If he loved her, he would've found some opportunity to mention it during the last two years. If he loved her, he would never have dated Carina, much less proposed to the woman.

Steph's sensible side screamed at her. *Why didn't you turn him down flat?* She should've insisted they seek a divorce as soon as possible. But how could she be expected to make an intelligent decision? After not one, but two, mind-altering kisses—tender and sweet, yet full of passion and restrained power—how could she think at all? Her iron will felt a lot like gelatin.

Declaring his love was one thing, but when his fingers read her face and he declared her beautiful with genuine wonder in his voice, her brain turned to warm goo. Nothing made sense. She was only certain of one thing... for all eternity, he'd ruined her for any other man.

"Are you going to bet?" Cole's voice brought her back to the present.

With only twenty minutes left in the tournament, many of the participants had abandoned the casino for the celebration party next door. Most of those who remained were clustered around two craps tables in the back of the room. Jarrett and Finn stood on the opposite side of their table, beside Branson, to whom Carina clung like a second skin. Stephanie had turned off her microphone thirty minutes ago. Bran certainly didn't act nervous, and she was tired of watching Carina hang all over him.

"No, I'm done betting. I think I'll go upstairs. My ankle hurts."

"But you have a lot left." With his neon hand, he pointed to the chips in front of her.

"Yeah." She stared unenthusiastically at the large stacks of chips. Upon her return to the casino an hour ago, she'd been surprised to learn she'd actually doubled her money earlier at the slot machines. Must've been that last angry push of the button before she stomped off after Carina.

At first she'd been enthusiastic about her newfound wealth and had relayed the news to Branson via her microphone, before hobbling back to the craps tables, ready to play. Yet, seeing Branson and Carina together turned her stomach, though she knew it was coming. It reminded her what a good actor he was.

She groped her vacant ring finger, thinking of the simple gold band at the bottom of her purse, while Carina's diamond engagement ring sparkled in the casino lights. She ought to throw it away, along with the marriage license she'd stashed in the zipper pocket.

"You can't leave now." Cole continued his protest. "What about all those chips?"

"I don't really feel like playing. Why don't you take them?"

"Are you kidding? Jarrett and I are both cold as ice tonight, but you're hot—in more ways than one." His eyebrows danced a jig, coercing a reluctant smile. "Anyway, house rules… contestants aren't allowed to transfer chips to each other. That'd be cheating."

"I still think I'll call it a night."

"Wait." His hand gripped her arm as she turned to go.

"Why not make a few big bets? If you lose, you lose. But you might accidentally win enough to get ahead of Finn and Branson. Think how they'd hate having to admit you bested them the first time you ever played craps."

"That would be fun," she agreed, though instead of Finn and Bran, she pictured Carina's shocked expression. "What should I do?"

"To start, take maybe a fourth of your chips and bet them on the Pass Line with this new shooter. You've been doing well with that bet."

She pushed a large stack of chips forward. Two rolls of the dice later, her chip stack had grown a bit bigger. Across the table, Carina flicked her blond locks behind her shoulder, laughing at something clever that passed between her and Bran. From the haughty expression in her eyes, Steph wondered if the comment was at her expense.

Steph bit her lip so hard she tasted blood. She had to get away from everyone, before she lost it.

"Hey, Cole." She swallowed hard, hating the way her voice trembled. "Can I add a bigger bet to my Pass Line?"

"You can, but the casino has rules about how much you can add." He motioned for the boxman and relayed the question. "Good news. There's no limit to the Odds bet, for the tournament. But you might want to go easy with a four as the opening roll. I wouldn't bet too much."

"I'm betting it all." Before Cole could stop her, Steph pushed her chips forward, in hopes of ending her torturous evening. She couldn't handle any more stress. Right now, all she wanted was to be home with Ellie, away from Branson Knight and his beautiful fiancée. To be hopelessly in love with her boss had been painful before... now it was excruciating.

Suddenly, her feet were dangling in the air as the room turned in circles. Cole cheered and hollered, spinning her around and sending her crutches crashing to the floor. "You did it! You doubled up!"

"Can't breathe," she wheezed. "Put me down."

Obediently, he let her slide to the floor and steadied her while retrieving her crutches. His expression was full of merriment as he waved across the table, calling out, "Eat our dust!"

It took every ounce of energy Steph had to muster a small fake smile.

Oblivious, Cole said, "Let's go cash you in before you bet again and lose it all. Finn and Bran are going to lose their shirts trying to catch up with you, now."

Daring a surreptitious glance across the table, she found Finn's mouth hanging open and Branson wearing a confused frown. But it was Carina who caught her gaze. Her steely eyes skewered Steph like a pinned butterfly. She could only watch as Carina slowly caressed Branson's arm with her delicate, manicured fingers. Then she planted a slow, deliberate kiss on his neck, leaving a red slash of lipstick behind.

The air turned caustic. It hurt to breathe. Steph twisted and hobbled after Cole, blinking through watery eyes. Carina had made one thing perfectly clear. She had staked a prior claim on Branson Knight, married or not.

Branson accepted the drink Carina shoved into his hand, but he couldn't make himself take a swallow. Sitting on a barstool at a round table, surrounded by hundreds of celebrants, most of whom already sounded drunk, he felt like a man adrift in an ocean.

"Finn," he called, hearing his friend's voice in the crowd a short distance away.

"Finn's not here. What do you need?" Carina's petulant tone had begun to irritate him like a festering splinter.

"Since I called Finn's name, I might want to speak to him."

"Why not talk to me instead? Especially since you ignored me the entire evening."

"Ignored you? Where do you get off saying that? I spent the last two hours with you."

"Yes, but you didn't hear a single thing I said."

He wanted to deny it, but this time, she was right. When he came downstairs with Cole and Stephanie, he'd split his attention between wagering at craps and Stephanie's conversation in his ear, rather than listening to Carina's babbling. He'd hoped she wouldn't notice. When Steph turned off the mic, he'd been too worried to give Carina his undivided attention. And Fordham's phone message was driving him to distraction, as well.

"I didn't mean to hurt your feelings, Carina. There was a lot of noise, and I had to listen carefully to keep up the action on the craps table."

"What's your excuse now?" was her sarcastic response.

"I'm talking to you, aren't I?"

"Yes, but you're still grouchy. Why aren't you drinking your champagne? I waited in a long line to get it for you. The least you could do is drink it."

One drink. Why not? After all he'd been through in less than twenty-four hours, he needed it. Bran picked up the glass and took a sip, wincing at the unpleasant taste. He'd never cared for champagne, but then he didn't really like the taste of any alcohol, except dry red wines. *Might as well get it over with.* He upended the glass flute, gulping it down and ignoring the tickling bubbles in his nose.

"Satisfied?" he snapped.

"You know what?" Her frigid voice could've made icicles form where her breath landed. "I'm going to find someone else to talk to. Someone who won't bite my head off. I'll come back after that drink has time to work."

Before Bran had time to apologize, she was gone. He strained his ears, but failed to hear any of his friends in the milling crowd and Stephanie was still maintaining radio silence. He was about ready to get out his cell phone, when someone wedged beside him at the table.

"Hey," said Cole.

"I'm glad you're here," Bran said. "Do you know what happened to Stephanie?"

"She went back upstairs. I couldn't make her stay down here, even though she might've won the whole tournament."

"I thought she'd at least come talk to me before she disappeared."

"Really? You were busy with Carina, so why would you care if Steph went to her room. You know, Steph was watching the whole time. The longer Carina hung on your arm like a dog in heat, the quieter she got."

"I had no idea it looked that bad." Bran wadded up the cocktail napkin in his fist. "You think Stephanie's upset?"

"In short... yes. Because I think she has a thing for you.

Correction. She *had* a thing for you. Before she left, she asked me to give you a message."

"What?" His heart stopped as he waited.

"She said, 'Tell Bran the answer is no.'"

An expletive slipped out before he could stop it.

Cole let out a low whistle. "Branson Knight said a curse word. It just dropped below thirty-two in hell."

"Shut up, Cole."

"Guess this means you're not denying it anymore?"

"Denying what?"

"That you're in love with Stephanie."

"It's complicated," Bran sputtered. "I need to go talk to her. Can you keep Carina occupied? I thought she would've gotten tipsy and gone to bed a long time ago. I can't believe she's still awake."

"Maybe she's afraid to let her guard down. I haven't seen her take a drink of alcohol this entire trip. She probably thinks something's going on between you and Stephanie."

Branson's gut churned. This weekend, he'd lost control of everything in his life.

"What's up, guys?" Finn arrived and a drink slid into Branson's hand. "I got you a martini. You look like you could use it."

"You're right." Bran lifted the glass and took a swallow. "But this makes two drinks for me. That's my limit."

"See ya later," said Cole. "Met a pretty little filly who likes my lime green hand. Turns out she's a sci-fi fan."

"Don't do anything I wouldn't do," Finn quipped.

"That's not saying much," Cole retorted, his voice receding.

Bran drained his drink and plopped his glass back on the table with more force than necessary. "You have some explaining to do."

"Me?" Finn faked an innocent tone.

"We agreed on a plan, and it didn't include putting Stephanie and me on the same marriage license."

Finn chuckled, unapologetically. "You found out, huh? It's no big deal. I thought it would be funny. Plus, I was afraid the clerk would ask questions if I did it the other way. Carina and Stephanie weren't acting very chummy at the office."

Bran debated telling him about the wedding ceremony, but decided against it. He didn't want Finn turning his marriage into a joke. "You could've told me before Stephanie discovered it by accident."

"Don't worry. I'll explain it to her tomorrow. I hear she's already gone upstairs. That's too bad."

"Maybe it's good she's away from Carina," Branson muttered. "I haven't told you about Fordham's voice mail."

"You heard back already? What did he find out?"

"Not much." Branson fingered his empty glass. "But he did say her story about the impending hostile takeover is a lie… or at least an exaggeration. Fordham says someone besides me has been gobbling up stocks, but they didn't make a deal with Aston, like Carina claimed."

"She made that up so you'd want to rush the marriage? I don't get it."

"Neither do I." The wheels turned in Bran's head. "What possible motive could she have?"

"Maybe something happened at Parker-Aston," Finn mused. "Maybe a lawsuit or a failed contract. Maybe the stock value is about to drop, so she wants to make the deal before you find out."

"Hadn't thought of that. I'll put Fordham on it. If something's going on, he'll find it."

"Whatever Carina's motivation, if she tries to get a bogus signature on that marriage license, she's in for a surprise," Finn boasted. "I have to say, I enjoyed pulling that off. I'm looking forward to having her chew me out for it."

"If she thinks I'm going to get drunk and rush out for a quickie wedding, she'll find out the hard way I always stick to my limits."

"Guess it was a good thing we got you drunk at camp that one time."

"Nothing makes a lasting impression like puking up your guts," Branson agreed. Almost as if responding to the memory, his stomach began to roil. Feeling a little dizzy, he gripped the table. "What was in that drink you gave me? Was it a double?"

"No way. I wouldn't do that to you." Finn's voice, heavy with concern, sounded as if it came from a tunnel. "You're white as a sheet. Are you feeling sick?"

"Yeah. Maybe alcohol on an empty stomach." The world spun in one direction while Bran's body twisted the other. He clung to the table for dear life as swirls of nausea hit him. His rapid pulse drummed inside his ear. "I… something's wrong… I feel crazy."

"What's the matter with Branson?" *Carina's voice.*

"I don't know. A reaction to alcohol, maybe. But he's only had two drinks."

Branson opened his mouth to say something, but his legs wobbled and gave way. Finn's voice cried out, and Bran felt his body sliding slowly to the floor, which seemed like a rotating merry-go-round.

"I'll take care of him," Carina crooned.

"You can't handle him by yourself," said Finn. "Me and the guys will get him upstairs."

The noise and the voices faded into nothingness.

CHAPTER 18

With damp hair and flannel PJs, Stephanie responded to the persistent knocking at her door, expecting to find Cole. Instead, there stood Carina, rubbing her hands together in frantic fashion.

"Branson's had a drug reaction. Finn wants you to come."

Her heart stopped, but only for a moment. Then a cool calmness overtook her. She couldn't afford to panic. She had to keep her head, to take care of Branson. He needed her.

"Is he at the hospital? Let me get my purse and some shoes." She hopped on one foot toward her bedroom.

"He's next door. We got him in bed."

"I'm coming." She grabbed her crutches and swung her purse over her shoulder, following Carina in bare feet. "What happened? Bran doesn't use drugs. How did he have a reaction?"

"It was an accident."

Steph didn't bother to ask any more questions. She didn't trust Carina's answers, anyway.

Cole let them inside Branson's room, sporting an equally anxious look that almost destroyed her calm façade. *Think, Stephanie. Think. Bran is okay. If he were dying, they would have him at the emergency room.*

She heard yelling and turned to see Jarrett and Finn standing on either side of the bed, trying to hold down a thrashing Branson.

"What's wrong with him?" She tottered into the bedroom as fast as her crutches would go, trying to make sense of Branson's shouts. "Is he having a seizure?"

"No," Jarrett replied, gritting his teeth with effort. "He thinks you've been murdered."

"Would you please tell him you're alive?" Finn requested, out of breath. "He's determined to call the police."

"Branson!" Stephanie pushed as close as she could while the guys held him still. "It's me... Stephanie. I'm alive. I'm right here."

"You're not Stephanie. Cole killed her!" Bran swiped at Finn's imprisoning hands. "Listen to me. Why won't anyone listen to me? Cole took her away and came back without her. Her voice was there, and it went *away*. She's *gone*. She's *dead*."

Understanding dawned, and she stepped back, grappling inside her purse to flip on the transmitter. "Branson? Can you hear me? Bran? It's Stephanie."

Bran continued to struggle and shout.

Of course... I'm not wearing the microphone.

Steph wriggled her way next to the bed and lowered her mouth to his ear. "Branson, can you hear me?"

"Stephanie?" Bran froze. "Is it really you?"

"It's me. It's Stephanie."

His head fell back against the pillow, and moisture

trickled from the corner of his eye. His voice dipped to a hoarse whisper. "Are you dead?"

"I'm alive." She put her hands on either side of his face, tears blurring her vision. "I'm right here."

Finn and Jarrett released him and stepped away, groaning from their sustained efforts.

"Stephanie?" His hands covered hers and groped their way up to her face, cupping her cheeks. "You're not dead?"

"Not the last time I checked." She chuckled, dabbing a sleeve at her watery eyes as she straightened.

Bran's hand grasped her wrist. "Please. Don't go."

"I'm right here. I'm not leaving." She sat stiffly on the edge of the bed, hoping no one would read more into their relationship than the dependent boss that he was.

Jarrett collapsed in a nearby chair, wiping the sweat off his forehead. "Thanks for your help, Cole," he hollered in a sarcastic voice, ripping off his tux coat and loosening his tie. He leaned back and closed his eyes, propping up his feet.

"I couldn't help," Cole objected from the outer room. "Branson would've killed me."

"Cole?" Branson's face hardened as he jerked upward. "Where is that son-of—"

Steph jumped to cover his mouth with her hand. "I'm alive, Branson. Cole didn't do anything."

His brows furrowed in confusion as he flopped back against the pillow again.

"Will someone explain to me what's going on?" Steph demanded. "How did he get like this? I thought you guys were watching after him."

"Carina can tell you all about it." Finn kicked Jarrett's feet aside and dropped onto the footstool. "Go ahead, Carina. Tell Stephanie how you put cannabis in Branson's drink."

"Cannabis? You mean marijuana? Isn't that illegal?" Steph wondered if they had filed a report.

"It's legal in Nevada." Carina leaned against the bedroom door, as if she wasn't sure she was welcome inside the room.

"It's legal to buy it and consume it in a private residence," Finn clarified. "It wasn't legal for her to bring it in the hotel or put it in his drink."

"Were you trying to kill him?" Stephanie's muscles trembled from head to toe. How she wanted to spring at Carina and rip out her hair!

"I only put in a couple of droppersful. How was I supposed to know he'd have a bad reaction?" She ventured around the perimeter of the room, moving to the other side of the bed to stare down at Bran.

Steph tried to cross her arms, but Branson held fast to her wrist. "Why put anything in his drink at all?"

"To help him relax, so we could have a *private* conversation." Carina's contrite expression vanished in an instant. Her eyes sent daggers Steph's direction.

"I'm assuming he didn't give you permission to drug him. Isn't that a crime of some sort? Assault, maybe?"

"You're right, Stephanie." Finn regarded Carina with narrowed eyes. "Maybe we ought to call the police."

Branson broke the tense mood with a sonorous snore, and Steph pulled her hand free.

"Carina..." Cole sauntered into the room. "Why don't you share the real reason you tried to make Branson fly high as a kite? I don't believe for a minute you only wanted to talk to him."

"And while you're at it," Jarrett added, "you can tell us why you're so anxious to get married. What girl wants a quickie wedding instead of a big deal with a long white dress and all the trimmings?"

To Stephanie's utter amazement, Carina started crying. "Fine! I'll tell you why," she sobbed, "I wanted a quick wedding because I'm *pregnant.*"

The room darkened, and Stephanie gripped the bed cover, balling it in her hands. Her chest felt so tight, she could barely breathe.

Carina's pregnant. Steph should've known. No wonder her boobs looked bigger. And why else would she have been so desperate to rush the wedding? How she must've laughed while feeding Steph that story about not being able to have children. And Steph, trying to follow MawMaw's advice, had pitied her.

"Miraculous healing, Carina." Steph cleared her throat to steady the warble in her voice. "Earlier tonight you told me you couldn't get pregnant."

"I refuse to apologize." Carina sniffed, but her eyes looked suspiciously dry. "I did what I had to do to save my marriage. My baby needs a father."

"You don't look pregnant." Cole leaned back against the wall and folded his arms across his chest.

"I am. Here's the proof." She opened her small clutch and unfolded a paper, tossing it on the bed beside Steph. A sonogram.

Steph didn't want to look at it. Using her crutches, she moved across the room, as far as possible from the offensive paper. She pulled out a desk chair and plopped down.

What was left of her hopes went up in smoke. She and

Branson could never be together. He wasn't like Jeff. Bran would never abandon his child. She tried to keep an indifferent expression, though she felt like dying. It would've been better if Bran had never said those sweet things to her. If only she could forget his words. Instead, the scene would replay over and over in her brain, reminding her of what she almost had.

Finn stood, his shoulders stiff, stomped to the bed and picked up the sonogram, studying the image as if he could detect her subterfuge. His tone was accusing. "How far along are you?"

She hesitated. "Twenty-two weeks."

Steph's eyes dropped to Carina's flat abdomen. It wasn't fair she was that far along and not showing, but tall women had an advantage. With her short torso, Steph's tummy started expanding early, almost the day she conceived.

"I'm not surprised." Jarrett counted on his fingers. "I have four older sisters, six nieces and two nephews, so I learned more than I ever wanted to know about pregnancy and childbirth. I noticed you ordered a salad at lunch, but only ate saltines. My youngest sister lived on saltine crackers the first twelve weeks she was pregnant."

"Exactly. Is that enough proof for you?" Carina pushed her already-plumped-up lips into a pout.

"It's not us you have to convince—it's Branson." Finn offered a hand to Jarrett, who rose from his comfortable chair with a reluctant wince. Finn continued, "You can explain everything to him tomorrow morning, assuming he's awake and in his right mind. He'll decide whether or not he wants to file charges."

With disheveled hair and his tux coat across his arm, Jarrett moved to stand beside Cole. "Wonder if he'll do it."

Finn shrugged. "Who knows?"

"You think Branson would press charges against the mother of his child? No way," Carina scoffed. "Once he finds out he's going to be a father, I expect he'll decide to make good use of that marriage license while we're here in Vegas."

Stephanie exchanged a glance with Finn. It was even more impossible than he knew.

"Still no reason to do it here, this weekend," Finn argued, leaning over the bedside to stare at his friend, whose chest rose and fell in peaceful sleep. "I know Branson, and he doesn't like being pressured into anything."

"Why didn't you tell him before, Carina?" Jarrett asked. "You must've known for a while."

"I had personal reasons," she answered, tersely. "The important thing is I'm pregnant with Branson's child, and we should get married immediately."

"You're not considering an abortion?" asked Cole in an acid tone.

"I suppose I might, if Branson doesn't marry me. I'm not planning to be a single mom."

Cole's face reddened. He whipped around and strode toward the door. "That's it. I'm outta here. See you guys later."

"Cole, wait!" Jarrett went after him, and the door closed behind them.

"What's wrong with *him*?" Carina asked.

"He's not a fan of abortions. It's a personal thing." Finn took off his tux coat and laid it across the chair. Then he sat on the footstool and untied his shoes, kicking them off.

"What are you doing?" Carina asked, crossing her arms.

"Getting comfortable." He took off his tie and began to unbutton his shirt, exposing a well-muscled chest. "I'm spending the night on that couch."

"We don't need you anymore," she argued. "Bran is fine. I'll stay with him while he sleeps it off."

Finn's answering glare was fierce. "After what you did tonight, there's no way I'm leaving my friend alone with you. So you might as well go to your room and get your beauty sleep."

Stephanie's tense muscles uncoiled. With Finn on guard, Branson wouldn't reveal their secret—at least not to Carina. As the adrenaline faded from her system, she remembered she'd come next door with wet hair and no makeup. In contrast, Carina appeared as fresh as when she first emerged from her room for the evening.

Steph's hands snaked up to smooth her damp tresses, and she tucked her chin toward her chest. Pushing up on her crutches, she hobbled toward the bedroom door. "Guess I'll head back to bed, since the crisis is averted."

"Don't leave yet. I want to speak to you alone." Finn sent a pointed look toward Carina.

"You can't make me leave," Carina sputtered, her cool composure cracking.

Finn's expression hardened to granite, and Steph caught a glimpse of the formidable man who'd built a multi-billion-dollar empire, along with his friends. She shuddered, glad his fury was aimed at Carina instead of her. "Try me," he growled.

Carina's nostrils flared. "Fine. I'll go. But I'll be back first thing in the morning. You can't keep us apart."

As the door clicked shut behind her, Finn's countenance softened. He pointed with a jerk of his chin. "Let's sit out here on the couch for a minute. How're you holding up?"

"Exhausted. Stressed." She limped after him and crumpled onto the sofa, fatigue settling deep into her bones. "But I'll be fine." *I have to be.*

Finn closed his eyes tight, like he was fighting a headache. "I hope you won't desert Bran. I think you've been good for him." He folded his hands in his lap and stared at his fingers. "But… this pregnancy—if Carina's not lying again—really throws a wrench in my plans. I thought he'd finally come to his senses. He was ready to back out of the relationship, but now…"

"He's going to marry her, isn't he?"

The muscles contracted along his jaw. "If he thinks it's the right thing to do, he'll do it. Even if it makes him miserable."

"You think it's the right thing to do?"

Both of Finn's shoulders lifted. "I don't know what I think. You might be able to influence him. Honestly, he could support this baby without marrying Carina."

"But that's not the only factor. He'll want to be in the baby's life, right?"

"For sure." Finn pinched the bridge of his nose. "I don't know what this means for you… for your job. If he marries her, I'm afraid Carina will make your life a living hell."

"It's okay," she said, as if she was blowing it all off. "I'd already planned to quit. Carina hates me, so I don't see how I could stay."

"Why not try to talk him out of the marriage, instead of leaving? He trusts you. He'll listen to you. And Monday morning, you'll have him all to yourself."

"I don't know. I'll think about it. I have to be able to sleep at night."

"By that reasoning, I guess Carina's a vampire." Finn chuckled. "You're the innocent one in all this... you and Ellie."

"And Laurie," Steph added. "I can only afford to pay her because of what Branson pays me."

He sat forward, resting his arms on his legs. "I was teasing, before, when I offered you a job. But this time, I'm not. If you have to quit, I'll match whatever Branson's paying you."

Steph was already shaking her head no. "I can't let you do that. You can't hire me because you feel sorry for me."

"Don't be ridiculous." He held up a silencing palm. "I may seem like a teddy bear, but I didn't get where I am making decisions based on sentiment. I'm certain you'd be an asset."

"We'll see." She refused to commit, though at least the job offer soothed her financial worries. And maybe Finn would have an "in" to get the new CF medicine cheaper. "Are you going to report this to the police?"

"I don't know. We'll see when Bran wakes up." He pushed his hair off his forehead. "For now, I want to protect him in case he ends up in a custody battle. We should keep that marriage certificate out of Carina's hands. I think she could use that as an argument against him in court. Last night, I thought it would be a funny joke, but now..." He twisted his mouth in a grimace. "Now, not so much."

"She won't find it. I've got it."

"Maybe you should give it to me and let me destroy it."

No way that's happening. She pursed her lips. "It's safe with me."

His eyebrows lifted. "Okay. I get it. You don't trust me because of the whole marriage license trick."

She tried to laugh, but it came out as an irritated cough. "It wasn't a pleasant surprise to discover both our names on there."

"Mad at me?"

She squinted at him from the corner of her eye. "Let's just say, you might want to hire a food-taster until I cool off a bit."

His familiar grin was back. "Yeah, Branson was steamed, too. It wasn't intentional, though. I couldn't follow my original plan. With Carina staring daggers at you, I thought the clerk might wonder why you two were getting married."

A huge yawn escaped before she could cover her mouth. *Maybe I'm already asleep, and I'll wake up and find out this was only a nightmare.* "I think I better go to bed before I pass out right here on this couch." She struggled to her feet.

"I plan to tell Branson the news when he wakes up, before Carina can spring it on him. I'll personally guarantee they won't be getting married here in Las Vegas."

You got that right. Unless Bran is into polygamy.

"Whatever. He made his bed, so to speak. I guess he can lie in it." She pretended her heart hadn't been ripped out of her chest and tossed on the ground.

Finn's sympathetic expression told her he wasn't buying her indifferent attitude. He walked beside her to the front door and held it open while she clomped into the hallway on her crutches.

"For what it's worth, Steph, I'm sorry you got caught in the middle of this mess."

"Not as sorry as I am."

CHAPTER 19

Stumbling on a dead body in the dark, Steph's blood pressure skyrocketed. On the outside, she held it to a gasp, but inside she screamed, adrenaline coursing through her veins. The audiobook playing through her earbuds was the only thing that kept her sane on the plane ride home.

Even with what should've been a riveting story in her ears, she watched Branson from the corner of her eye. Finn chose a seat beside him, never allowing Carina a moment's privacy with her fiancé. It seemed Finn still opposed the marriage, though Stephanie was resigned to it.

I'll be fine. I don't need him.

Hadn't she gotten along fine before she met Branson? She didn't need *any* man in order to survive. Her first husband had taught her never to put her trust in someone else. She'd been so enamored with Bran, she'd almost forgotten that lesson. Luckily, Carina's big reveal had reminded Steph she could only rely on herself.

She allowed the terror of the story to envelop her mind and distract her from depressing thoughts for the next hour. The bump of the plane touching down on the private landing strip jerked her back to the real world. Within ten minutes, the driver delivered them to the estate complex, allowing her to escape without having a single conversation with Branson. *Thank goodness.* Her sham composure would've crumpled if he'd confronted her. She counted on the next twelve hours to pull herself together so she could face him in the morning, at work.

Elated to see her mom, and even more excited about the picture of Elvis with a personalized message, Ellie never questioned Steph's mood. Laurie, on the other hand, challenged her the moment Ellie went to bed.

"Okay, what happened?"

"I told you," Steph opened her eyes wide. "I twisted my ankle."

"You know I'm not talking about your foot. What was it? Did you and Carina have a knock-down-drag-out fight in Las Vegas?"

Laurie patted the couch cushion beside her, and Steph hobbled over and dropped onto it like a sack of stones.

"Nothing happened. Nothing important."

"Then tell me what *unimportant* thing happened to make your eye twitch like it always does when you're upset."

Steph rubbed at her eyes with the backs of her hands. "Everything's fine. I'm mostly tired."

Laurie's perfectly arched brows pulled low over eyes so dark her pupils disappeared. Any attempt to escape without spilling her guts to her best friend would be futile. For the next hour, Steph spewed out the whole story. Well, *almost* the whole story. She omitted a few pertinent details, such as the part about Elvis and the wedding chapel. Nor did she mention Bran's kiss or the declaration of love.

When Steph finished the tale, Laurie's mouth hung open so wide Stephanie could see her tonsils. "Carina's pregnant?"

"Yes, and she made it quite clear she detests me with every fiber of her skinny little body. Do you think I'm an awful person for hoping she gets really bad stretch marks?"

Laurie shook her head, a glower shadowing her usually animated face. "No one deserves to look that perfect."

"But she's going to be the mother of Branson's child. I can't wish bad things on her."

"Why not? A little creative ill-wishing might lift your spirits. Only on Carina, not the baby."

"Hmmm..." A grin pushed its way onto Steph's lips. "My face broke out like crazy when I was pregnant. I'm thinking a blemish or two for Carina would be nice."

"Forget that. I'm praying for a plague of boils."

Steph snorted through her fingers. "Good one. You're so much more inventive than I am."

"While we're at it, let's go for some swelling. Give her fat feet with sausage toes." Laurie stretched her arms wide to illustrate the enlargement goal.

"Yes!" Steph cried, caught up in the contagious enthusiasm. "Perfect."

"And hemorrhoids," Laurie pointed a finger to the sky.

"You're inspired." Steph gave a mock bow. "I'm awed by your presence."

"Thanks." Laurie lifted her chin, accepting the accolades. "I try."

Steph laughed and then fell into contemplative silence. "Finn offered me a job."

Laurie sucked in a loud breath, turning to face her. "Carina got you fired?"

"Not yet. But I can tell from the weekend, I won't be able to stay if they get married."

"I'm sorry, Stephanie. Even though you call it a crush, I think you've been in love with him a long time. It has to hurt."

Steph threw her hands up in the air, in an effort to appear blasé. "Nah. I was never serious. I knew it was only a pipe dream."

"Maybe he won't marry her. He could still support the baby, even if they weren't married. Especially if he doesn't like to be around kids." Laurie put a comforting hand on her shoulder, which only served to make tears spring to her eyes.

"It's possible." Steph swiped her sleeve across her face. "But Finn thinks he'll feel obligated to marry her."

"Branson might listen to you, though. He trusts you. Maybe you could suggest they shouldn't get married. You shouldn't have to give up your job." Laurie angled her head. "By the way... where would we be moving if you took the job with Finn?"

"New York City."

"New York?" Laurie danced a seated victory jig, pumping her hands in the air. "I've always wanted to live in New York. That's awesome. My classes are online, so I can live anywhere. We'd have so much..." Her voice trailed off. Her lips turned down, and her brown eyes turned puddly. "Sorry. I know you don't want to leave Branson. We'll just pray they don't get married."

Steph nodded, swallowing her tears, as a surge of nausea hit. "I think the stress may be getting to me, because my stomach feels terrible. Or maybe it's something I ate."

"You could have a stomach virus." Laurie wrinkled her nose. "Ellie threw up all day yesterday."

"Oh no." The meager contents of her stomach rolled around to confirm the diagnosis. "The school nurse warned us there was something going around, but I thought we'd escaped it. Why didn't you call me?"

"You know I would've called if it had been a respiratory bug. But I knew her CF didn't make a stomach bug particularly dangerous."

"Poor thing. Can't believe she's so peppy today. She didn't even mention being sick."

"It didn't last long. She was feeling better by bedtime and was fine when she woke up this morning. Maybe a twelve-hour bug. Ran a little fever. I guess you'll know all about it, soon."

"I hate throwing up." Stephanie clamped her hand over her mouth. "This is going to be a long night."

Laurie disappeared into the other room and emerged with a white spray bottle. "Here goes the Lysol, again."

"I hope you don't get it, too."

"You and me both." Laurie looked like she was considering drinking the Lysol. "If you don't mind, I think I'll go hide out in my suite. But I'll come over in the morning and get Ellie ready for school, so you can sleep in."

"Sounds good." Steph barely got the words out before limping to the bathroom, her only comfort in knowing she would have another day before she had to face Bran.

BRANSON FUMBLED about in the huge kitchen, grumbling that nothing was where he remembered it. He shouldn't be surprised, since he hadn't cooked anything for himself in the past two years. At two a.m., all his culinary employees were sound asleep, but it wouldn't have made a difference. He had to do this alone.

He'd been lying in bed awake when Stephanie's text came in. *Stomach virus. Will take sick day tomorrow.*

He'd immediately fired back a text informing her of his intention to bring her a cup of ginger tea for the nausea. She protested, but he was determined. He was equally determined to make it himself, without any help from the staff. This meant smelling each box of tea to locate one with ginger flavor.

After every open package failed the sniff test, he considered calling on his cell for a late-night grocery delivery.

He fumed. *Sixteen different flavors of tea in the drawer, and none of them are ginger.* Then he remembered the cook's special tea tin inside the pantry. Fortune smiled on him as he opened the lid and breathed in. *Ginger!*

Filtered water in the electric pot took a few minutes to boil—enough time to locate a mug. In the back of the cabinet, he felt his special cup, a textured mug he'd acquired from New Zealand when he'd done his first bungee jump.

Still waiting for the pot to whistle, he considered Stephanie's text. In the two years since she'd started working, she'd never been ill enough to miss a day of work. Though Ellie had frequent health issues, Steph had a strong constitution and a stronger work ethic. If she hadn't been so utterly honest, he'd have suspected she made up the stomach flu story to avoid working with him the next day.

The pot whistled, and he poured the hot water over the tea bag, using a thumb to feel when the cup was full. He set a timer, removing the tea bag after precisely three minutes. Satisfied that his nausea remedy was as perfect as possible, he made his way down the west wing corridor, around the corner, counting until he reached the tenth doorway on the right. A quick inspection of the Braille numbers on the door told him he'd reached the right suite. Afraid he would wake Ellie if he knocked on the door, he sent a text to Steph.

I'm in the hall outside your door. Have ginger tea.

A few seconds passed before Steph's response came. *Too sick to let you in. Told you not to come.*

Have a master key. Can open door.

A short pause followed, then another text. *No. Not dressed.*

Doesn't matter. I'm blind.

A minute passed, and he thought she might've fallen back asleep. Maybe he could let himself in and leave the ginger tea on the table. Then his phone vibrated with another message. *Hugging toilet. Leave tea outside.*

As he thought of her on the bathroom floor, suffering all alone, he sent a final text. *Coming in. Be right there.*

He ignored the phone, which vibrated angrily in his pocket, while he opened the door and slipped inside, carrying his magical ginger tea concoction. Uncertain which direction to go, he stopped to listen. He was soon rewarded for his efforts when he heard a coughing sound straight ahead. As he navigated slowly down the hallway, his white cane checking for obstacles, he strained his ears to locate her.

At last he came to the end of the hallway, where another series of coughs filtered through the closed door. He tucked his cane under his arm and tested the door handle. It swung open, and he stepped inside, noting the familiar sour odor of bile. Though he was particularly sensitive to smells, his concern for Steph outweighed his stomach's response. A low groan came from his left.

"Why are you here?" she rasped.

"I'm going to take care of you." He used a don't-argue-with-me tone, though she sounded too weak to put up much of a fight, anyway.

Probing with his cane, he located the vanity counter, glad he'd chosen to make the layout of each guest suite identical. As he set the tea down, he heard gagging noises. He ached to make her feel better, hating his powerlessness.

"Do you have a cool, wet cloth for your face?" he asked.

"No," she croaked. "Branson you don't have to do this."

"I want to," he replied, as he probed the vanity cabinet. "This is empty. Where are your washcloths?"

"In the laundry," she replied. "It's okay. I don't need a rag."

"Yes, you do." He ripped his clean T-shirt off, wetting it in the sink.

Another groan. *She must be hurting.* He hastened his efforts.

―

STEPH'S FACE BURNED, but not with fever from her flu. She wasn't sure which was more embarrassing—that she was retching in front of Branson or that she'd moaned out loud when he took off his shirt. Why was God torturing her with a view of those broad shoulders and incredible abs that could never be hers? Wasn't it enough that she'd thrown up so much her stomach had turned inside out?

He moved toward the toilet and knelt beside her, his rippling muscles momentarily distracting her from her misery. With the wet shirt across his jean-clad knees, his hands found her shoulders and moved up to her hair, his fingers sweeping the strands off her face.

Shocked that tingles of pleasure shot through her system in spite of her sickness, she closed her eyes and leaned into him. The cool cloth caressed her face, swiping gently across her forehead and returning to stroke down her neck. Again and again, he brushed her skin, soothing it with the soft, damp shirt that smelled like a mixture of fabric softener and Branson. If she hadn't felt like dying, she would've been swooning in his arms. Instead, she collapsed against him like a lifeless ragdoll.

She had no idea how much time passed before he spoke, the rumbling voice in his chest vibrating in her ear and startling her awake.

"Let's get you into bed."

"Okay." Her voice came out a hoarse whisper through her parched mouth.

He stood and scooped his hands under her arms, lifting her to her feet. But for his steadying arm around her waist, her legs would've collapsed. He helped her to the sink to wash out her mouth. Then, supporting her weight, he moved unerringly through the door that led directly to her bedroom. The fleeting thought occurred that any other time she would've relished the feel of his bare chest against her cheek. But, for the moment, survival was foremost on her mind.

When they reached the bed, he helped her climb in, tucking the covers around her and fluffing her pillow. His hands lingered on either side of her face, his expression unreadable in the dim light filtering from the bathroom.

"Can't let you get dehydrated. I'll get a glass of water and heat up your ginger tea. It's stone cold by now."

Too weak to object, she nodded her head. Fading in and out of sleep, she woke to his gentle touch on her forehead. "You're burning up. Can you drink some water? Maybe sip some tea?"

She struggled to raise her head, but flopped back, with a moan. His hand slipped under her shoulders, lifting her forward. He held the glass in front of her and she guided it to her lips to take a few swallows. Her stomach cramped, and she pushed it away, thinking she'd never make it back to the bathroom in time.

"No more. Makes me sick."

"Let's try the ginger tea."

"Can't. Help me to the bathroom," she panted. "Quick."

"I brought this big bowl." In seconds he was sitting on the edge of the bed, cradling her against his chest and holding the vessel under her chin.

Queasiness washed over her, but she didn't throw up. After a few minutes, he set the bowl aside and retrieved a mug from the bedside table.

"Try a swallow of this. It helps. I promise."

She accepted the cup, blowing before she took a sip. The light, spicy flavor was pleasant, and the warm liquid soothed her throat and stomach. At his urging, she drank a few more swallows, rested a while, and then drank a bit more. As her queasiness improved, chills descended, her body shaking from head to toe.

Heavy with guilt, she begged him to leave, through chattering teeth. "You n-need to get away. You're going to c-catch this from m-me."

"Too late," he said, tightening his hold and settling back against the head of the bed. "I kissed you yesterday. Twice. I'm already exposed." As if to make a point, he pressed his lips to the top of her head.

"S-stubborn m-man," she said, wrapping her arms around his delicious chest and burrowing against him for warmth. She blinked heavy eyes while composing another argument in her mind, but her words were lost in a thick fog.

CHAPTER 20

"Mommy! Who's that?"

A child's voice jolted Branson awake. *Where am I?*

Beside him in the bed, someone jerked and screamed, "Oh my gosh!"

The female screamer shoved at his side and, two seconds later, he slid to the floor, face down, taking the sheet with him.

"Well, well, well." A second woman spoke, from somewhere above him. "What have we here?"

"Mommy, are you married now?" asked the child.

"No!" came the shouted response.

As Bran's mind began to clear, he recognized Steph's voice.

"But you told me grownups only sleep together if they're married."

The child, he now knew to be Ellie, was close, as if she were leaning over to inspect him.

The second woman, who must be Laurie, the babysitter, laughed out loud. "Try to talk your way out of that one, Stephanie."

As Bran struggled to free himself from the tangle of covers, Steph's voice came from the bed above him. "I'm sorry I pushed you on the floor, Bran. It was a reflex."

"No problem." He managed to yank one hand free.

"I think I need to get to the toilet, again.. I… Oops!" A hard boot landed on his back, followed by the rest of her, tumbling off the bed, along with more covers. "Sorry. Lost my balance." She wrestled with the blanket, then she rolled off, her air cast clunking toward the restroom. "You explain it, Bran. Tell them what happened."

As Bran freed his other hand, he realized he'd come over in the middle of the night without putting in his prosthetic eyes. His heart rate skyrocketed. No one saw him without his eyes in place.

"I need my cane. It's white. Do you see it anywhere?" He kept his face aimed toward the floor.

"Are you my mommy's boss? The blind man?"

"Ellie, don't be rude," Laurie scolded.

"I see it," Ellie exclaimed. "It's underneath you. A white stick."

He groped on the floor under the sheet and blanket, sighing with relief as his fingers closed around the cane.

"I came over last night to bring your mother some ginger tea to fight nausea," he clarified, as he pushed up on his elbows, careful to face away from Ellie and Laurie. "I helped her get back in bed after she threw up. Then, I accidentally fell asleep."

That sounded lame. I should've thought up a better story.

"Why did you take off your clothes?" Ellie probed, her innocent question prompting a snicker from Laurie.

"I didn't," he sputtered, trying to wriggle out of the twisted sheet to demonstrate. "Just my shirt. I have my jeans on."

"Oh." She sounded confused. "Why did you take off your shirt?"

The truth seemed implausible, as did every other response that came to mind. For Bran's part, he was simply grateful he hadn't removed any more clothing in his sleep, especially since he was accustomed to sleeping in the nude.

"Don't you need to be leaving for school?" he asked, hoping for distraction.

"Not yet," Ellie declared, her words distorted as if her lower lip protruded in a pout. "Aunt Laurie told me I could say goodbye to Mommy, first."

"Yes," Laurie agreed. "But you've done that. We should get going now."

"Nuh-uh," Ellie argued. "Mommy left before I got to talk to her."

Laurie exhaled heavily. "Fine. Run in the bathroom and tell her bye. Hurry up. We don't want to be late."

"Okay."

As Ellie's footsteps pattered into the bathroom, Branson extricated himself from the sheet and climbed to his feet, hoping to make a quick escape. He turned toward the doorway, keeping his chin tucked low, his eyelids closed tight.

"A word of caution, Mr. Knight." Laurie's voice lost all its lighthearted cheer. "I don't take kindly to people who hurt my friend. In spite of everything Steph's been through, she's still sweet and forgiving. But I'm not."

"I'll keep that in mind," Branson replied, with his face averted. "Not that I like being threatened, but I'm glad she has a friend like you."

"Not that I need your approval, but it's a good thing you understand what I'm saying." Her voice transformed to an angelic tone as she called toward the bathroom. "*El-lie*. Time to go."

"Coming." Humming a wordless tune, Ellie skipped back into the bedroom. Then her small body impacted his legs, almost knocking him off balance. Her arms wrapped around his waist and squeezed.

"What's that for?" Laurie asked the question he was too shocked to voice.

"Mommy said Mr. Knight was lonely, and he needed a hug. That's why she had her arm around him when they were in the bed."

"That's sweet," said Laurie, though her tone indicated the opposite. "Now go grab your lunch and meet me at the door."

Bran lifted his hand to cover his eyes. He felt Laurie's disapproving gaze slicing him like a razor before she spoke again.

"It's one thing that Ellie caught you in bed with Stephanie, without a shirt on. I know she was sick, and nothing actually happened. But Mr. Knight…"

She paused, and he squirmed in place, resigned to the castigation he knew was coming. "Yes?"

When she continued, her words came out like a Rottweiler's warning growl. "When you're around Steph, you better keep your pants on."

THE BILLIONAIRE'S SECRET MARRIAGE

∼

Though her stomach was still a bit queasy, Steph didn't throw up. She moved to the mirror, afraid of what would greet her there. As expected, her pale, blotchy face and dark-circled eyes gave testimony to the tumultuous night.

Thank goodness Branson is blind. I'd hate for him to see me like this. But his nose works fine.

She squeezed a generous glob of toothpaste on her toothbrush and scrubbed hard. After a few splashes of water on her face, she felt ten times better, though still wobbly and weak. Perhaps the virus had run its course, or maybe Branson's ginger tea had done the trick.

Despite begging him not to come last night, she had to admit he'd saved her. He'd also let his cloak down, revealing a tender side that broke her heart, along with her resolve. And as his wall came down, she realized he might love her after all.

Not that it mattered. How could they ever be together? She could beg him to buy a small island in the Caribbean. They could all move there—she and Branson, Ellie and Laurie—and forget about Carina, the baby, and the rest of the world.

Ha! As long as I'm at it, I might as well dream that Ellie would be cured of cystic fibrosis and live a normal life.

She was powerless to fix this problem. And so was Branson. What's done was done. He had to take care of Carina and his unborn child. And Stephanie would go on with her life, apart from Bran, and tend to Ellie.

But Steph could give him one parting gift—to tell him how she really felt. She'd thought to hide the truth, to spare him the pain of realizing how close they'd come to having a real marriage. She'd loved him too much to cause him such regrets.

Yet, that was before he'd confessed his belief that no one could ever love him. That idea was eating away at him, destroying the kind and selfless man she knew as Branson Knight. If she did nothing else, she would give him the knowledge of her love, despite the fact nothing would ever come of it.

With fresh determination, she emerged from the bathroom in time to see Laurie stomp out and slam the door so hard the pictures rattled on the walls. Branson stood beside the bed, achingly handsome, his chest bare and a pair of jeans slung low on his hips. Yet he looked as forlorn as a lost puppy.

"Sorry about Laurie," Steph said. "She can be a little protective where Ellie and I are concerned."

Bran stiffened and turned his back. "I should go. Give you some privacy."

"Kind of late for that," she quipped. "I have on the same flannel PJs as last night, so you can face me. I don't mind."

Still facing away, he edged sideways, his cane sweeping the floor. "All the same, I need to get back."

"As long as you're here, maybe we should talk... you know... about Carina and stuff."

"Maybe later."

As he shuffled closer to the door, she moved to intercept him. "Bran, you're making this more awkward than it already is." Grasping his arm, she attempted to whip him around to face her.

He jerked away. "I told you I have to go. Get out of my way."

He refused to look at her. Not that he could see, but he'd always shown his respect and attentiveness by facing her square on.

Leaning against the door, she refused to budge. "Why won't you look at me? What's wrong with you?"

"Why must you always be so obstinate?" He rotated toward her, and she saw his face, a mask of rage, with his hand across his eyes. "I'm trying to protect you."

"From what?"

"From me. From *this*." He indicated his hidden eyes. "You don't want to see it."

"Bran." Her soul cried for him. "I told you, already... I don't care. I love your eyes. They're blue and beautiful. I don't even think about them being prosthetic."

She tried to pull his hand down, but he pushed her away. "Please... don't."

The agony in his voice tore at her. She had to tell him now. It was the only way he would believe her.

"Come sit with me for a minute. Let's talk." She tugged on his arm, like a gnat trying to move a boulder.

"We can talk tomorrow."

"I need to sit. Feel weak, like I might pass out." It was true. The room seemed to narrow, and her stomach complained about her continued upright position.

Bran's disposition transformed in an instant. He dropped his cane and looped his arm around her, though he was too mulish to uncover his eyes. "You should be in bed. You take care of everyone else, but you don't take care of yourself."

"Not the bed. Help me get to the loveseat. It's on the other side of—"

"I know where it is. All the suites are identical—it's my design."

She sagged against him, willing herself not to stumble as they walked around the bed to the small sofa. He sat down with her, and she closed her eyes until the room stopped spinning. "Okay. At least I don't feel like I'm at an amusement park anymore."

"Have you had anything to drink this morning?"

"A little water. But Laurie said she put some ginger ale in the fridge. I don't suppose—"

"I'll get it." Bran was up in a flash, snagging his cane as he went.

Tempted to lie down, Steph resisted, lest she fall asleep and give Bran an excuse to leave. Now was her best chance to explain, before she lost her nerve. Drowsiness threatened to overcome her, and she pinched her arm to wake up. But fatigue won the battle, and she nodded off where she sat. She woke to the shake of gentle hands.

"Here's your ginger ale."

She took a few sips and handed the glass back. "Bran, I need to tell you something."

He shook his head, still refusing to face her. Why was he being so paranoid about his eyes today?

She took a deep breath and blurted it out before she lost her nerve. "Bran, I love you."

"No, you don't."

"Hey!" She shot him an ineffectual look of outrage. "Don't tell me what I feel. It took me a long time to get up the nerve to tell you."

"That's not love, you feel—it's guilt. I was nice to you, and now you feel sorry for me."

"For once, will you shut up and listen?"

"Fine." He perched on the edge of the loveseat with his back toward her. It would've been off-putting, if she hadn't been tempted to trace the lines of his muscles with her finger. "I'm listening," he said.

She breathed a long, loud sigh, designed to let him know he was trying her patience. "Bran, I've been in love with you for most of the two years we've been together. You are, bar none, the most handsome man I've ever seen, and I'm well aware you're way out of my league."

"You have that backwards—"

"Be quiet! I'm not listening to you unless you turn around and say it to my face."

"I can't." The words seemed to be extruded through his gritted teeth.

"You mean, you *won't*."

His shoulders drooped. "I guess it doesn't matter. We can't really be married, anyway. I couldn't hide it from you forever."

He rotated slowly until his face was visible. Something was strange about his eyes. Not as full as before. They looked white, instead of blue.

"You see, now." His face twisted in agony. "This is the real me. Even scarier than the prosthetic eyes."

The lightbulb finally switched on in her hazy brain. "Is that what this is all about? You thought I'd be freaked out by your ocular implants?"

"You aren't?" The fragile uncertainty in his voice brought tears to her eyes.

"Of course not." She swiped her face on her sleeve. "I know what they look like. Googled it two years ago, the day I met you."

"They don't bother you at all?" His lips stretched in a rapturous smile, flashing his even white teeth.

"Nope."

"And you love me?" His voice became gravelly, and he leaned closer.

"Yes, I do." She put a hand to his face to stop his progress. "But we can't kiss again."

He frowned. "Why not? We love each other. We're married. Why can't we kiss?"

"Have you forgotten about Carina?"

"No, but I'd like to." He straightened, pushing his fingers through his hair, sending it in crazy directions. "I can't live like this. The moment we start to make progress, you jerk the rug out from under us."

"I beg your pardon," she spat. "It's not my fault Carina is in the middle of all this. That's one hundred percent on you."

He twisted to face her, his eyes closed and his hands folded, as if in prayer. "Just say the word, and I'll tell Carina we're married. I'll pay my child support and stay out of her life. Let her have full custody." He found one of Steph's hands and turned it over to press a kiss against her palm, making rows of goosebumps on her arm. "We'll start now and build a life together—you, me and Ellie. What do you say?"

He laid out her dream on a silver platter, as enticing as his ripped physique. She wanted it. She wanted it so badly she could barely breathe. Her eyes filled with tears, even before she choked out her answer. The word ripped from her raw throat, a bare whisper that echoed for eternity.

"No."

A tear leaked from the corner of his eye and rolled down his cheek.

"Please."

"We can't, Bran." Each word cut her like a knife. Her lifeblood ebbed away. "You'd be miserable. Not at first, but eventually you'd regret it. You've spent your whole life trying to be a better man than your father. That means being present in your child's life."

He turned away, his throat convulsing. "How long, then? How long before we can be together?"

"It doesn't work that way." She steadied her quavering voice. "You need to work out things between you and Carina. You're going to be a father, and that's the most important thing. I think it's best if I leave. I'd only be a distraction."

"No." He groped to find her hand and clasped it tightly. "Please don't leave me."

"I have to, Bran. How could I bear being here if you and Carina are together? I could hardly stand watching the two of you this weekend. When I saw you coming out of her room, I felt like I'd been stabbed."

"I'm so sorry." Bran clenched his eyes shut, rubbing his temples. "Nothing happened—I promise. I didn't sleep with her."

"You obviously slept with her at least once."

Bran's silence spoke volumes. When he finally answered, he seemed resigned. "Can I kiss you? One last time?"

"I don't know..."

Those three words obviously translated to *yes* in whatever world Branson lived, because his hands slid behind her head, fingers tangling in her hair as his mouth descended. His lips brushed across her lips. Soft as a feather. Then harder. Demanding. Her hands flattened on the hard planes of his chest. Short of breath, she felt lightheaded, like she was in a dream. The gentle caress of his lips made her ache for what could have been. She trembled as his fingers trailed down her neck, leaving a fiery brand in their wake. He followed with his mouth, pressing a kiss into the hollow of her neck until lights flashed under her eyelids. As his mouth found hers again, she tasted the salt of their mingled tears, and she hugged him close, as if she could make the moment last through eternity.

But it didn't.

Tearing herself away left a gaping hole in her chest—forever empty—the place where her heart used to be.

CHAPTER 21

"I've looked at it from every angle, Mr. Knight. I still believe a marriage would be the best way to assert your parental rights."

Bran massaged his temples, hoping to rub away the headache that ibuprofen hadn't diminished. *I need a workout.* He'd been back home since Sunday and hadn't worked out the last three mornings. Though still a bit weak after his bout with the short-term virus, he knew that wasn't the main issue. His life was completely off-kilter without Stephanie as his personal assistant. He forced down a sip of his now-tepid coffee.

"I can't see how it would make a difference, Johnson. I'm the child's father whether or not we're married."

"Yes, but the decision is made by a human, and most humans have a tendency to favor the mother. Carina can truthfully claim you were engaged and called off the wedding after you learned of the pregnancy."

Bran slammed his fist on the desk. "I can't believe she can corner me into this marriage. There must be another way."

"I'm afraid not."

His lungs deflated, along with his spirit. "I'm not ready to sign the new prenup. And there's certainly no reason to rush the marriage. She's only twenty-two weeks along."

"It's not wise to offend Carina's pride, Mr. Knight. She's more likely to sign the new agreement without arguing if you accommodate her on the timing. If you marry now, you could initiate the divorce shortly after the baby is born."

Mark Johnson didn't know Branson was married to Stephanie. Bran started to tell him multiple times, but something inside his gut stopped the words from coming out. He couldn't explain it, but he didn't entirely trust the man.

"Johnson, how long have you worked for me?"

"My firm has served you for almost two years, Mr. Knight. I hope you've been more than satisfied with our work. We always try to provide exemplary service, with absolute confidentiality."

Branson couldn't argue his point. Johnson had made himself available at any time, day or night, and toiled tirelessly on every project Branson gave him. His work had always been flawless. Yet there was something about him… something he couldn't put his finger on.

Two years! A bilious feeling formed in the pit of his stomach. When Branson's attorney of seven years suddenly took ill, Mark Johnson had applied for the position. His credentials and recommendations unmatched, Branson hired him on the spot. Yet, unlike most of his close employees, the two had never spoken on a first-name basis.

THE BILLIONAIRE'S SECRET MARRIAGE

Branson had written it off as Mark's formal manner, but it was more than that. In Bran's gut, he simply didn't trust the man.

Branson pushed back from his desk and rose to his feet. He heard the sounds of movement as Mark matched his posture.

"Thank you for coming, Johnson."

"But... don't you want to..." Mark made a strangled coughing noise. "Very well, Mr. Knight. But I recommend approving the final copy of this document today. Would you like for me to start the paperwork for the marriage license? Of course, you and Carina will have to go to the clerk's office to sign it."

Branson strode to the door, unconsciously counting the steps. "I'll be in touch later today, Johnson."

"Yes, sir. Perhaps I'll check back at one o'clock?"

"That sounds perfect, as always." Though Bran's tone and manner dismissed the man, he still resisted.

"When this matter is settled, you'll feel much better about it, Mr. Knight. I'll do everything I can to expedite the proceedings. What else can I do to allay your fears?"

"My current fear, Mr. Johnson, is another round of that stomach virus coming on. Unless you'd like to experience it for yourself, I suggest you give me some privacy."

The man shot out of the room like a rocket, mumbling under his breath. By the time the door clicked shut, Bran had already dialed his cell phone.

"Fordham... I need a new lawyer."

∼

"If he's associated with your father, he's hidden it well." Fordham's calm demeanor didn't fool Bran for an instant. He'd never cared for Mark Johnson, and he was ecstatic that Branson now agreed with him. He would dig until he discovered dirt on Johnson, and Bran felt certain it was there.

Though Fordham had acted as Bran's primary caretaker when he was growing up, his true value was his sharp mind. He'd been Branson's best behind-the-scenes advisor, rewarded for his efforts with a lucrative profit-sharing plan. He still acted the part of Bran's personal butler, drawing a nice salary that was a pittance, compared to his accumulated wealth.

"It makes so much sense." Bran drummed his fingers on the desk. "I don't know why I didn't suspect him before. He showed up less than twenty-four hours after Cal got sick. Now I wonder if Dad didn't have something to do with that as well."

"A stiff accusation," Fordham remarked, "but I wouldn't put it past him."

Fordham's loyalty had always been with Bran, even though his father had signed the paychecks when Bran was a child.

"Let's think about this." Bran stopped to take a sip of fresh coffee, the pungent aroma calming his nerves. "We still don't know why Carina wants to get married so quickly. It's like there's something she's hiding. Something time sensitive."

"The pregnancy?" Fordham suggested.

"Can't see where a few days makes a difference where the baby is concerned." He chewed his lower lip. "Something happened while we were in Vegas. Something that made her panic. She wanted us married as soon as possible."

The room went quiet, but for a light tapping from Fordham's direction, where he sat facing Bran's desk.

"Let's try a different approach," said Fordham. "If your dad is involved in this, what would he do? What's his motivation?"

"Dad? He'd like to ruin me." Branson gave a harsh chuckle. "Especially since I founded Escapade Resorts two years ago, and it's already toppled his resort empire. I even lured away some of his board members."

"I'm certain that stings his pride," said Fordham. "He would've made more money if he'd bought stock in your company."

Ice water poured into Bran's veins. "What did you say?"

"He would've made more money if he'd..." Fordham gasped. "We need to check the activity on Escapade. What's Carina's cut in the prenuptial agreement?"

"Ten percent."

In the ensuing silence, Bran considered all the implications.

"And what if those board members you *lured away* are still in your dad's pocket?" Fordham proposed. "He's shrewd. He gathers a lot of information about everyone he comes in contact with and keeps it hidden away in his safe to use as future leverage."

"Blackmail?" Bran hadn't been aware of this aspect of his father's persona.

"He called it *influencing behavior*." Fordham sounded like he'd swallowed nasty medicine.

"So, Carina's in league with my father." Branson's fury smoldered beneath the surface.

"More likely," Fordham said, "she's under his *influence*."

"Why didn't he do the same to you?"

"Contrary to popular belief, not everyone has a skeleton in the closet. There's a lot to be said for integrity." Fordham paused before speaking again, this time with uncharacteristic emotion. "That's how I raised you, Branson. You've made me proud."

Though he knew in his heart Fordham loved him, Bran had never received such direct verbal affirmation before. He could hardly speak around the lump in his throat.

"I couldn't have asked for a better father."

"I only wish your father could see you for who you are," Fordham murmured. "He's far more blind than you will ever be."

∼

With worries about Carina, his father, Johnson, and Escapade Resorts jamming the circuits in his brain, Branson couldn't concentrate. He closed his laptop. The backlog of emails would have to wait.

Anticipating a good long workout, he headed to his suite and changed clothes. When he stepped into the hallway and turned toward his private gym, he heard something—a quick intake of breath.

He froze, listening. "Who's there?"

Silence.

"I know you're there. Who is it?"

A slight rustling noise. Or was it his imagination? *I'm getting paranoid.*

"This hallway's monitored with security cameras. We have your face recorded already. One phone call, and you'll be in jail." It was a bluff, but a plausible one.

He heard a sniff. Then a small, trembly voice said, "I'm sorry. Please don't send me to jail."

"Ellie?"

"Yes." She sniffed again. "I didn't mean to come here. I got lost."

"Why aren't you at school?"

"Mommy said I could stay home today, on account of we're moving tomorrow."

His throat constricted. He had no idea Steph would move out that fast. He'd hoped he had time to convince her to stay. How could she afford it? How would she take care of Ellie?

"Are you going to call the police?"

"I won't." He gave her what he hoped was a pleasant smile, to soothe her nerves. "Want me to show you the way back to your rooms?"

"No, not yet. Mom told me not to come back for an hour."

"Why not?"

"Because, she's talking to my dad."

She wants an hour alone with her ex? Inside my estate? I don't think so.

∼

"How did you find me?"

Stephanie stood, gripping the back of the chair, to hide her trembling fingers from Jeff's sharp eyes.

"Someone told me where you were and what you're up to. What's the matter, baby? You act like you aren't happy to see me."

"Why are you here?" She mustered all the bravado she could find. "And don't tell me you're here to see Ellie. You don't even believe she's your daughter."

"I miss you, sweetie. Thought maybe you miss me, too."

With his feet propped on the coffee table, he leaned back on the couch and stretched his arms over his head. Steph remembered when she used to admire his biceps and swoon over his six-pack. She'd been so enamored with his outward appearance, she'd brushed certain behaviors under the rug. Constantly questioning her whereabouts. Accusing her of cheating. Criticizing her appearance. Controlling her outside contacts. She hadn't realized how oppressed and alone she felt until he left her with a sick child. She'd all but lost touch with her old friends. Laurie, however, stuck with her through it all, and made no secret of celebrating when the marriage ended. Though he'd never been violent before, his sudden appearance made Steph nervous. She took comfort knowing, if she screamed, Laurie would come running over from next door and likely beat the man to a pulp… or at least call nine-one-one.

"Sorry to disappoint. I don't miss you. Not at all." Steph swept her hand toward the door. "Time to go."

He gave her a smarmy smile. "I don't think so. Not until I get what I came for."

"Spit it out, Jeff. I don't have time for this."

"I want in."

She blinked. What on earth was he talking about? Ellie?

"It's too late. Ellie doesn't want anything to do with you."

He stood up, slinking closer, while her heart thumped a machine gun rhythm in her chest.

"I don't care about your defective kid. I want a cut of the extra dough you're getting from your blind boyfriend."

"There is no extra dough. I worked for Mr. Knight and got paid a salary. I live paycheck to paycheck, trying to cover Ellie's medical bills. And I think you should leave before I decide to sue you for the child support you've never paid."

His eyes rolled up to the ceiling. "You expect me to believe that billionaire isn't paying you a little extra for his booty calls?"

Steam spewed out with her words. "There are no booty calls. And why would you think I would ever give you a dime, anyway?"

With a blur of movement, her wrist was cinched in his painful grasp. "Either you pay up, or I'll tell him all about you. I'll tell him what a slut you are. I'll tell him how you wiped out my savings account."

"I told you a thousand times, I never cheated on you. And I used *our* savings to pay some of Ellie's medical bills. That's all." She jerked against his relentless grip, so tight it brought tears to her eyes.

Evil gleamed from his eyes as his lips spread to expose his teeth. A shiver rippled down her spine. He'd been so sweet and romantic when they were dating. How could this dark personality have been so well hidden? Was it obvious all the time, or did he change after they married?

"That's not the way I remember it, baby." Ripe and foul, his hot breath hit her face.

"It doesn't matter." She tugged again, to no avail. "I quit my job. I'm moving away tomorrow."

The corner of his lip twitched. Suddenly, her arm was wrenched down and around, behind her back. She cried out in pain, but he lifted it high, forcing her head down. She couldn't take a deep enough breath to scream for help.

"You're not leaving here until you pay me back. You married me and slept around and took my money. Did you think I'd let you get away scot-free?"

"I don't have any money." Her voice came out a barely audible gasp, the pain in her arm intense as she waited for it to twist out of its socket.

"We'll find a different way for you to pay."

"No!" Her rasping protest sounded almost as terrified as she felt.

He's out of his mind. Totally crazy.

Her arm bent further, pushing her to the floor. Adrenaline surged through her system as she watched for an opportunity to fight back. His weight fell on her back, trapping one arm beneath her and squeezing the air from her lungs.

With her arms pinned, she could only flail about, the clunky boot on her foot impeding her efforts. Then his weight shifted. He flipped her over and trapped both arms over her head, sending stabbing agony to her shoulders. Her legs were still trapped, but her mouth and lungs were free.

One deep breath later, she screamed for all she was worth and prayed Laurie would call nine-one-one. When his hand clamped over her mouth, she opened her jaw as wide as possible. A finger slipped inside, and she bit, hard. He answered with a shriek of pain, his wild eyes growing even wider. Something that felt like a chunk of lead impacted the side of her head and, for a second, she saw stars.

All at once, his weight lifted, and he gave a yelp of surprise. His body tumbled sideways to the floor. In his place stood Branson, chest heaving, expression dark with fury.

"Mommy! Mommy!" Ellie bounded over and fell to her knees beside Stephanie, tears streaking her face.

Steph scooted and crawled, backing as far as possible away from Jeff, who was already climbing to his feet, his cheeks red, veins pulsing on the side of his face.

Hopefully, Jeff would take one look at Bran, with his formidable height and bulging muscles, and decide to make a run for it.

"What's wrong? Afraid to fight someone your own size?" Bran jeered. "One of those guys who beats up on women because he's too chicken to fight a real man?"

"Bran. *No.*" He was taunting an insane man. He could get himself killed.

As she backed against the wall, Steph maneuvered onto her feet, a difficult task with her air cast in place. She whispered in Ellie's ear and sent her running for help.

"Are you the guy who's been sleeping with my slutty wife?" Jeff gave a harsh laugh as he marched up to Branson, giving him the once over. "Believe me, she's not worth fighting over."

"Maybe I disagree."

Bran stood like a target, a sitting duck, hands at his side. Stephanie didn't know what to do. If Jeff beat him up, it would be her fault.

Relaxed and smiling, Jeff shook his index finger at Stephanie. "I'll come back to you in a minute, babe."

In a blink, Jeff's head snapped backwards, and his body

teetered, tilting to the rear. Then, Branson sent a side kick to his belly, and he folded, landing with a thud.

Bran rubbed the knuckles on his right hand. "No, you won't."

Steph tiptoed closer to Jeff's unmoving body, wary that he might jump up at any minute, brandishing a knife or a gun, as in every action movie she'd ever seen. From a distance of ten feet, she could see his chest rise and fall and decided she'd come far enough.

"I can't believe you knocked him out. He's alive, though." She fanned herself with her hand, pushing her sleeves up to her elbows. "I was so scared when he got close to you. I thought he might kill you. Why did you taunt him like that?"

"Thanks for the ego boost. Thought, after all this time, you wouldn't expect so little from me, just because I'm blind." His eyebrows knitted together, and his jaw flexed. "If you really want to know, taunting makes an opponent talk. It's a lot easier to hit my target while he's speaking, especially if I'm aiming for his chin."

"Oh. Right. Uhmm… makes sense." The complete awkwardness of the entire situation settled in. Other than sending a single text asking for "space," she'd ignored Branson's attempts at communication. In an effort to avoid him at all costs, she'd located a short-term, low-rent sublease in Monee, a suburb of Chicago, where the three of them could stay until she made arrangements to go to New York. That was assuming everything worked out with Finn, whom she hadn't yet contacted.

Now she felt like a complete heel, even though she'd pushed him away for his own good. She didn't even know if he'd come down with the stomach virus. The last two nights, she'd laid awake with nothing but Branson on her mind. When morning came she would crawl out of bed, splash water on her face, and struggle through the day, explaining away her bloodshot eyes and dark circles as a cold. From the way Laurie reacted, pressing her lips together and watching her with a sympathetic gaze, Steph assumed she wasn't buying the excuse.

As if I didn't owe Branson enough already, he went and saved my life, or at least saved me from a horrible experience. I have to say something.

"Thanks for... coming to my rescue. Thought I could handle him, but he's never been like that before. Maybe he was on something."

His expression softened. "Stephanie, I—"

"*Dang-it!*" Laurie galloped into the room, past Stephanie and Bran, until she reached Jeff's crumpled form. "I *missed* it."

CHAPTER 22

*B*ranson's fingers had scanned the same line at least ten times. He still couldn't make his brain concentrate on what he was reading. How could he get any work done, knowing Stephanie was moving out of the estate today? Even worse, he was scheduled to meet with Carina later that afternoon, and he wasn't ready. She'd lied about the Parker-Aston stocks and slipped drugs into his drink, which certainly justified breaking off the marriage. Bran was convinced Carina was somehow involved in a plot with his father, though he hadn't found any evidence to support his theory.

He jumped when his cell phone rang.

"Hey, Finn." He didn't wait for his friend to respond. "I planned to call this afternoon and give you another update. It's just like we thought. A lot of activity on the Escapade stocks. Someone's been buying them up under the umbrella of various shell companies. Fordham hasn't been able to prove my father's behind it... not yet."

"What about Carina? Is she wrapped up in the Escapade deal, or is that a coincidence?"

"No way to tell. The information she gave on the Parker-Aston stocks was bogus. But she claims she lied to talk me into rushing the marriage because she didn't want me to find out she was pregnant. She'll be here in a few minutes, and I've basically got nothing."

"Your life is so screwed up right now." Finn gave an audible sigh. "I gotta ask you, Bran. How did this happen? You're so careful about everything. I can't even understand why you would go out with Carina, much less sleep with her."

"She was different when we first started dating. She can be charming when she wants to." The ever-present knots in Bran's intestines drew tighter. "One stupid mistake. I wish it hadn't happened, but it did. I took precautions, but I guess it wasn't enough."

"So maybe the baby isn't yours?" Finn's voice was hopeful.

"I wish I knew. The timing is right, though. Twenty-two weeks would be about right. Guess I can't prove anything until the baby comes. And meanwhile, I'm losing my personal assistant over this."

"Your personal assistant?" From his harsh tone, Finn's exasperation was obvious. "If that's all Stephanie is to you, I'll send you a list of qualified applicants to replace her. You can have a new employee in that position by tomorrow."

All the feelings Bran had been pushing into the background tumbled out at once, covering him like an avalanche of depression.

"I love her," Bran whispered, though admitting it aloud felt like salt on his raw emotions.

"Finally!" Finn declared, then paused, making a funny sound in his throat. "Which brings me to the reason I called. Stephanie contacted me this morning, asking for a job."

"What?" Bran took a swig of coffee, wincing when he realized it was tepid. He swallowed anyway, needing the caffeine boost. "I assume you already turned her down. Why would she call you, in the first place?"

"Uhmm… Eh-hem…" Finn's voice was barely audible. "Maybe because I kind of promised her a job if she needed it."

"I can't believe this!" Bran exploded. "You're supposed to be my friend."

"I was thinking it'd be a good thing if she worked for me. At least I could keep tabs on her, and you'd know she was okay."

Bran replied with a word Stephanie wouldn't have liked.

"Okay," Finn remarked, a hint of humor back in his voice. "Something tells me you're a bit unhappy."

"She doesn't need to go anywhere." Bran felt like hitting something. Or someone. He resolved to go back to the gym and skip dinner. "I plan to keep paying her salary. I'm going to take care of her and Ellie, no matter what."

"Perhaps you should mention that to her," Finn suggested.

"I tried!" Bran shouted. "She won't talk to me. She blocked my calls. She wouldn't answer the door. And yesterday, if I hadn't used my key to let myself in her suite, her ex might've killed her. I pulled him off her and cleaned his clock. She barely had time to say thank you before everyone descended on us, including the police."

"You beat up her ex?" asked Finn. "Can't wait to hear this story."

"Never mind that," Bran fumed. "The important thing is I haven't been able to talk to her. How can I stop her from moving to New York?"

"I'm afraid it's too late for that. She's already on her way."

"How could that be? She just moved out this morning." His chest burned with excess acid.

"Seems the place she was planning to sub-lease was infested with little critters—namely roaches and mice. What could I do? I told them to come. I've got an empty apartment in my building, although I had a high-paying leaser lined up. Since you planned to take care of Steph and Ellie, I'll let you reimburse me for the apartment."

"You take Stephanie away from me, and I pay you for the privilege?" Branson was too stunned to be angry.

"If you don't like it, I suggest you do something about it. Insist on a paternity test. Why wait 'til the baby comes? Do it now."

"Ha! I wish."

"I think it can be done. Google it."

A box on Bran's desk buzzed, indicating someone was at his office door. "I don't have time. Carina's already here. Mind looking it up for me?"

"Sure. Guess it's the least I can do for the guy who's paying my new assistant's salary and housing."

"I didn't agree to pay for—"

"Want me to send a text as soon as I find out the answer?"

Outside the door, his visitor demonstrated her impatience with persistent knocking. "Branson, let me in."

Bran gritted his teeth and murmured into the phone. "Yes, please. And hurry."

As he disconnected the call, he pressed a button to unlock the door. She marched inside, complaining as she came. "First, you insist I make an appointment, just to talk to you. Me—your fiancée. Why should I need an appointment to speak to my husband-to-be? And then, when I come, you make me stand outside and wait. I don't know what you think about our relationship, but I can tell you I'm not putting up with this kind of thing. I deserve to be treated with respect."

Branson imagined her standing with her hand on her hips, looking down on him as if she thought herself superior in every way. He waited until her tirade dwindled to nothing, then leaned forward with his elbows on his desk, folding his hands to support his chin.

"Good afternoon, Carina. Thank you for coming."

"Thank *me* for coming? *I'm* the one who insisted we talk. You've been avoiding me all week, treating me like I'm nobody, instead of your fiancée."

He shook his head slowly from side to side. "Not sure your title is still *fiancée*. That would imply we're getting married."

He heard a sharp intake of breath. "Are you threatening me?"

"Not at all." He forced his lips to smile. "I'm simply explaining to the woman who lied to me and drugged me that I'm not sure she possesses the qualities I'm seeking in a wife."

"That was only out of desperation." Her voice went shaky. "It was all for the baby. He needs his father."

"About that… I've been thinking…" Branson let his words hang, stalling for time. *Hurry up, Finn. What did you find?* "I'm thinking perhaps the baby needs his or her father, but that might not be me."

"How dare you!" Carina's outrage didn't convince Branson of anything.

"Sorry to offend you, Carina." He yawned and stretched as he rose from his desk and strolled to the coffee maker in the corner of the room. "Yet, I seem to remember a conversation where you expressed that we needn't be exclusive, even if we were married. Doesn't give me a lot of confidence in the child's paternity. There's that, and the fact that I took precautions."

"Precautions aren't one hundred percent effective," she declared. "Hope you don't plan to wait until your child is born before we get married."

It occurred to Branson she might not be pregnant at all. She'd flashed a sonogram at his friends, but what proof did he have that it was hers? In his pocket, his cell phone vibrated. He slid it out and checked the message from Finn. Then his lips curled into the first genuine smile he'd worn all day.

"Carina, why don't you sit down for a minute? You're pregnant, so you shouldn't be on your feet, right?"

"Fine," she grumbled, settling heavily into the chair across the desk. "At least you're showing some consideration… for the *first time*."

"Have you seen the newest version of the prenup agreement? The one that nullifies any exchange of property in the event the child's paternity isn't confirmed."

He heard the surprise in her voice. "Mark didn't say anything—" She coughed, an awkward choking noise. "No, I haven't seen the new one."

"Mark? Since when are you on a first-name basis with my attorney?"

Or should he say *ex-attorney*. Mark Johnson had left at least a dozen messages since yesterday, urging immediate action and proposing alternate solutions, all of which involved a quick marriage.

"We've exchanged a lot of phone calls and emails over the past few weeks," she defended.

Had Mark and Carina exchanged more than phone calls?

"I mentioned the paternity test, because I've decided I want one, immediately."

"Now?" she squeaked. "You can't do that. Not without risking the baby's life."

"Actually, there's a simple test available. If the results say I'm the father, I'll marry you within a week. I want my son or daughter to be legitimate."

No sound answered him, except her rapid breaths. Then a sniffle. And another.

"It's not fair," she cried. "I didn't ask for any of this. I didn't want to be pregnant."

"The test won't hurt," he elaborated. "It uses a blood sample from the pregnant mother and a cheek swab from the father."

"And I'm stuck being a single mom with a baby I never wanted." She sniffed and took a shuddery breath. "That's what's going to happen."

His chest clenched. *What if this is truly my son or daughter?*

"I'll take the baby," he blurted out. "I'll be the primary caregiver, and you can go back to your normal life. I'll take custody."

"No, you won't," she sobbed. "It's not even yours. I wish it was, but it isn't."

"You're positive I'm not the father?" His heart flew about, beating against his ribcage.

"I'm only twelve weeks along."

I'm not the baby's father. An incredible feeling spread throughout his system—elation. He was free. Free to be with Stephanie. Free to love her and be loved by her. He couldn't wait to get Carina out of the room so he could call Steph. Nothing else mattered. Not the Parker-Aston stocks or his father or the attempted takeover of his own company. Nothing mattered except being married to Stephanie.

"I'm sorry this happened to you," he said, incredulous to find he meant it. Now that he was free of her, he had no desire to hold her sins against her.

"You're a good man," she said, her voice cracking. "If the baby was yours, I'd give you custody. I know you'd be a good father."

"Maybe the baby's real father will marry you," he suggested. Perhaps, if Mark was the father, Bran could put pressure on him to marry her. The man might be on the take from Bran's father, but he still ought to take responsibility for his actions. "Have I met this man?"

"You could say that." She gave a bitter laugh. "He said he loved me. He made me feel special. You never did that."

"Neither one of us was in love."

"I think..." Her voice dropped to a low murmur. "I think I could've loved you. I tried not to, because... you know... my pride was hurt. You rejected me, Bran. I pretended not to care, but I did. Guess that made me vulnerable when someone came along and said the words I wanted to hear. Only, he was lying."

"I'm sorry, Carina." How could he have been so thoughtless? He prided himself on being hyper aware of people's emotions, interpreting the slightest change in tone. "I've tried to be honest."

"Yes, I know," she admitted. "But it's too late, now. I suppose I could get an abortion, but I don't feel good about it."

A repulsive thought occurred. She'd mentioned Stephanie's ex-husband one time, speaking as if she'd heard personal testimony from him. And someone had told Jeff where he could find Stephanie. If Carina believed Bran had been sleeping with Steph all this time, she might've slept with Jeff in retribution.

He swallowed, steeling himself against the answer before he asked the question. "Jeff Caldwell? Was it him?"

"No. He's attractive, but I knew he wasn't going anywhere. No goals. No aspirations."

Good. He let out the breath he was holding. "Then... was it Mark Johnson?"

She didn't respond.

"I promise it won't make any difference to me if Mark's the father," he assured her. "I've already decided to do business with a different law firm."

"It's not him."

Then who? From her attitude about Jeff's future, Bran knew it wasn't one of his employees. Obviously, it must be someone he didn't know well.

"That's okay. I don't need to know."

"I'm so alone," she whispered. "I don't want to be a single mother. Who's going to marry me when I have a kid?"

"If someone loves you, it won't matter to him that you have a kid." Bran thought of Ellie. He barely knew the child but already loved her, simply because she belonged to Steph.

"That's not how it works in *our* social circle. You should know that. People are so judgmental."

"You'll find another circle," he encouraged. "A better one."

"My family will disown me," she said in a flat tone, pronouncing an inevitable death sentence. "Their position in society is everything. Dad really wanted this match with the Knight family. I thought I was going to give it to him."

"I can't marry you, Carina. You know that, whether you admit it or not."

"I know." She sounded like she was already dead.

"Maybe you should talk to a counselor."

"It wouldn't help." Her trembly tone told him she was on the verge of tears again. "He said he loved me, and I believed him. He said I was beautiful. Exquisite. He said he'd been looking for me all his life. He was going to marry me. Then I got pregnant, and everything changed."

"You deserve better, Carina. Good riddance to him." *I can't believe I'm comforting her, after all she did.*

She ranted on, sniffling between phrases. "He got this bright idea that we could pass the baby off as yours. He said we could still be together after you and I divorced."

Her rambling didn't make any sense. "Why would he do that? If he was planning to marry you anyway, why would he want you to marry me first? Was he hoping I'd pay child support?"

"It was all about you. Grabbing the stocks. Public

humiliation. Everything. It was all about hurting you." A raw sob escaped. "It was never about me. Only you. I thought he loved me, but he didn't care at all."

"Who was it?" The words tumbled from his wooden mouth in a garble. In his gut, he already knew the answer.

"Martin Knight," she whimpered. "Your father."

CHAPTER 23

Steph planted a tender kiss on her sleeping daughter's cheek, tiptoed out, and shut the door with barely a sound. With a lingering tenderness in her ankle, she limped into the room and collapsed on the couch. She noted Finn and Laurie, standing nose to nose—as much as possible, considering their height disparity—glaring at each other, their furious expressions a mirror image, but for the sharp contrast between Finn's fair complexion and Laurie's golden brown.

"What's going on?" Steph asked, wondering how Laurie had the energy to stand up after their grueling fourteen-hour drive. She couldn't begin to guess why her friend was angry at Finn, who'd been gracious enough to meet them at the complex at one a.m. with a crew who had their car unloaded and in their apartment in fifteen minutes.

"I'll tell you what's going on." Laurie whipped her head around, coal black eyes flashing. "This man had the gall to blame you for Branson's problems. We all know that man brought this on himself. Having a disability doesn't give you a license to be careless and not take responsibility for your actions."

"I never said Steph was at fault." Finn's face glowed red to the tips of his ears, his hands flexing with tension. "I only said I think she's running away instead of dealing with the issues, and her timing is particularly bad."

"You called her a selfish coward," Laurie snapped her glower back to Finn. "Nobody calls my friend a selfish coward and gets away with it. If you knew half of what she's done, you'd never say that. She's braver than you'll ever be, and all that woman does is sacrifice herself, on a daily basis."

Finn lifted a finger. "No. I'm sorry. But you're wrong. I never called Stephanie a *selfish coward*. I simply said moving off to another state without even giving him a chance to talk to her was a *selfish act of cowardice*. I was referring to something she did, not calling her a name. Those are two entirely different things."

Stephanie yawned and stretched. "Hey, can we put this World War III off until tomorrow? We're all exhausted, and Finn probably has to work tomorrow."

"Fine by me." Laurie stepped back and crossed her arms. Her chin jerked toward the door. "See ya later, Finn."

"Are you going to tell her what I told you?" Finn asked, his chin lifted in defiance.

"It can wait until tomorrow," Laurie snapped.

"What?" Steph was suddenly awake, adrenaline surging through her arteries. "Did something happen to Branson?"

"Yes," Finn said.

"Nothing important," Laurie added. "All week you told me Branson was better off without you there. You said he had a lot of decisions to make, and he needed to make them without you. You told me if you were there, he would just feel guilty, and he might make the wrong choice."

"Yes, but—"

"If you hadn't convinced me this was the right thing to do, I never would've let you drive us all the way to New York City."

Stephanie groaned. "Yes, but that doesn't mean I don't care what happens to him."

"You can't fix this," Laurie said with a note of finality. "There's nothing you could do, even if you were there."

"What happened?" Her mouth went dry.

"I'll tell you." Finn stepped in front of Laurie. "He found out he's not the father of Carina's baby."

Steph almost clapped her hands for joy, but something in Finn's eyes told her there was more. "And?" she asked, holding her breath.

"The baby's father is Bran's dad."

Steph slapped both hands over her mouth and moaned, "No. Oh, poor Bran." Before she realized what she was doing, she was on her feet, hobbling down the hall to find her purse. "I need my keys. Laurie, you stay here with Ellie, I'll be back as soon as I can. Better pray that hunk of metal doesn't break down on the drive."

"No, no, no, no, no." Laurie blocked the way, grasping both her arms. "Be sensible about this. You can't go back there. You made a decision, and you have to stick to it. Anyway, you're in no condition to drive, right now. You're exhausted. You'd fall asleep on the highway and kill yourself. And probably kill someone else, too."

"You can go with me. I'm flying out in the morning." Finn wore a smug grin that seemed to irritate Laurie.

"Finn... you *weasel*! I'm not letting her go. Not unless you promise you're bringing her back with you. I can't handle moving three times in two weeks." As her hands flailed about, she scanned the room. Then she dashed off and returned, holding out a magazine. "Swear on this. Swear you'll bring her back. Right now. Do it."

"On a Good Housekeeping magazine?" His mouth curled with merriment.

"You're going to have to pretend it's a Bible."

Her eyes narrowed to dark slits, and Finn's face sobered. He laid his left palm on the magazine and lifted his right hand. "I do solemnly swear, when this short trip is concluded, I will reunite Stephanie with her family, forthwith. How's that?"

Laurie threw the magazine into the air, spun on one foot, and flounced down the hallway, calling, "I know you're up to something, Finn Anderson. You better not double cross me."

"I take that as more of a challenge than a threat," Finn quipped, his laughter following after her.

Steph put a hand on his arm. "Tell me the truth... How's he doing? I know how he feels about his father. I'm sure this is killing him."

"No. *You* killed him, Stephanie. You killed him when you left him. You took the air right out of his lungs."

"That's not fair. I left him so he could do what's best for him without worrying about me."

"Stupidest thing I've ever heard." Finn's eyes rolled to the ceiling. "He loves you. What could possibly be best for him without you in it?"

She rubbed her temples, trying to relieve the throbbing behind her eyes. "I'm too tired to argue about this. My head hurts. My foot hurts. And I haven't slept in a week. So listen to me... I'm going with you tomorrow because Branson needs me right now. But you have to keep your promise and bring me back here."

"I promised no such thing. I vowed to reunite you with your family. If I'm not mistaken," Finn said, with a wink, "that would include your *husband*."

⁓

"Tsk, tsk, tsk. Are you going to lie in bed all day, Mr. Knight?" Fordham's voice could hardly be heard over the blaring bagpipe and drum corps music he'd apparently chosen as Branson's wakeup call.

"It's ten a.m., Fordham," Branson shouted, pulling a pillow over his ears. "That hardly qualifies as 'all day.'"

The volume dropped a few notches. "You have a point. Yet, I feel compelled to bother you, like a proverbial burr in your saddle, until you stop wallowing in self-pity."

"Leave me alone. I like wallowing."

"It's more than five hours past your normal wakening time. I believe that's sufficient time to consider all the ways life has dealt you a raw deal. It's time to rise and play the game, Mr. Knight, while you still have opportunity to win."

"I'm afraid my father has flopped the nuts," said Branson, hoping to throw him off with unfamiliar jargon.

"You believe your dad has drawn an unbeatable hand?" Fordham responded without hesitation. "How can you say that when so many parts of his plan have failed? He didn't manage to purchase enough shares of Escapade Resorts to attain voting control or pull off a hostile takeover. Nor did he acquire the needed shares through Carina. You have broken the relationship with both Carina and Mark Johnson, both of whom, we presume, have provided your father with inside information."

"Yes, but he fathered a child with Carina. That's enough. A slap in the face. He succeeded in the place where it hurts me most."

"You are piteous indeed if you cannot see where that plan has not only failed to achieve its purpose, but also saved you from marital disaster." The music quieted, and Fordham continued. "Had Carina not pushed you toward a rapid matrimony, you might have continued with your original plan to marry her in exchange for controlling stock shares in Parker-Aston—a foolish scheme which you conjured without any help whatsoever from your father."

"It would never have happened." Bran sat up in bed and threw his feet over the side. "Not after I realized—" He stopped in mid-sentence, before accidentally revealing too much. Only Finn knew the truth about Stephanie.

"I assume you were about to say something regarding Ms. Caldwell. Am I correct?"

"Fordham, sometimes it's creepy when you read my mind like that."

"I'm no mind-reader, Mr. Knight. The entire staff is well-aware of your foul mood, which has risen in direct correlation with the length of time since Stephanie resigned as your personal assistant."

"She'll be difficult to replace," Branson muttered, as he trudged into his closet to find his clothes.

"I agree. And as such, I'd recommend you not do so."

"I need an assistant, Fordham. You can't do all the things Steph did for me." Branson raised his voice to be heard outside the closet.

"Nor would I ever desire to do so," he replied, drolly. "I'm afraid I'm not physically attracted to you, in the least."

"Very funny." Bran didn't affirm or deny Fordham's implication as he emerged from the closet, with his shirt unbuttoned, and sat down to put on his socks and shoes. "What am I supposed to do, if I can't replace her?"

"What to do. Indeed, that is the question. Perhaps you should anticipate your father's next move."

"Next move? He's already played his hand." The moment Bran made the statement, he realized how shortsighted he'd been. Of course his father wouldn't make a play without a backup plan.

"Though the game may be over for you, I seriously doubt your father feels the same. I've been vigilant on your account, but he's escalated the scope of his attack. I believe Jeff Caldwell's appearance is a prime example."

"Stephanie's ex? Think Dad had something to do with that slimeball showing up here?"

"Seems more probable than not. We know Carina contacted him at some point."

"Caldwell's in custody now," Bran mused, as he buttoned his shirt.

"Makes one wonder what your father will do next, in an attempt to hurt the one you love."

Fordham's contemplative words sent a shudder of dread down Bran's spine. He didn't bother to defend against Fordham's assumption that he was in love with Stephanie.

He could only wonder how far his father would go in a game that was spinning out of control. What Branson had started, in an effort to prove himself to his father, had now put Stephanie and Ellie in danger. Did his dad know where she was? Bran's heart accelerated, breaths coming faster. He had to warn Stephanie. He retrieved his cell phone then remembered Steph had blocked him. Instead, he dialed Finn, but the call went to voicemail. His fingers trembled as he pushed them through his hair.

"Mr. Knight," said Fordham. "I believe you've misbuttoned your shirt."

"Never mind that." Bran leapt to his feet. "Fordham, contact my pilot. Tell him we're leaving for New York in fifteen minutes."

"An excellent plan, Mr. Knight."

Branson could hear the smile in Fordham's voice. It matched the one on his own face. *I'm bringing Stephanie home.*

～

"I still can't believe he told you about the wedding," Steph commented over the low rumble of jet engines.

Finn glanced up from his paperback. "I think he let it slip because he was upset about his dad." His eyes twinkled. "Where are you going for your honeymoon?"

"Stop it. It's not a real marriage."

"It was a real wedding. So it could be a real marriage, if you wanted."

"That's *not* why I'm going to see him."

"If you say so." He turned back to his book.

"Really. I mean it."

"Okay." Finn mumbled the way people do when they're pretending to listen but actually paying attention to something else altogether.

"Finn? Did you hear me?"

"Huh? What?"

"I said I wish you'd quit talking about the wedding."

"You're kidding, right?" He closed his book, shoulders sagging. "Since you're the one bringing it up?"

"Of course I'm kidding. I want to talk about it. I *need* to talk about it. I'm legally married, and I haven't been able to tell a soul about it. Do you have any idea how hard it's been for me? It would be hard for anybody. But for me, it was excruciating. Look at me, I'm so desperate to talk about it, I'm forcing a bored man I hardly know to listen to me."

Finn chuckled. "Can't claim you hardly know me. We dated for a while."

"True. We were quite an item for a few hours."

"And, I was practically the best man at your wedding."

"The accidental wedding to a man who was engaged to someone else. The marriage I've had to keep secret *forever*."

Finn tilted his head, scrunching his nose. "It's only been a week."

"The longest week in history!" she ranted. "I got married, got a stomach virus, got attacked by my ex-husband and rescued by my current husband, quit my job, moved to a house to which the furry and six-legged inhabitants refused to relinquish the rights, and drove all the way to New York City in a car so full of stuff we could barely squeeze inside. So I was in the car for fourteen hours with my best friend, and I couldn't even tell her I was married."

"Why didn't you just tell her?"

"Because..." Steph slapped her armrest. "Branson said we weren't telling anyone. Then he up and told you all about it. Out of the blue. Why does he get to do that?"

"Guess you can tell Laurie, now."

"Oh my gosh. She's going to be so mad I didn't tell her when it happened. I may just keep it a secret until we get divorced, rather than face her fury."

"Yeah." His smile spread so wide all his teeth showed. "Laurie's a ball of fire."

"You did a number on her last night. I've never seen her so bent out of shape."

"It was awesome fun." His dimples flashed in impish fashion.

"She's a good friend in a tight spot. But be careful... you don't want to be on her bad side."

"I'm willing to risk it." One eyebrow kicked up on his forehead. "From what I've seen, she doesn't have a bad side."

Finn's reaction made Steph wonder exactly what had transpired while she was putting Ellie to bed. She jotted a mental note to question Laurie as soon as she got the chance.

"This wedding mess is all your fault, Finn. You and that stupid idea about the marriage certificates. None of this would've happened, if it weren't for you."

"*You're welcome*," he bantered. "I accept gift cards and money orders."

She shoved his arm. "It's not funny. Do you know how complicated you've made our lives?"

"I can't take all the credit." He slapped his hand over his heart in mock humility. "I couldn't have done it without the help of my leading lady... Destiny."

She battled to keep an answering smile away. "Are you ever serious?"

"Hardly." His mouth twisted to one side. "Only for the big stuff. You know… hurricanes, earthquakes, Bubonic Plague… that sort of thing."

Finn returned to his paperback and left Steph alone with her thoughts. She flipped through a book on her phone, though none of the words registered with her brain.

"One more question." She tapped Finn's shoulder. "How upset was Branson when he called you last night?"

This time Finn didn't smile. "I told you. He sounded depressed."

"Had he been to the gym?"

"Fifteen-mile run." He stared ahead at nothing, his empty gaze hardening. "Still depressed."

Steph chewed on the inside of her cheek. Finn's expression indicated this was a bad situation—*Bubonic Plague* bad.

"But he knows we're coming, right?" *What if Bran doesn't want me there? What if I make it worse?*

"I told him I'd be there as soon as I could. You'll be a surprise. A nice one." His head nodded as if he were certain of this fact. She hoped Finn knew his friend as well as he thought he did. "Bran probably doesn't expect me 'til tomorrow. But he'll be there—he never leaves the estate, anymore."

CHAPTER 24

Branson was too worried about Steph to be nervous about traveling away from home. He'd thrown a few items in an overnight bag, in case he had to stay a few days. But he had every intention of bringing Steph and Ellie back to Chicago where he could protect them.

As the jet lifted into the sky, Bran rehearsed his speech. Should he explain the threat his father posed and justify the need for Steph to stay close? Would that make her want to cling to him for protection or run as far away as possible? Should he address the fact that Carina might need physical help raising his little half-brother or sister? Would she be able to handle the child's intrusion into their lives or would she insist on a divorce?

With a growl of frustration, he realized Stephanie deserved much better than the life he could offer, fraught with complications, stress, and danger. He hated himself for bringing more sadness into her life. But he couldn't live without her—he knew that now. He would do everything in his power to keep her safe and make up for the hurt he caused her.

Perhaps he should hire a bodyguard. *Wasn't there a movie about a woman with a bodyguard? Didn't she fall in love with her protector? Scratch that idea. I'll do it myself.*

Fifteen minutes into the flight, the pilot's voice came over the loud speaker. "Mr. Knight, I've just received a radio communication from home base. They wanted me to inform you Mr. Anderson's jet is landing at the estate, even as we speak."

If Finn was in Illinois, that meant Stephanie was alone in New York. *Is she at risk? Surely my father hasn't been able to locate her in less than twenty-four hours.*

Branson made his way to the front of the plane and opened the cockpit door.

"Hey, Bran." Hosea, his long-time pilot and friend, fell into casual speech as he shouted over the noise. "Want to fly the plane for a bit?"

Bran grinned, in spite of his anxiety. Hosea had let him *fly* the plane, much as an adult allows a kid to *drive* a car. "No, thanks." Careful not to bump the controls, he slid into the copilot's seat, empty for the short, one-hour flight.

"Are we turning back?" Hosea asked.

"No. Stay on course."

"Whatever you say, boss. Want the headphones? They're hanging up and to your right."

As he slipped the headphones on, rock music began to play in his ears. "Seventies music," Bran commented into the mic. "My favorite."

"I remembered," Hosea remarked. "It's been a long time. You and I used to spend a lot of hours up here. You were always going places. Some new adventure. Never knew what was next. I really missed that these last couple of years. Nice to have you back."

"It's nice to *be* back."

At once, Bran realized exactly how close his father had come to destroying his life. Branson had given up everything he enjoyed to prove he could beat his father at his own game. Yet, Bran would never find joy in winning, because he hated that game. The only way to win was not to play.

Wasn't that what he'd learned when his friends roped him into the Vegas trip? The few moments he forgot all about achieving his new goals—the ones designed to stick it to his dad—those were the times he felt like himself again. He'd neglected the relationships that meant most, trying to build ties with people he hated.

How could I be so blind? At that, he chuckled, knowing it was the kind of tongue-in-cheek remark Fordham would make. Come to think of it, Fordham had been nagging at him about this issue for the past two years, though Bran refused to listen.

The radio squawked, Fordham's voice speaking. "Please inform Mr. Knight he no longer needs to fly to New York. Stephanie Caldwell is here."

A weight lifted from Bran's shoulders, and he couldn't help laughing. He felt giddy and light, like he could fly without the plane. As Hosea banked the jet into a one-eighty, Bran sang along with the music in his ears. "The boys are back in town…"

STEPHANIE PACED in front of the glass doors, waiting for the transport van to bring Branson back to the estate. According to Fordham, he'd been flying to New York to talk her into moving back. Evidently, he feared his father might cause her physical harm. The idea sounded absurd, but Fordham believed it was possible.

It seemed Branson was now dealing with both depression and anxiety. Her heart hurt for him. As much as she loved him, she knew she couldn't fix everything in his life. All she could do was hug him and remind him he had people who loved him.

"Could you please sit down?" Finn complained from the bench on the side. "You're making my eyes cross. He'll be here in a minute."

"I think I see him coming." Steph stepped outside, shading her eyes with her hand as she peered into the distance.

"A black Suburban?" Finn joined her, outside. "Yeah, that's it."

As the SUV skidded to a stop, Branson jumped out of the passenger side door.

"Stephanie?" he called. "Are you here?"

Before she could respond, Finn shouted. "I'm here. Your best friend. Don't you want to see me?"

Branson threw his head back and let out a belly laugh. "I don't want you, Finn. I want the present you brought me from New York."

He doesn't act depressed. Maybe he's hiding his pain.

"I'm here, Bran." She limped toward him, her clutch still

tucked under her arm. "I'm so sorry about what happened. I know you must be—"

He took two steps, dropped his cane, and hoisted her into the air, in a bear hug, spinning her in circles, her legs dangling. Her purse went flying, and she squealed, beating playfully on his chest. "Put me down, you beast."

"Never," he replied, relaxing the circle of his arms until she slid down, their faces level. "From now on, I'm not wasting another minute of my life. Since any minute without you in my arms is a waste, I'm never going to let you go."

Her pulse throbbed in her ears, racing faster and faster, as he nuzzled her neck. "You smell so good." His lips brushed along the line of her jaw, taking her breath away. "You feel good, too." He peppered her face with tiny kisses, moving closer to her hungering lips. "Let's see how you taste."

His mouth slanted across hers, lips crashing together in an explosion of burning fire and icy tingles. Her world narrowed until nothing was left but Branson—his spicy scent, his sultry voice, his urgent lips, his gentle hands. The power of his kiss left her thirsty for more.

As her feet touched the ground, his embrace gave her no chance to escape. Not that she wanted to.

"I love you." He breathed the words into her mouth. "More than life."

"I love you, too."

"Never leave me," he demanded, though his kiss turned gentle and pleading, its tenderness her undoing.

"I won't." She pulled away to respond, panting for air, then dove back for more, wishing she could somehow get closer.

"Did I mention I love you?" he asked, his mouth still caressing her lips.

"Yes, but you can say it again," she whispered.

"I love you, Stephanie Knight," he murmured in her ear, making chill bumps rise on her arms.

"Please," she begged, though she had no idea what she needed. She only knew Branson was the sole source of it.

He murmured, "Yes," as he nipped at the hollow place under her jaw.

His arms closed tighter, holding her so close she could barely breathe. Given the choice, she would've picked his arms over oxygen, anyway. Then reality inched its way into her mind.

"What about your father? And Carina? And the baby?"

"I don't know, but I'm not going to worry. Not anymore."

He caressed her lips with a gentle kiss that drew her anxiety away and covered it with a soft blanket of peace.

"I love you so much, Stephanie Knight."

Her heart did a flip. "That's really my name," she said, in a breathy tone.

"I realized something when I was on that plane. By trying to prove I was better than my dad, I was becoming exactly like him. I was so obsessed with success, I almost missed the best thing that ever happened to me... *you*."

"I don't know why you would want me. I come with a lot of baggage. An unfinished degree. A ton of debt. A daughter with cystic fibrosis. A psycho ex-husband."

He grinned. "That's exactly why I fell in love with you. Despite everything that happened, you still have a kind heart. Sure, maybe you're a bit too trusting, but I'm cynical enough for both of us. I love that you forgive people, even when they don't deserve it."

Steph kissed each of his eyelids. "You know what I love about you?"

"Tell me," he mumbled, while nuzzling her neck in the most distracting way.

"I can't think when you're doing that," she complained.

"Are you saying I make you mindless with desire?" His eyebrows bobbed up and down.

"Ha! Yes, but that's not the reason I love you. It's because you give to people who can't give back. People like me."

"You're so wrong. You've given me more than you'll ever know," Bran declared. "You've given me hope. You've given me a reason to live. You've—"

"Ah... excuse me." Finn broke into their conversation, leaning against a pillar and tapping his foot. "Are we about finished here? I think you've established that she's given you lots of stuff. But you're giving *me* a headache."

"You could go away and stop eavesdropping," Steph suggested.

"Or," Finn countered, "You could wrap up this mutual admiration session and we could all go to lunch."

"Put your fingers in your ears," Branson said, "because I've got one more thing to say."

"Just kill me." Finn rolled his eyes and covered his ears with his hands.

"I can't promise a life without problems or stress." Bran smoothed her hair away from her face. "But I can promise my love is bigger than those things. We'll run, not to get away from our trouble, but for the joy of running. We'll fly away, not to hide, but to find grand adventures. In each other's arms, we'll escape the world. Hand in hand, we'll face it."

The breeze felt cool on her damp cheeks. "That's so beautiful."

"I think I'm going to be sick," Finn goaded. "Maybe you two should get a room."

Branson smiled and pressed his ravenous lips to hers. "That's an excellent idea."

CHAPTER 25

"I don't understand why you can't just tell people we're married. Wouldn't that take care of everything?" Steph paced around Branson's bedroom like a lion in a cage. At the estate, only Laurie and Fordham knew the truth, so Steph and Bran had to sneak around like teenagers in order to be together. "It's been a week, already. I hate keeping it a secret." *And it makes me feel insecure, but I don't want to sound needy.*

"Come here." Branson sat up against the headboard and patted the bed beside him. "Please?"

Yanking her gaze away from his well-muscled chest, she climbed in bed and snuggled against him. "I'm still waiting for an answer, Bran."

He ignored the question. "I love this sexy outfit you have on. This baggy sweatshirt is my absolute *favorite*. What color is it?"

"Grey." She held back a chuckle, biting her lips.

"Grey—that's my *favorite* color. I like it so much better

than red or green or pink or black. Did you put this on just for me?"

"Just for you." She couldn't keep the corners of her mouth from curving up.

"I knew it. You're the best. Have I told you I love you, yet today?"

"No," she answered, though it wasn't true. He'd said those words at least ten times since the sun rose that morning, but she knew it was the answer he wanted.

"*E-gads*! I've been remiss. I hereby proclaim that you, Stephanie Knight, Guardian of My Heart, are the love of my life."

"Hmmm… I'm not sure saying I'm the love of your life is the same as saying you love me. After all, one is passive and the other is active."

"You're so right." His voice dropped an octave and filled with gravel. "I much prefer the active kind of love to the passive kind." He nuzzled behind her ear, kissing along her jaw and making stars explode under her eyelids.

She pushed his face away. "Stop distracting me. I want to know why the marriage still has to be a secret."

The air escaped his lungs in a long, heavy breath. "I need you to be patient a little while longer. I've got my new attorney working on some important things."

A prenuptial agreement. I should've known. She'd gladly sign any document giving up rights to Bran's money, but it still stung, knowing he didn't trust her any more than he'd trusted Carina.

"Okay. I can wait. It's just that Ellie's asking questions."

"But you always wait until she's asleep to sneak up to my room. Right?"

"Not always. I've missed a few of her breathing treatments so I could be with you. She's always a little pouty when Laurie does the nighttime one." Her chest hurt, tight with guilt.

"Are you missing it now?" His brows drew together.

"Yes, but it's okay. Ellie will—"

"Let's go." He threw the covers back and stepped into his pants.

"You want to help with her CF therapy?"

"Sure I do. If I'm going to be Ellie's dad, I need to know how to give her breathing treatments."

As she crawled out of the bed to get dressed, she tried to respond. She opened her mouth, intending to tell him how sweet he was. She wanted to tell him he'd make a great dad, but the only thing that came out of her mouth was a sob.

"Shhh..." His arms went around her, holding her against his chest, one hand stroking her hair. His deep voice rumbled in her ear. "It's okay. I love Ellie almost as much as I love her mother."

She swallowed hard. "I don't deserve you."

"No, you don't." His voice was quaky. "You deserve better—so much better than me. I'm trying hard to be what you deserve, but I'm broken, Steph. I'm so screwed up."

"That's not true, Branson. You're—"

His lips silenced her protest. His kiss seemed to cry out in a desperation that matched her own, as his hands tangled in her hair. When he drew away, her lips mourned—a soft, wordless cry.

"Come." His hand slipped to the small of her back and moved her toward the door. "Teach me how to be a real dad."

∼

Branson tightened his hands on the arms of his desk chair, trying to push his temper back.

"Mr. Parker—"

"Horace. Call me Horace."

He sucked in a lungful of air and held it, counting to ten. "Horace, Carina is a beautiful woman. But more importantly, she's a strong, intelligent person."

Horace's chair legs screeched, moving closer to the desk, so close his smoker's breath came across with his words. "So, you'll marry her, then?"

"No, Mr. Parker. Carina and I decided to go our separate ways."

He spat out a vulgar curse word. "I wouldn't have this problem if she wasn't such a *slut*."

"*Mr. Parker—*"

"She slept with two Knights, got knocked up by one, and neither one wants her." His coarse laugh sounded more like a bark. "I get it. I don't want her, either."

"You don't mean that. Carina's your daughter."

"I *know* she's my daughter." A slam on his desk made Bran jump out of his skin. "That's why I have this problem. If she'd been a *son*, we wouldn't be having this conversation today. She was a disappointment from the day she was born."

"I don't even know what to say to that," Bran replied, as his heart returned to its normal pace. "Surely her mom would disagree with you."

"My wife doesn't often have enough sober minutes in the day to form a lucid thought." His voice came out strangled, like someone was choking him. "But when she finds out

Carina was so stupid and selfish she got herself pregnant, she'll tell me to kick her butt to the street like the tramp she is."

"Horace..." Bran tried another approach. "Since my father is responsible for the child, Carina will have plenty of money to take care of the baby. All she needs is family to help her raise your grandchild."

"Your dad denies being the father." Horace sounded resigned. "We could take him to court, but it would ruin the family's reputation."

"That hardly seems important right now."

"What would you know? You had everything handed to you on a silver platter. I had to work to get where I am."

Bran didn't bother to tell him he'd rejected his inheritance to prove he could make it on his own. Horace wouldn't believe him, anyway. "What's more important— your position in society or your daughter?"

"If you think Carina's so important, you can have her." Horace's chair scraped again as he rose to his feet. "I told her to get an abortion, but she refused. So as far as I'm concerned, she made her choice."

~

"No, leave it on." Carina lifted her chin, red-rimmed eyes brimming with tears. "I asked Bran to let me hear it."

Stephanie slowly withdrew her hand from the switch that would've silenced the speaker. She studied her fingernails, pretending she wasn't paying attention to Horace Parker's hurtful speech.

Branson asked Stephanie to sit with Carina to ensure she

didn't come blasting into the room. But if Steph had known this would happen, she would've run the other direction. After an eternity, a door slammed, and the torture was over.

Carina sat like a statue, staring at the wall, tear-tracks staining her perfect complexion.

You were right, MawMaw. I almost feel bad for hating her, but I'm not as good a person as you.

"I'm sure he didn't mean it." Steph struggled to find something encouraging to say. "He didn't know you were listening. He was probably blowing off steam."

Carina's blank expression was etched in stone. "I've never pleased him. Nothing I ever accomplished was worth anything. My life was a total failure until I started dating Branson, but I couldn't even do that right."

Steph couldn't stand the haunted look on her face, so she dropped her gaze back to her fingernails. "What are you going to do?"

"I don't know. What's it matter to you?" Her flat tone was eerie, like she was dead, or wishing she was.

"I'll help you with the baby." *Why did I say that? It's too late to take it back. Maybe she'll say no.*

"Really? I suppose you've got a huge stash of money somewhere? Or is Branson giving you a big raise, soon?"

"I meant I'd help you take care of the baby. I could sit for you sometimes… give you a break." She slid a box of tissues across the table.

"I can pay for a sitter. I'm going to sue Martin for child support. Why should I care if it ruins my family's reputation?"

Steph shrugged, relieved she was off the hook. "Sounds like a good idea."

Carina snatched a tissue and patted her face dry, careful not to smear her mascara. She stood up, smoothed the wrinkles from her upscale dress and glided to the door on designer heels. As her hand reached for the handle, she paused and looked down.

"I guess I won't be wearing these heels much longer. My feet are starting to swell."

"Yeah, I had a lot of swelling when I was pregnant."

"I could probably use some baby advice." Her hand dropped down to rub the small bump on her belly. "Can I buy you a cup of coffee sometime?"

"Uhmm…" Steph swallowed, but her mouth was dry. "Sure, I guess."

"I'll call you."

The door clicked shut behind her. Steph sat frozen in shock, feeling like she was in a weird dream.

"Shut up, MawMaw. I know you're up there laughing at me."

∽

"Are you sure you want me down there in the meeting?" Stephanie wished she'd worn an antiperspirant instead of just a deodorant. When Bran told her to dress up for a big date after the Escapades board meeting, she hadn't worried how she would look. She'd put on the nicest dress she owned —the white one she'd worn in Las Vegas—and taken extra care with her hair and makeup.

Maybe tonight's the big night. Maybe he'll tell me he's got the prenuptial agreement ready, and we can be married for real. A prenup might not sound romantic to most people, but to her, it was better than a diamond ring.

"Yes, I'm sure." Branson swept his hand forward and waited for her to step onto the private elevator before joining her and pushing the button for the third floor conference room.

"But I feel so self-conscious. You'll look like all the other men, wearing a coat and tie, but none of the other women will have on evening gowns. Why can't I take notes from next door, like I always do?" She'd transcribed the proceedings of countless board meetings, while watching the broadcast from the adjacent room.

"I need you to be my eyes today. I want you to tell me which board members are against me. And anyway, you're the reason we're here. You're the one who did all the background research on every board member and followed all the leads. Why should you have to hide in the side room as if you were an ordinary personal assistant? You're so much more than that. You helped me build Escapades from the ground up."

How could she explain it? *It's not enough that you're proud of how well I do my job... I want you to be proud that I'm your wife.* Aloud, she said, "I just wish you would've warned me, so I wouldn't have worn this dress."

He lifted her left hand and kissed the backs of her fingers, empty of any identifying rings. "I've been told you look stunning in that dress, and it so happens I want to show you off today."

"How can you show me off? No one even knows we're together." She tried to keep her resentment from showing.

He groped the elevator panel, pushed a button, and the elevator jerked to a stop.

"What's wrong, Steph? Am I in trouble for something?"

Darn him for looking so sweet and concerned. She felt petty for being upset.

"No, it's nothing."

"Seems like it might be something, instead of nothing. If we're going to make this relationship work, you have to talk to me." He ducked his head away. "I try to get your cues, but I guess I'm not very good at it."

I'm a jerk. Of course it's hard for him to understand when something upsets me, without any visual cues.

"I'm sorry, Bran. I didn't want to say anything, because... well... because I didn't want you to feel rushed. Or I thought maybe you changed your mind."

His eyebrows knitted together. "Changed my mind about what?"

"About being married. We've been secretly married for weeks, now. The only reason I can think that you haven't told people by now is you've changed your mind."

He held her shoulders the way he always did when he wanted to be certain he faced her. "Haven't I told you I love you, every day? Haven't I said I'm the luckiest man in the world to have you as my wife? Don't I come every night to help you give Ellie her breathing treatment?" The muscles worked in his throat. "Can you not tell how I feel about you when we make love?"

So much for my great makeup job. She dabbed at her wet face with her hand, determined to keep mascara tears from dripping on her white dress.

"Sure, when we're alone together, it seems like everything

is perfect. But I don't understand why we can't tell people." She sniffed, long and hard, making a horrible sound that probably grossed him out. *No, he's already heard me throw up.*

He opened his arms, and she fell against him. His hand traced her spine in soothing strokes. "I'm sorry, Steph. I'm so sorry. I'm not good at this. I thought I was protecting you by not telling you."

"What? What haven't you told me?"

"That I don't trust my father." He squeezed her so tight she could barely breathe. "Right now he's angry, and from what Carina told me, he's more ruthless than I've ever seen him. He seems determined to destroy me, and I'm afraid that might apply to anything or anyone who's important to me. I didn't want to take the chance that he might hurt you."

"I can't live like this, Branson. I can't keep pretending you're nothing but my boss, and then sneaking around with you every night. When is it going to stop?"

"A week or two, at most. I need to take care of this thing with my father. I'm counting on Bernstein. He said Dad's going to crash the board meeting this afternoon. That's why I need you in there with me."

"What if your plan doesn't work?"

"It'll work. It has to."

Dread settled in her stomach, knowing all the things that could go wrong. Bran was the type that wanted his life in perfect order. He might not be able to commit to her as long as his father remained a threat. She shoved that thought to the back of her mind. What else could be holding him back?

"Did you finish the prenuptial agreement?"

"What prenuptial agreement?" He furrowed his brows even deeper. Then his eyes flew open wide. "Oh, right... the prenup... *our* prenup. Yes. Yes, it's done. I haven't had time to look over it, but Phillip took care of it. Technically, it's not a *prenup*tial agreement, since we're already married."

His forced chuckle didn't fool her for a minute. He was lying to her—she could sense it deep inside. She couldn't put her finger on which part was untrue, but she knew he was covering something up. It felt like the beginning of the end. This might be their last night together.

"We're going to be late for the meeting." Teetering on the edge of control, she reached around him to start the elevator, barely able to see the numbers through her tears. If his beautiful blue eyes could actually see, he would've known she was holding herself together with masking tape and paper clips. But he had no idea, and she was glad he didn't. He didn't need any distractions during this meeting. If it was the last thing she ever did for him—and it just might be—she would help him beat his father at his own game.

The boardroom fell silent when they entered. Though some eyebrows raised at her atypical dress, something in Bran's authoritative aura commanded their attention. Eighteen sets of eyes fixed on Branson's sightless ones as he moved to the head of the long table. She felt a warm glow of pride in him, despite her hurt. Settling into the empty chair beside him, she opened her laptop and attempted to shrink until she was invisible.

"Ladies. Gentlemen." Branson seemed totally at ease, turning his head to face each side of the table. "I believe congratulations are in order. We've had a stellar quarter at Escapades Resorts, expanding from our eco-adventure resorts into the luxury hotel market and swallowing the competition. I'm happy to report the value of our shares has increased by four percent."

Polite clapping spread around the table like a wave. As he continued his speech, quoting the statistics he'd memorized and arguing for optimism in the face of a recent adjustment in the stock prices, Steph made notes about the expressions of each of the board members, rather than transcribing the meeting, as those present must've assumed.

William Bernstein, their secret informant, twisted and twirled a pen in his hand. His eyes were fixed on Branson, though they seemed unfocused. The grey-haired man claimed to have shifted his loyalty from Martin to Branson, but Steph worried it might be yet another ploy of Branson's father.

Ester Martel's loyalty was an unknown, but Steph noted she was flipping through her handout, rather than watching Branson. Stephanie went down the line, recording every eye twitch, chewed fingernail and fidgeting hand, along with a few board members who gazed at the table or out the window or anywhere other than the man they should be listening to.

"The successful acquisition of Harrison Hotels and Resorts has increased our cash flow, while—"

The heavy wooden doors burst open, and Bran's father stomped into the room, amid gasps of surprise. Steph's heart thundered in her chest, but she kept her cool, watching the board members with hawk eyes.

"Good morning." Martin strode all the way down the long table to stand beside Bran, glancing from one startled board member to another, like a king surveying his servants.

"Good to see you, Branson. I only wish it could be under better circumstances."

"What are you doing here?" Bran growled, rising from his chair. "This is a private board meeting. Do I need to call the guards to escort you out of here?"

Steph's tongue stuck to the roof of her mouth, seeing the two men side by side, Martin's salt and pepper hair the only thing that set him apart from his son, thirty-five years his junior.

"I don't think that's going to happen," said Martin. "You don't know it yet, but you'll be the one escorted out."

Steph fumed, wishing she could wipe Martin's smug expression off his face, but she kept her mouth zipped.

"I'm not going anywhere," Bran said. "Not only do I have the controlling shares of this company, which I started from the ground up, two years ago, but I'm also the CEO."

"Not for long," Martin said. "As the second largest shareholder, I have the right to call for a vote for a *new* CEO."

"Second largest shareholder?" Branson raised his voice to be heard over the loud objections. "I would've known if any single buyer had purchased that many shares."

A number of the board members barked with outrage. Others had worried frowns, while a few were smiling as if they'd expected this announcement. Stephanie made quick notes of the board members who seemed to support Bran's father.

Martin gloated so much, his cheeks seemed to puff out. "There's a lot you don't know about me, such as the names of every ghost company I own."

"Call for a vote and get this over with." The voice belonged to Bernie Miles, a rather rotund man with a bald head and grey mustache. Steph marked his name on the list—he was obviously in the know.

"Very well," said Martin, a frown flickering over his face as his sharp gaze rested momentarily on Stephanie. Something sick fluttered in her gut, but she lifted her chin and refused to break eye contact. He turned to look down the long conference table. "I nominate Reagan Cooper as the new CEO of Escapade Resorts."

Reagan stood and moved to stand behind Martin. With blond, thinning hair and a weak chin, he flashed a leering smile that gave Steph the creeps. A low grumble rippled across the boardroom.

"All in favor raise your right hand." Martin's glare swept the room.

Two or three hands shot into the air, while others joined more reluctantly, like someone was pointing a gun at their heads. Stephanie was furiously typing names when Martin's low voiced growled, "Mr. Bernstein? Is there something you've forgotten?"

Bernstein slowly rose from his chair, his jaw muscles bulging. "No, Martin. I remember everything. Every threat. Every manipulation. Every convoluted business deal."

"You're judging me? Ha!" Martin made a grating noise that sounded more like a scream of frustration than a laugh. "You weren't complaining when I made you millions of dollars."

"I'm not proud of everything I've done, but I've never broken any laws." Bernstein's face was the color of a ripe plum. "This personal vendetta of yours has taken you across the legal line, and you're not taking me with you."

"You're making the biggest mistake of your life." Martin's hand balled into a fist so tight his knuckles blanched.

Bernstein shook his head, his eyes softening. "I'm sorry, Martin..."

The doors opened again, and two men with badges strode inside, moving to flank Bran's father. The first man spoke.

"Martin Knight, you're under arrest for violations of the Federal Trade Commission Act. You have the right to remain silent. Anything you say can and will be used against you in a court of law. You have the right to legal representation. Do you understand your rights?"

Steph couldn't help feeling sad for Martin, whose face turned so white she thought he might pass out. "How dare you! Do you know who I am?"

"If you come along quietly, we won't have to use the cuffs, Mr. Knight."

The two men ushered Bran's still-protesting father from the room. Silence covered the room like a funeral pall. Reagan Cooper looked like he'd eaten something that had spoiled weeks ago. Pivoting on one foot, Branson faced the board members and cleared his throat.

"If you voted with my father, it's time for you to leave. I expect your resignations on my desk in twenty-four hours. Stephanie, do you have the list?"

Steph retrieved the list on her laptop and read off the names she'd recorded during the vote.

When one of those named muttered an objection, Branson added, "Don't forget that every meeting has a digital video recording." He pointed toward the window, and Steph redirected his arm until his finger was aimed at the camera.

"Thanks, sweetheart." He beamed at her, as if his father

hadn't just torn a huge hole in his soul. "We make a great team, don't we?"

She felt a little thrill that he used her pet name in public. While half the board members filed out, Branson called someone on his cell.

When the door closed behind the last person Branson put his phone away and rubbed his hands briskly together. "That's it. The meeting's adjourned, but don't leave yet."

"But Mr. Knight?" Ester Martel raised her hand. Then she seemed to remember Bran couldn't see and lowered it, her face reddening. "What are we supposed to do?"

Still worried that some traitors might not have been detected, Steph continued to note the nervous reactions of the remaining board members.

Steph could see the tension of the past two weeks was finally gone when a wide smile split Bran's face. "Stay for the party."

The door opened again, and Finn's face appeared. "Are you ready, Bran?"

"Ready as I'll ever be."

"What's going on?" Steph stopped, her fingers still poised over her laptop keyboard. "Why is Finn here?"

Strains of music began to play over the room's audio speaker, and a deep voice sang, with thick vibrato. "Wise men say... Only fools rush in..."

"What's going on, Bran? Why are you playing Elvis music?"

Branson lifted her by the elbow and edged her away from the table until they stood, facing the door on the other end of the room. "I thought Ellie ought to see it in person."

Right on cue, Ellie stepped inside, dressed in a beautiful coral chiffon dress, and carrying a basket with a white ribbon. She took a few halting steps, before breaking into a run. She crashed into Steph's arms, sending rose petals flying.

"Mom, I got to skip school and I got a new dress and—"

"Shhh..." Branson was on his knees, his hand on Ellie's shoulder. "Remember... don't spoil the surprise."

Ellie's arms switched from Steph's waist to Branson's neck, and he lifted her up, securing her on his hip.

Laurie came through the door in a simple satin gown, the same color as Ellie's. Stephanie knew without a doubt Laurie had chosen the dresses, since it was her favorite color—simultaneously contrasting with her dark skin and making it glow.

"Traitor," Steph whispered, as Laurie took her place beside her. "How long have you known about this?"

Her dark eyes sparkled with humor as she shot back, "Not as long as you waited to tell me you got married in Vegas."

As Elvis' voice continued to croon over the speakers, Finn, Cole, and Jarrett strolled inside. Finn wore what Steph now recognized as his customary expression—a grin that said he was in the midst of a great practical joke, which seemed to be his ultimate goal in life.

When Fordham materialized in the doorway, Steph expected him to follow the other men down the aisle. Instead, he motioned with his hand at someone out in the hallway. *Who else are we expecting? Hopefully, not Carina. She's been a lot nicer lately, but I don't want her at my wedding.*

The first thing Steph saw was a mass of red curls, then a

blue velvet dress with an ample bosom spilling out below massive shoulders.

"Priscilla?" Steph slapped both hands over her mouth. "Oh my gosh! Branson, what have you done?"

As Priscilla moved forward, Steph could see Billy waltzing toward them, microphone in hand, poured into a white bell-bottomed suit that sparkled in the conference room lights. George followed behind, beaming with excitement, probably because Bran had paid them more than the chapel made in a year.

She felt Branson's warm breath in her ear. "I'm sorry I kept you waiting, but I wanted it to be the perfect surprise. Forgive me?" His lips nibbled on her earlobe, ripples of pleasure shooting all the way down into her toes.

"You're cheating." What was meant to sound stern came out weak and breathless. "You're forgiven, but only if you promise this is the last surprise."

"Then, I'm afraid we're both out of luck."

With Priscilla poised to begin the ceremony, Branson dropped to one knee. "Stephanie Knight, love of my life…"

Time stopped—no one breathing, no heart beating. The second hand froze in place. Though Branson's lips moved, no sound penetrated Steph's ears. She didn't see the diamond engagement ring he slid onto her finger. For one single moment, she was blinded to all but one thing… she glimpsed into the soul of the man who loved her. The soul who refused to reject the society who rejected him. The soul who loved with his whole heart, even though his heart had been broken. The soul who saw her, with all her flaws, and called it beautiful. She saw a lovely thing—a treasure—Branson's soul, offered into her hands for safekeeping.

As cheers and clapping broke into her cocoon, Bran kissed her hand, then turned to Ellie. From his coat pocket he retrieved a folded paper, which he handed up to Stephanie, while opening a small black jewelry case in front of Ellie.

"Ellie, will you do me the honor of being my daughter? I promise to—"

"*Yes,*" she cried as she jumped against him, her arms strangling his neck.

Not an eye was dry in the room, as Branson promised to love Ellie and be the best possible father he could be, over Ellie's tearful wails. Stephanie unfolded the paper and almost choked when she recognized what she held in her hands—a legal form with Jeff's signature. Her ex had given up his parental rights, paving the way for Branson to legally adopt Ellie.

"Surprise!" whispered Branson, as he stood up beside her. "Told you I couldn't make any promises about that. Sorry it took me so long to get all this legal stuff done."

"So it's all done?" she murmured. "Because I'd like to sign that prenup and get that behind us."

"Don't you realize I trust you, by now? The only thing you need to sign is our will. It's pretty simple. If I die, I'm leaving everything to you and Ellie."

"But—"

His mouth descended in a kiss that made her toes curl.

A hand tapped her shoulder. She opened her eyes to find Priscilla peering at them, her toothy smile accented with bright pink lips. "Are we ready to start the wedding?"

"I am." Branson stole another kiss. It was easy for him, since he couldn't see George raise a disapproving eyebrow.

This time, when Branson spoke his vows, Steph knew he meant them as much as she did. Ellie was bouncing on her toes as Billy sang *Love Me Tender* to end the ceremony.

Ellie tugged on Branson's sleeve, and he scooped her up to watch from a perch on his shoulder. "This is way cooler than a picture. It's the real thing."

Steph gazed at the two people who owned her heart. "Yes, it is."

Within the crush of hugs at the wedding's end, Fordham pushed his way forward and pulled the two of them aside. He handed a manila envelope to Branson.

"What is this?" Bran asked, extracting the enclosed papers. Finding no identifying Braille, he handed the pages to Stephanie. She stared, trying to make sense of the documents.

"It's your wedding present," Fordham told Bran. "I've been collecting these for the past year and a half, since you first realized you wanted to make that cystic fibrosis drug more affordable. I believe these shares of Parker-Aston should be enough to give you a controlling interest."

Bran shook the empty envelope in his face. "Why didn't you tell me all along? You let me almost marry Carina trying to get these stock shares."

"Ironically, when you were acting a fool, willing to do whatever it took to get your hands on those stocks, I didn't trust you with them. Why, when you could afford to buy the drug at any cost, would you feel compelled to marry Carina to control the price?"

Bran ducked his head. "Because I thought being married to Carina would help me get over Stephanie."

Steph gave Bran a playful punch in the arm. "*Really?* You

put me through all that misery because you wanted to get *over* me?"

"Because I knew I wasn't good enough for you, and never would be." Bran grabbed her hands and held them tight.

"That's ridiculous."

"No it's true. No one is good enough for you, me included. But I realized something else… something more important. Nobody else loves you the way I do. I'll become the man you deserve, or die trying."

Fordham clapped him on the back, his lips making a wobbly smile. "That's why you're getting the stocks. You're stubborn as a mule, but eventually you learn."

Steph stood on her toes to give Fordham a kiss on the cheek. "I have a feeling I owe you a lot," she whispered.

"For the stocks?" His brows lifted.

"No, I mean for making Branson into the man he is. You're the best father he could ever have. I don't know how I can ever repay you."

Fordham returned the kiss on her forehead. "You just did."

EPILOGUE

ELEVEN MONTHS LATER

"Morning, Sleepyhead." Bran's warm lips pressed against her cheek.

Stephanie stretched and rubbed her eyes open to find her husband standing next to the bed, an affectionate smile on his face. Cradled in his muscular arms, a sleeping baby wriggled against his bare chest.

"That would make a sweet picture," she said, blinking at sudden tears.

"I tried to let you sleep in as long as possible. I know you were up a lot last night."

"Your baby sister has her days and nights mixed up. She's determined to give me dark circles under my eyes."

"Did you hear that, Lilly?" He bent to kiss the baby's soft curls. "You mustn't keep Steph awake at night. What's that? You're excited because it's your four-month birthday? I understand, but Stephanie needs her beauty sleep."

"It's not like Lilly's the only reason I have dark circles." She smiled, thinking Branson was even more attractive when

EPILOGUE

he was holding a baby. Something about a brawny man showing tenderness just tugged at the heart strings. "Anyway, I can catch cat naps today. You're the one who has to go to work and keep our family fed."

"Did you forget it's Saturday?"

"Saturday!" She threw off the covers. "Finn's coming over to tour the apartment, and it's a wreck."

"Relax." He pushed her back against the pillows. "Stay in bed and drink your coffee. I put it on the bedside table. Laurie said she'd get the place ready for Finn's visit."

Steph groaned. "What's she going to do? Set up booby traps for him?"

He snorted with laughter, startling Lilly, but managed to rock her back to sleep.

Their new home, the entire upstairs of a converted warehouse, was huge by New York City standards. Branson had divided it into two apartments—a large one for them and a small one for Laurie, next door.

"Are you and Finn stepping on each other's toes, now that you work in the same building all the time?" Stephanie rearranged the pillows, so she could sit up. "This is the most time you've ever spent together."

"Not really." Branson shrugged his scrumptious, broad shoulders, and Steph smiled, enjoying the view. "I've always had a private office suite here, just like the others. We each handle our part of the business, as usual. Honestly, I only run into him once or twice a week, unless we schedule a conference call with Cole and Jarrett."

"Wish the other three guys were married, too." She lifted the coffee mug and breathed in the rich aroma before taking

EPILOGUE

a swallow. "Think how fun it would be if you all had babies at the same time."

Bran's lips stretched in a grimace. "Whatever you do, don't say that out loud. Those guys are afraid to commit to a second date, much less marriage. If you suggest having kids, they'll probably move to Antarctica."

"I was hoping they'd all move to New York City, with us."

"Doubt you'll blast Cole out of Texas. And Jarrett isn't about to give up skiing 150 days a year."

"Guess we're lucky Carina's in love with New York—she was happy to move, even though she has a love/hate relationship with me." Steph drank some more coffee before setting her mug down.

"Carina can't figure you out," he said. "She knows how horrible she was to you, but you've been nice to her. She's jealous of you, but she loves that you take care of Lilly, so she can pretend she's not a single mom."

"How is her latest boyfriend? Think he'll last more than two weeks?"

"Doubt it." Bran rocked back and forth, soothing Lilly as she began to fuss.

"Have you mentioned anything to Carina about letting us have Lilly on a permanent basis? Do you think, maybe..." Stephanie bit her lip. She'd tried not to get attached, but it was impossible.

"One day at a time, Steph. That's all we can do. Right now, Lilly's here more days than she's with Carina. We can be thankful for that. We may never get full, legal custody. We knew that from the start."

"But I didn't know how hard it would be." She sniffed, wishing she wasn't so emotional.

EPILOGUE

His awesome abs flexed as he bent to kiss her forehead while holding Lilly in his arms.

"You're incredible, Steph. Do you know that? I still can't believe you'd want to care for Carina's child, after all that happened. You're the most selfless person I know."

"I still get mad at Carina, but Lilly's your sister—a sweet, innocent baby. It's impossible not to love her. I still worry your dad's going to find a way to use Lilly to hurt you. Like he may suddenly decide to assert his parental rights and take her away." Steph pushed her chin forward, pursing her lips. "It's too bad he ended up with financial penalties instead of going to prison."

"He got hit where it hurt most—in his pocketbook and his pride. He lost control of his company, and his friends disappeared like roaches running from the light."

Steph tilted her head, squinting at him. "How do you know what roaches do in the light?"

He lifted one shoulder. "I read a lot."

He still surprises me.

Bran's lips pressed together in a flat line. "But I refuse to let my dad keep me from being a part of Lilly's life."

A knock on the door barely preceded it flinging open. "Dad-dy," Ellie sang his name. "It's Saturday. Will you make chocolate chip waffles for breakfast?"

"That depends," Branson said, pretending to debate the question, though he cooked them every Saturday without fail. "Are you going to get all the ingredients out for me?"

"I already did." Ellie bounced on her toes and grabbed his elbow, tugging him from the room. "Come on."

He let her drag him out, grabbing a t-shirt from the hook on the back of the door.

EPILOGUE

Darn. He's going to cover up that six-pack.

∽

After a leisurely shower, Stephanie emerged from the bedroom. Branson, adorable in his apron and chef's hat, was busy in the perfectly ordered kitchen, producing heavenly smells that wafted throughout the room and elicited a grumble from Steph's tummy.

"Where is everybody? Finn hasn't gotten here yet?" Steph leaned back against the kitchen counter, watching Branson bustle about.

"Finn's here. He already ate a half dozen waffles. Ellie dragged him back into the playroom, and Laurie's putting Lilly down for a nap." Bran unplugged the waffle iron and wiped his hands on his apron. "I waited to eat with you."

"A romantic breakfast for two?"

He moved in front of her, placing his hands on either side of her swollen belly, and leaned over to kiss it. "Breakfast for *three*. How's my boy today?"

"Ford has been pretty quiet, lately. Oh! Did you feel that? First time I've felt him move today. I think he responds to your voice."

"I felt it. I can't wait to see him in person." He grinned, planting another kiss on her tummy. Then his expression turned serious. "Are you really okay with all this? We already have Ellie, and Ford will be here in two weeks. Maybe we need to tell Carina to get a full-time nanny. With the money she got in the settlement, she can afford it."

"I'm fine. I'm more than fine." She put her hands over his, where they rested on her tummy. "Just the fact you love Ellie

EPILOGUE

would be enough to make me happy. Now, we're going to have a baby together. I can hardly believe how blessed I am. And Lilly is like a ray of sunshine—a perfect gift."

Bran's hands moved to caress her face. "You really are the most beautiful woman in the world."

Her heart warmed. "You always make me feel that way."

"You know what?" Brans tone turned sultry. "We have a few seconds together."

"Probably not long." Steph glanced down the hallway toward the nursery. "They could come back any minute."

"We have long enough to do this…" His hand slid behind her head, and she lifted her chin toward him. His lips descended, worshiping hers, as hungry as the first time they kissed. She shuddered at the fiery touch of his fingers, lightly tracing the outlines of her face.

"Not *again*." Finn's voice came from the hallway. "Get a room!"

Branson pulled back. Grinning, he tilted his head and swept his hand toward the bedroom.

"Shall we?"

ACKNOWLEDGMENTS

I can't thank my *Remarkable Romance Readers* enough. They lived through this story as it developed, encouraged me to keep writing, and gave suggestions that literally changed Bran's and Stephanie's lives. Thank you, Wanda Liendro, Jessica Dismukes, Tabitha Kocsis, Rennae McIntosh, Jennifer Chastain, Stephanie Adams, Barb Gill, Eleni Datsika, and Nadine Peterse-Vrijhof. And undying thanks to my beta readers and *ARC Team*, as well.

Thanks to my awesome cover designer, Agape Author Services, and my fabulous editor, Laurie Penner.

As always, I can't thank my sweet husband enough, for giving me the time to write and edit and for taking care of me while I did it. (Dear Bruce... Submarine!)

ABOUT THE AUTHOR

Tamie Dearen lives in Texas with her incredibly romantic husband and two dogs. She hates dusting and exercising and loves anything musical or artistic. When she's not writing books, you might find her playing with her grandkids or drilling on someone's tooth.

Contact Tamie on her website at TamieDearen.com.

BOOKS BY TAMIE DEAREN

Sweet Romance

Underground Granny Matchmakers Series:

I Love Rock and Roll

Carry on Wayward Son (Coming Soon)

The Best Girls Series:

Sweet Adventure (Prequel)

Her Best Match

Best Dating Rules

Best Foot Forward

Best Laid Plans

Best Intentions

Sweet Romance

A Rose in Bloom

Restoring Romance

Cherished by the Cowboy

Sweet Adventure

Sweet Inspirational Romance

The Billionaire's Secret Marriage

The Billionaire's Reckless Marriage

The Billionaire's Temporary Marriage

The Billionaire's Alternate Marriage

The Billionaire's Bodyguard

The Billionaire's Practice Kiss

Christian Romance

Promise of Love

Promise of Hope

Promise of Faith

The Alora Series

YA/Fantasy

Alora: The Wander-Jewel

Alora: The Portal

Alora: The Maladorn Scroll

Subscribe to TamieDearen.com and get your free books!

Follow on Facebook: Tamie Dearen Author

Follow on Twitter: @TamieDearen

Made in United States
Orlando, FL
03 June 2023